International praise for *The Girls Who Saw Everything*

'A postmodern novel about the members of a Montreal book club who find themselves involuntarily acting out *The Epic of Gilgamesh* may not sound like a crowd-pleaser, but playwright and banjo enthusiast Sean Dixon's debut novel has been a surprise success ... The pleasure of the book comes from Dixon's deft handling of his weightier literary themes, making it reminiscent of the kind of irrepressibly mischievous and literary novels that John Barth used to write. Call it populist poindexterism.'
— *Quill & Quire*, selecting it as one of the top 15 books of 2007

'[A] sweet, unpredictable novel, ingenious and openly written.'
— *Time Out London*

'It takes a gifted writer to bring back the days when some of us were gawky college kids, loud and pretentious and arty. Canadian Sean Dixon draws readers into a complex circle of people lurching into their 20s ... [a] remarkably original new story.'
— *St. Petersburg Times*

'A clever little book! You'll love it.' — *Daily Express*

'A giant, sprawling tale condensed to the barest emotional bones of a story about the bonds that books form, and destroy, between people.' — *Baby Got Books*

'What makes Sean Dixon's first novel so electrifyingly smart and charming is its abundant passion.' — *Georgia Straight*

The Girls Who Saw Everything

EVERYTHING

SEAN DIXON

COACH HOUSE BOOKS | TORONTO

Published with the assistance of the Canada Council for the Arts and the Ontario Arts Council. Coach House also acknowledges the assistance of the Government of Ontario through the Ontario Book Publishing Tax Credit Program and the Government of Canada through the Book Publishing Industry Development Program.

LIBRARY AND ARCHIVES CANADA CATALOGUING IN PUBLICATION

Dixon, Sean
    The girls who saw everything / Sean Dixon.
ISBN 978-1-55245-184-7
    I. Title.
PS8557.197G57 2007   c813'.54   C2007-902253-7

This book is for the two bugs: Kat and Lida.

(Let's start with the epitaph.)

(Oh no. Categorically no. This should become well-established as an adventure story before anybody ever dies and anything ever changes.)

(But it's a beautiful quote!)

(You mean the epigraph.)

(Yes, let's begin with the epigraph. And don't tell anyone I made that mistake.)

(It's called a malapropism.)

(I know!)

(And by the epigraph, are you suggesting the quote by Ezra Pound?)

(Yes!)

(Who, I might point out, is a man.)

(So?)

(Not to mention a damned fascist.)

(Don't you like the quote?)

(I like the quote very much. I love the quote.)

(… (?))

'What thou lov'st well
shall not be reft from thee.'

(Yes, just like that. That's the perfect epitaph.)

PART ONE

Chapter One
Runner's Fall (i)

When Runner Coghill fell through the ceiling, she interrupted what we can only call a domestic quarrel.

Of the arguers in question, the young man's name was Dumuzi, though his name has been changed to protect the innocent (that is, Dumuzi). Moments before, he had been huffing and puffing from the cold, for which he was wilfully underdressed, and standing with his sometimes girlfriend Anna inside the front entrance to the warehouse at 5819 Saint-Laurent, a building that, against all probability, she owned.

Anna had called him, out of the blue, on what he thought was the first warmish day of the year, although that had turned out to be an illusion propagated by the phone call and Anna's attention; in fact, it was cold, but Anna was bored and looking for company to walk around downtown. They had met in the early afternoon and walked down the hill into the late afternoon, Anna telling him about her classes — a bit of philosophy, a bit of English, the only thing she liked was anthropology, or at least she liked the idea of anthropology, though the reality of anthropology was boring and more boring. The sound of her voice so soothed his chronic spikes of sexual anxiety — brought on by her arbitrary pattern of granting and withholding affection — that he began to question whether he'd ever felt them in any serious way.

Now it was freezing raining and it was evening, and Anna, who was wet, wanted to go inside and find a clean corner where the two of them would be able to pile some remnants of her grandfather's old shmatte emporium into something that might resemble a bed and a blanket, beside a pale beam of streetlight they could roll into when they were done. Her other conditions included a solid ceiling above their heads and no turds, human or otherwise, at least not nearby. She didn't mind a little dust and dirt though, since, as Du had noticed, she hadn't washed for some time, either her clothes or her person, and had embarked on a more animal form of grooming.

It was a slow negotiation, because Anna was offering Du what he'd been pining after through the entire winter; that is to say, she was offering sex, in a warehouse that suddenly didn't seem so filthy because of the way the light filtered out of the darkness and the dust and the endorphins that were suddenly released into Dumuzi's brain. But she wanted him to pay her for it. To see what it was like. And her proposal was slowing him down.

A little note about Dumuzi: his hormones were raging, but he tried to be polite about it. He was a big squarish guy, but when you looked at him you got the whole picture. He wasn't a bobbing Adam's apple or a collar or a grin. There was nothing about his maleness that was easily Atwoodian. It would be unfair to describe him like that, even though he was a boy and the reader might not like boys.[1] He tried to keep tidy. He wore clean lines. He was a whole guy, albeit a young guy who just needed, very desperately, to get laid. Where Anna was concerned, he definitely did not like who he became when he was with her, but still he wanted to be with her and wished only to change who he was and how and what he thought.

He asked Anna where she'd gotten the idea and she told him how earlier in the day an elderly gentleman had mistaken her for a prostitute and propositioned her while Du was buying gum. This shocked him almost as much as the proposal itself and he looked away, shuffling in a head-bowed, punch-drunk silence.

(Eventually.) 'You like this place?'

---

1 We weren't fond of boys ourselves, but our opinion here is not relevant.

She said, 'Yeah, why not.'

He tried to speed up his thoughts. 'Well, I don't know about all this love of decay and dark dripping warehouses. I mean, you might try to take out your contacts every once in a while if you don't want to go blind, and you might want to change your clothes every once in a while, and, yeah, this new obsession of yours is really going to help, although, although I think any dirty old man on Saint-Laurent would lose his erection if he was standing downwind of you and your – '

'I doubt it.'

'Sure.' He deflated. 'Sure. Me too. Anyway, this place is falling apart. There must be a million squatters living here.'

'I can't afford to fix it. I'm warehouse poor.'

'Oh.'

'Dumuzi … I'm going to let you sleep with me.'

'But you want me to pay you, Anna.'

'So just forget about that part.'

'Anna, you want me to pay you a lot of money.'

'Let's say you don't have to pay me all that much. I'm only asking you to pay for what most men think they have the god-given right to get for free.'

'So why shouldn't I think that too?'

'Don't you think that's a little arrogant?'

'You think it's good for men to pay for sex? Wow.'

'I'm saying it might be good for me to get paid for sex. It might fulfill some sort of destiny.'

'Oh, I can't stand it!'

And this is when Dumuzi's fist hit the pillar, compromising, it would appear, the integrity of the building, and that's when Runner fell through the ceiling above and landed behind them in a bunch of cardboard boxes.[2]

---

2 It might be of interest as well to note how, on this day, on the other side of the world from there, everyone who could was getting out of Baghdad, filling the outlying cities of Rawa and Anna. Water was scarce and the American dollar was worth 2,700 Iraqi dinars. According to the Blogger of Baghdad. (Aline's note.)

✛

A new quality Du was beginning to notice about himself was his capacity to be grateful for events that reasonable people might find abhorrent or tragic, as long as these events deflected the attention of his tormentors. The truth is that he would have preferred the whole city to come down on their heads in that moment, but he had to make do with Runner Coghill, falling like debris. He unshouldered his backpack and ran over to the crumpled girl set like a small broken mannequin among the boxes and the stones. She was screaming, though Du realized as he got closer that she was shouting not incoherent pain so much as the name of a boy: 'NEIL! NEIL! I'M HURT!'

The girl paused to reflect, loud enough for Du to hear, 'Oh I don't think a dose of Prozac is going to help this kind of pain.' She was talking over his head though, aiming her thoughts straight for Anna.

'Oh. Hi. I guess that came as a shock to you. I seem to have — '

Anna interrupted her, having forgotten her former business, and was trying to figure out uh what this intruder uh was uh doing here.

'Well, I don't really mean to be here. Upstairs is where I — '

Interrupted by Anna again, who meant to say, 'The uh building. How did you come to be in the uh building?'

'Cool it, sister. Don't hate me because I'm beautiful.'

Now, Runner Coghill was not exactly a looker, not by any stretch of the imagination and certainly not to Dumuzi. Runner was small. She looked like a Grey Nun out on a day pass — you could imagine her in a wimple. She was almost weightless, with translucent skin, a haughty nose — a pig nose she sometimes called it in her own garment-rending arias of despair, which were private and known to us only because they were occasionally gossiped about in fits of envy of which we are not proud. And she let her hair grow more thickly over her bumps, to try and cover

14

them up, though this practice only augmented them. They were called pilar cysts. She insisted that everyone know what they were called even though she was supposedly trying to hide them. That is the way she was. She boasted about her minor ailments while keeping the most prominent one — the actual life-threatening one — entirely to herself. We are still amazed to report that she kept it a secret, though the primary sign, the tell-tale one, would have been obvious to a medically minded person had there ever been one in the group — this primary sign being that her eyes popped right out of her head, more so with every passing month, so much so that you might think she was staring even when she was not, though she did sometimes stare. It was disconcerting to some, most immediately to Dumuzi, who felt a little Gordian knot of fear every time he caught her eye, even though he was literally twice her size.

So when this wreckage of a girl, crumpled up in a coat, having fallen through the ceiling seconds before, said, to the perfect Anna, 'Don't hate me because I'm beautiful,' Du, after a moment's uncomprehending shock, laughed, a sort of stunned laugh. And that's when the girl noticed him for the first time.

Being broken in the presence of the male gaze would have made Runner feel overwhelmed under normal circumstances, but, beyond a few fleeting thoughts,[3] she was in too much of a hurry to be overwhelmed at the moment. Still, it was fortunate she'd got some warning, because a second later Du swooped in and crouched very close to her, examining her, opening her coat, uncovering her, touching her leg. She gasped for air with a little

3 His cheeks were stubbled, like the bark of a tree ... the hair on his head grew thick as laundry ... his beauty was consummate. He was tall! He was magnificent! He was terrible! He would scour [Runner's] body in search of life and coax it toward maturity! He would dig from [Runner's] most shadowy slopes the deepest well of pure water, out of which an ocean would spring, and he would cross that ocean to the sunrise beyond, arrive on some future morn when [Runner] was hale and adult and smiling fully in his arms, in the bedroom of a third-storey flat in Mile End! (From Runner's notebook.)

yelp that she hoped sounded like an expression of pain and not its opposite, and squeezed her eyes shut.

'Anna, I think she's broken her leg.'

Anna swore. Runner drew a breath and let it exhale without speaking. And then drew another.

And then began to explain patiently to them — well, to Anna, still ignoring Du despite the temperance he'd suddenly inspired in her — about her ailments. She said that she was sorry, that she had a mild form of osteoporosis which, she felt, made a bad combination with her epileptic tendencies (which tendencies she was fabricating for the first time in that very moment), but that she was also really quite grateful for it, her osteoporosis, because it made her a very modern thinker. It forced her to think about the body in art and the world. Like, for instance, how was she going to get her body, broken leg and all, up to the fifth floor of this building, if she had willed herself already up to the second and it had brought her, of its own volition, right back down to the first? How was she going to get this useless shell of a body, this inattentive and ungrateful husk, back up to the second, and beyond to the third, fourth and finally fifth, especially when faced with such a pair of uncomprehending and unsympathetic faces as now looked down upon her?

Anna kept her eye on the ball: 'What's up on the fifth floor?'

Runner took a deep breath and sighed, as if to say that these two were just not going to get it. When she spoke again, however, there was a green blade of hope in her voice: 'Have you ever heard of the Lacuna Cabal?'

'No.'

'Well … it's … a very exclusive … book club, and I'm sure … '

Du, who was a devoted student of every thought and mood that flickered across Anna's face, here observed her try to imagine the possibility of a book club on the fifth floor of the Jacob Lighter Building.

'… and I'm sure it doesn't interest you, but there are six

women up there right now who at this moment are finishing up the last book and are about to launch into proposals for the next, at which point I have to make an entrance.'

Anna's instinct of ownership kicked in. 'But this is my building!'

'I see you fail to see the bigger picture.'

'How long has this been going on?'

'I tell you, I need to get upstairs!'

'I don't care.'

Du recognized the expression that now came over Runner's face. It allied him to her, at least for the moment, fellow recipient of the chill wind from Anna. The girl saw first that Anna didn't care, and then she saw that, really, really, she didn't care. It was an obstacle. It was a challenge. Runner launched in, like Churchill convincing an island to make war.

'Kid,' she said, addressing Anna, for how else do you address someone young in years who has revealed herself to be as jaded as a dead thing, except to appeal to the part of her that is still young, the bright shiny package that contains her, her skin? 'Kid,' she called her, and went on to ask her if she'd ever felt anything for a cause that was bigger than herself, if she'd ever wanted to throw herself behind such a cause, for the sheer bumfuckery of it, if she'd ever been curious about …

Anna's uppercut in the microsecond's lull: 'I don't care.'

'Please,' Runner said. 'Those girls up there don't expect to ever be caught by anything even remotely resembling the owner of a building. You're missing a great opportunity here, for, believe me, they are far, far more deserving of your goddess-like wrath than I — '

'I don't c— ' Anna had not expected that. Goddess-like wrath? For one moment she didn't speak. And then another. Dumuzi could see that the broken-legged girl had hit pay dirt, found a weak spot he didn't even know was there. He made a mental note: 'goddess.' And then the girl on the floor went on.

17

'Association with this club, which I now offer to you in defiance — '

'Who says I want — ?'

'— of our heartless executive, will expose you to the damaged masterpiece I am about to propose. That's right, sister, I can see that you're a bit of a damaged masterpiece yourself, aren't you? Though you're strong and beautiful and everything I'm not.'

Anna looked squarely at the girl. She was thinking that she did often feel like a damaged masterpiece. Quite often, in fact. Regularly. She gave sudden rein to the thought that this girl knew ... she knew ... what did she know? She knew something. Something about her. Perhaps ... everything. Perhaps she was wise in all matters. Shit, man, Anna couldn't even make her 8:30 classes. This girl, though, she obviously had it together. Anna had always wanted ... Her eyes drifted up to the hole in the ceiling. Du's, mystified, uncomprehending, followed. For a moment, considering the stranger's words, Anna suddenly felt that she was not confused at all. She felt that she had been confused, but was, for this precious instant, pretty smart, pretty witty, pretty pretty, not dead. Gloriously defeated by the girl with the broken leg, on the floor.

But did any of this show up on Anna's face? Nope. She was tough. She was tough as nails. The only indication of a change of heart was the gesture for Du to pick the chick up.

As for Runner, she had been relishing her victory until she saw Du's hands zeroing in, getting closer and larger. She had a fit of sneezing. When that was through, she proceeded to lay herself bare before this boy's deepest cell of shame: 'Oh no, pal, not you. Her. Not you. If you touch me I'd have to ask you to fuck me, and if you said no then that would be humiliating for me, wouldn't it? It's been so long, I feel like a virgin. Really. Let's be honest, I am a virgin, that's not normal. And still you're going to let this brute put his hands on me?'

Runner's virgin status was not something she necessarily wanted to get rid of. But she did feel that the sexual act might just pull her flagging, barely post-adolescent body fully into the present and force it to grow up. As for shyness around the opposite sex, her wreckage of a body had just led her to an epiphany. She decided, right here and now, anticipating the strong arms of Dumuzi, to fully explore the archetype of the foul-mouthed shy person and take it to new heights.

At least that's what she decided deep down. On the surface she was screaming indignation that Anna was allowing a boy to lay hands on her.

Anna said, simply, sorry. She wasn't going to lift a finger for this girl. Maybe she felt a bond with her, but she sure wasn't about to show it.

Dumuzi, blushing pink, gathered Runner into his arms and picked her up. She was as small and light as a beanbag full of little bones, and she relaxed into his arms. As he swept her up she felt a sharp pain in her leg but ignored it. That is, her voice responded, practically bursting Du's eardrum, but her mind ignored it. She launched again into her protests and was in mid-aria when she suddenly remembered.

'Don't forget those.'

Those?

There at Du's feet, surrounding him like a toy rampart, were several irregularly shaped slabs of stone. They looked fragile, though none seemed to have broken in the fall. And they were marked all over, front and back, with tender notches of writing, presented in columns with a symmetry and order that nearly took Du's breath away. They looked old. Really old. She must have been carrying them when she fell through the floor.

Anna clapped eyes on them too. Ten of them. Looked like she would have to lift a finger after all. No idea what this crazy chick needed them for, but she didn't feel the need to question. Anyway, they were manageable. Weird. But small. Ish. She gathered them up, and they carried on, toward the stairs, and up, and into a bygone era.

✛

And then Neil appeared.

He'd seen Runner negotiate her way through this sort of accident before, and he knew she would survive it, this time at least, even if it wasn't clear that she wanted to. Earlier, he'd watched, on the second floor, as she gave herself freely over to the fall and disappeared into the floor with all ten tablets. It made him tired. He knew she would apologize when he saw her next, and that upset him and made him even more tired.

He'd been here on the first floor for quite some time, through the negotiations, having made his way quietly around the perimeter. When he finally appeared, though, you would not have imagined him capable of such stealth. He looked awkward in his clothes, which were old and badly fitting, and he wore a pair of large round-rimmed glasses without lenses, and his head was buried in a book even when he walked. It was a notebook, which he held open with his right hand, crooked in his elbow, while writing from time to time with his left. As he crept across the floor toward Du's backpack, he stopped to jot something down no fewer than five times, creating the impression of a time-lapse photograph or a Noh stage show. It seemed he had a running commentary going on the passing moments of his life.

If we were to have stood over him, in this moment, and peered down into his book, we would have seen the following entry as it emerged from his pen:

Once so strong she was … now so … crazy … accident-prone, and Neil … He carried the bag.

And then Neil bent over and with some effort picked up Du's bulky backpack, slung it over his shoulder and crept toward the stairs.

Chapter Two
The Lacuna Cabal

The Lacuna Cabal had not always met on the fifth floor of the Jacob Lighter Building at 5819 Saint-Laurent. In our efforts to keep moving, we tried cellars, garrets, walk-in closets and bell towers, with very little account given to our general welfare and comfort. Priority was given rather to the idea that the location should suit the book, the book the location. It went beyond re-enactment and into the realm of living out, as much as possible, the story of the book, in the hope that its experience would rub off on us. Thus we considered ourselves to be the premium reading club of the English-speaking world.

This method took some refinement. An early example: we once conducted a spontaneous public reading of a novel in verse called *Autobiography of Red* at the airport, for which we all painted ourselves top to toe for the occasion. It was later agreed, however, that we did not absorb a great deal from the presentation, beyond a bit of pigment, some skin rashes and a charge of public mischief (dismissed).

And another time, early on, we kidnapped the aging poet Irving Layton for four hours from the Maimonides Geriatric Centre in Côte-Saint-Luc and took him for an excursion up the mountain — a trip from which he was reported to have reappeared sporting a diadem of autumn leaves and looking immensely satisfied. That one made the papers. And the evening news. Still, it had been dangerous and seemed like a cheat to meet the poet himself rather than the words in his book.

In our second year, when our methods had acquired some clarity, we once headed down to Place des Arts on a Sunday and tried to depict the scene of the nun swinging from the bridge-builder's broken arm in *In the Skin of a Lion*.[4] One of our members nearly hanged herself. Accidentally, of course. But it was memorable and satisfying and we declared that book a success.

Our third year was characterized by a more traditional approach: we began to calm down as a group and seek out a more or less permanent meeting place.

There's an elongated little park just west of Saint-Denis on Laurier, north side, with a sandbox and small set of monkey bars.[5] We tried to meet there for a while, since someone had noticed that there never seemed to be any children. But when we started going, so did the children. The park stayed empty throughout the week and even on weekends, as long as we weren't there. But when we showed up, they were never far behind. And when we abandoned the place, so, again, did they.[6]

Eventually we found a beautiful warehouse on the waterfront, rumoured to have required rent — rent rumoured to have been paid by the wealthy father of our founder and president. There we felt safe from prying eyes and blessed with a view of the river.

But then, in the fall, someone in the Cabal died, and so we decided to move. We felt that the waterfront warehouse had lost its lustre and its luck. And when the general mood failed to brighten by November, we even decided to enlist a new member as a gesture of self-preservation — someone to push against the pall that had fallen over the group.

The Jacob Lighter Building was discovered in mid-December, during a well-needed Christmas hiatus, by Romy

---

4 If the reader isn't familiar with this particular novel, she might as well stop reading this book right now and go read that one. Or else dispense with the whole idea of reading altogether. *In the Skin of a Lion* is, officially, the Lacuna Cabal's favourite book.

5 Later note: No there isn't.

6 It's not there anymore. Somebody must have dreamt it. Unless our abandonment of it, along with the children's, caused it to fade away.

Childerhose, on one of her long walks. She tried the door by the loading dock for five days in a row and it was always open. She finally ventured into the building and bravely worked her way up through the darkness of the stairwell, floor by floor, finding that all evidence of squatter habitation — blankets and newspapers and washrooms that would have to be sealed off — ended on the third. Thinking it over, she felt that there must have been an instinct among squatters to be ready for a quick escape, although, if it had been her, she would have climbed as high as she could, like a squirrel with a nest, and kept her stuff near a window that could be opened so that everything might be hurled out and away, to be retrieved later. But it was clear that no one had lived here for quite some time.

Up on the fifth floor, the flappable Romy found things to be clean, spacious and empty. Though very, very cold. There was evidence that someone had begun to renovate the building up there — presumably Anna's rovingly entrepreneurial father — but the project had been abandoned. Drywall had all been ripped out and there was little or no insulation. We have long speculated that it might have been the general state of abandonment, by squatters on one side and developers on the other, that had so drawn Romy (who hailed from a city in Ontario which she referred to exclusively as 'Bingotown'). The building was a book — a weighty tome no less — that nobody wanted, neither for pleasure nor pillage, a gargantuan testament to wasted lives, like hers, like ours, like this book itself, whose leviathan bulk is a reflection more of waste than achievement.

When we moved into the fifth floor of the Jacob Lighter Building, it was decided by vote that we had to acquire a portable heater with a scary-looking flame and two enormous and truly frightening propane tanks, rented with the benefit of Missy's father's credit card. We called it 'the blue flame-thrower.' Some of us wondered how Missy's father could have allowed such a rental to be made by his daughter. Where paternal love was concerned, we could understand the silver Sunfire with its custom pull-down top, we clocked the purchase of the flat in Outremont and we appreciated the rent paid on our waterfront meeting place. But allowing a propane heater with an eternally flaming grill, like the burning bush except indoors and blue — this took parental indulgence to a new level and led some of us to wonder whether the man was paying any attention at all. What's more, there was a period wherein Missy erected a large tent up there — also acquired by the divine grace of her father's card — to try and contain the heat. So the blue flame was two times indoors, a fire hazard inside a fire hazard, at least until she pulled the tent down and returned it at the beginning of March.

We wonder, from the cool perspective of three or four years' distance, whether we didn't all share a funny latent death wish that one weird winter.

So we stayed on the fifth floor of the Jacob Lighter Building, 5819 Saint-Laurent, even though it did not provide us with the poetry of shelter from winter. Missy told us that we all had our respective homes for that. The readers of *Don Quixote*, she said, huddled shivering for centuries in cold places and still managed to get through the book. That book was present in point of fact, she added, all the way through the worst excesses of the Industrial Revolution. You can only imagine, she said, what kind of horrors people must have endured between bouts of reading Cervantes's book.

That's the thing about born leaders. They convince you that you're capable of doing — that you want to be doing — the craziest things. When they go too far, we suppose, is when you find yourself with a cult on your hands. And when they don't go far enough, they come across as carping, opinionated, pain-in-the-ass purveyors of sloppy thinking. Missy fluctuated between these two extremes. How could she not? She was young and only beginning to experiment with holding the reins of power. Anyway, it's no secret that the two primary writers of this book remained loyal to her and would have followed her anywhere except that point beyond which, according to the foundation principles of the Lacuna Cabal, we were expressedly forbidden to go.

✝

Which brings us finally to the call of the role. The sitting members of the Lacuna Cabal as of March 18th, 2003.

House left, stage right, in a semi-circle heading toward house right, stage left, books open in our laps, it goes as follows:

The first is one of us. One of the two of us. One of we two narrators or, if you prefer, glorified stage-direction readers. Missy liked to keep us separate so that her consolidation of power would not seem so obvious. So I, Jennifer, about whom the less said the better, sat at the farthest left, house left, all by myself, next to the newest member, whose name was (is)

Priya Underhay,

the aforementioned newest, the ray of hope and sunshine, meant to combat the gloom that had followed a death in the club — about whom we knew, at the time, very little. She was, not coincidentally when you consider Missy's motive for taking her on, a bit of a hippie. To us she seemed a little crazy and often could be overheard speaking in a low voice to — one could only assume — herself.

Priya, who carried a travel guitar with her wherever she went, missed the occasional meeting because she had the occasional commitment to play at the occasional small-time open-mike event. She called these 'alt-country nights,' whatever that meant. Such events were never attended by the Cabal, for two, no, three reasons:

1. They would have blown our cover.

2. We were declaratively interested in the written word, to the exclusion of every other art form, and would pay attention to a ballad only if it were written in a book.

3. An example of Priya's early song lyrics:

we are the fortunate ones, you and I,
who travel with the pelicans and the platypi …
'goodnight,' lisp the smiling, dozing sarcophagi
as we pass them by.
we are the delicate ones, though we do not cry
when we wound one another with the lash of an eye …
'and you think you'll live,' screech the dead sarcophagi
but they are out of earshot, by and by.

We'd like to meet some living sarcophagi.

(Allowing a folksinger into our ranks seemed, for the longest time, a very serious mistake.)

Priya kept her travel guitar in a slim tube designed to sling a yoga mat over her back. Rumour had it, or, rather, Romy had it, that she didn't need to carry the mat around because she used it for sleeping, that it was the only piece of furniture she owned. This wasn't quite true, since it emerged that she lived with her mother and a younger sister in a small flat in the eastern French section of the plateau — a very small ground-floor flat, although they were very close to the people who lived in the two above them, a French couple with a new baby who owned the whole building, and another single mother, who lived at the top with a one-year-old. They were all doctors and architects in a vertically oriented community, and Priya made most of her money from babysitting.

At the time when this story begins, Priya had written, by all accounts, upward of thirty songs, most of them incomprehensible, and suffered from the occasional nosebleed, one can only imagine because of her nocturnal flights with fellow folksinging witches.

Next to Priya sat

Romy Childerhose,

the aforementioned squirrel in her nest, who hailed from the so-named Bingotown and had felt drawn to the epic seediness of the Jacob Lighter building.

We have no desire to present a negative portrayal of Romy in this passage, as we feel it might cause pain and would not be commensurate with the esteem in which we currently hold her. This presents a problem for us because, during the time this story takes place, we felt nothing but contempt for her, and this account would be nothing if it did not present something resembling the truth. In confessing this dilemma to the subject in question, however, a solution presented itself: apparently, not surprisingly, our contempt was nothing compared to how Romy felt about herself.

Here, therefore, is Romy's introduction, in her own recently commissioned words. Characteristically, she has begun far earlier in her story than expected, and has included information that we were perhaps better off not knowing:

> I was born in a barn. I was. Just outside of Bingotown, Ontario, where my mother-to-be had been dropped in a field with her two older sisters, one of whom had vomited on the other two while their parents — my grandparents — were on their way to church in their Sunday best. They dropped the vomit-covered sisters in the field to wait out the hour while the clean ones — the younger boys and the parents — went off to do their churchly duty. It was just enough time to quietly induce labour, since the sisters were privy to the knowledge of my mother's condition and the vomit had in fact been purposely induced. My mother (did I mention that my mother was very large?) had managed to conceal her pregnancy from her extremely Catholic parents. And then, for several months after I was born, she managed to hide me. You've heard the story of Kaspar Hauser? Living beneath the

floorboards of a little house somewhere in Germany? Well, if I hadn't been discovered, I might have been the small-town Southwestern Ontario version of that poor kid. And in many respects, perhaps I was.

What's more, Romy felt that this was one of the two seminal stories of her childhood, the other one being a Homeric narrative on the subject of fatness and responsibility:

People get fat through an act of will. Don't they? It's instead of a callus. The emotion is all nestled inside, like a pig in a blanket, and, as with calluses, the blows don't land quite so hard. Is that why they do it? My mother was fat. She was a cement balloon sinking into the ocean, who held me by the ankles and pulled me down, like galoshes on a mobster who'd slept with the wrong moll. I was fat too, but my fat was an air pocket to try and keep me afloat, to try and stop my mother from consuming everything. When I was a kid I once purchased a mouse. A little white mouse. I bought it at a pet store downtown and took it home in a small cardboard box, with a big bagful of mouse food. It was in the middle of a particularly harsh winter. I don't know what I was thinking. When I got home, my mother flipped out. Another mouth to feed that was not her own. But I have food for it, I said. A whole bag. I'm sure it's not the kind of food that you would like, I said. Who's to say? she said, and took the food. Besides, there was no place for the little mouth to live. My mother occupied everything. I found a little fishbowl that had belonged to a long-ago goldfish. And I put the little mouth in there. And then I watched in horror as he scrabbled around the small bottom and tried to jump free. He would leap into the air and catch a small paw at the lip of the bowl, spin his legs frantically and then fall to the bottom again. It was horrifying. Only a matter of time before he mastered the leap. I considered putting a pile of books there, *at the top, to block the exit, but then he would have suffocated. I suppose I could have drilled some holes in the books, but I didn't have a drill and you don't treat books like that, do you? And besides, the goldfish bowl was way too small. It was way, way too small. There was a woodpile at the back of the yard. I gazed at the woodpile through a window, imagining that it might make a beautiful, spacious, multi-hallwayed new home for my little burden. No, said my mother, the poor thing will die out there in the cold. We have to return it to the store. But there's a no-return policy, I yelled. It says so on a big sign right on the door! But we drove downtown with the mouse in the box. And when they refused to take the mouse back, my mother revealed her secret weapon, dragging a desperate, sobbing, sorry little me in through the jingling door. And they took back the mouse.*

Romy on how she came to leave Bingotown:

Bingotown was not a colourful city in those days, though I haven't been there lately. I remember reading somewhere that nineteenth-century municipal laws restricted the use of colour in the urban environment. This was true all over the world at the time, but Bingotown still had no colour over a century later. And so I left finally and came to Montreal, which, I heard, had coloured gables and coloured spiral staircases. I asked somebody, 'What is the most colourful city in Canada?' and they told me to go to Montreal.

Romy was, in the days of the Lacuna Cabal, a proverbial deer in the headlights, which suggested she always had something else on her mind. Still, she had one outstanding feature that made her, in our eyes, a paragon of womanhood: the most beautiful flowing locks of auburn hair you can imagine, which did much to mitigate the effects of the earnest demeanour they framed. She towered over the rest of us, trying always (and unsuccessfully) to keep her larger-than-life feelings to herself.

Let's see, what else? Romy had a soft spot for children's literature — due, we hypothesized, to the arrested development that may have occurred as a result of not being allowed to look after that goddamned mouse — and tried to keep up to speed on its developments. She considered *Harry Potter* to be inferior to some book about a girl and a bear and atheism, the title of which we can't recall, and the first book she recommended to the group (summarily rejected), was *Shardik* by Richard Adams, not really children's literature at all but also somewhat intensely about a bear (though he had written more famously about rabbits). The trajectory from mouse to bear in Romy's imagination remains a mystery to us.

Oh yes, and she found the building. The saddest, greyest, ugliest building in the city of Montreal. That was her single contribution to the Lacuna Cabal Montreal Young Women's Book Club at the beginning of our story, a fact that is, we suppose, nothing to sneeze at.

Romy sat next to

Emmy Jones,

offering her constant comfort, due to a heartbreak that had occurred in Emmy's life at exactly the same time, almost to the day, as the death that had occurred in the Cabal the previous fall. Nobody was certain why Emmy continued to feel heartbroken six months after the fact, but the generous interpretation was that she had occasionally resumed torturous relations with the man in question. The primary casualty of this heartbreak, however, even considering her self-centredness during the season leading up to the new book, seems to have been her love of literature, which made a sudden and, it seems, permanent, exit.[7]

---

7 As a playwright, her highest ambition, according to a recent interview published in the *Mirror*, is to create a *théâtre verité* domestic drama in which not one word is spoken on the stage and all expression is made using only looks, small gestures and violence.

What's more, speaking now of the present, she resents, apparently, very deeply, being depicted in the 'exaggerated mythopoetic realm of this account,' and will not read it, will have nothing to do with it, will barely even acknowledge its existence. She stuck it out with the Lacuna Cabal's final book, she reports, out of loyalty to and concern for Runner's health and feelings, but was otherwise finished with fiction. She has, in fact, challenged us, through the intercession of a third party, to entirely remove her from this account. But after deep consideration afforded by many sleepless nights, we have determined that we cannot do that, at least not altogether. Many of the decisions Emmy made during the weeks in which this story takes place — decisions which, granted, may have arisen out of heartbroken self-destructiveness — rendered her de facto the catalyst for many other events, events that go to the very heart of our story. Emmy's private story is intertwined with the larger story of the Lacuna Cabal Montreal Young Women's Book Club, which fact renders it not exclusively her own. We're sorry. We're very, very sorry.

We considered changing her name, but that doesn't seem to go far enough in the case of Emmy Jones. We feel, given her concern and our deep regard for same, that we have to transform, somehow, her whole self. It's a difficult dilemma because we can't just replace her with a scarecrow with no past and no future, who merely commits the actions that are necessary for Emmy to commit in order to move ahead with our story. We also have to be careful to avoid becoming like the storied Islamic painter of the thirteenth century, who, having been told that he cannot depict Muhammad, begins to dream the Prophet in three glorious dimensions on canvas and so prefigures the Renaissance and the Enlightenment, depicting Muhammad and always Muhammad and only Muhammad. The last thing that we need to happen in this story is for us to become obsessed with depicting Emmy, holding up a mirror to reflect another mirror, casting Emmy forever and alone into infinity. We do not wish to be embraced by our repression, lest it bring forth monsters. We have therefore adopted a somewhat radical narrative strategy and decided to make Emmy a fictional character. And to make the fact of Emmy as a fictional character clear to the reader in every moment. In order to fulfill this mandate, we have determined to (ahem) make her striped. And to always comment on her actions and feelings with respect to the fact that she is striped.

Emmy was striped. Like a zebra. Except saying she was striped like a zebra is like saying Einstein was smart like a fox. It does not convey the truth of the matter. Also, we should stress that her stripes were not of the zebra (or tiger, etc.) variety at all. We know that, because they did not fan out from her spine, as they do in most of the natural world, but were rather more uniform, running horizontally all the way around her body. And her stripes changed width, colour and shade, depending on her mood. Still, no matter how they changed, one shade was always lighter and the other darker.[8] So, if you attended a very close eye, you would always perceive the stripes. Her mind in those days was a perpetual state of black and grey, but her skin was always projecting at least two colours, exquisitely matched. We wonder, under what circumstances would she mismatch? And was it an act of will that she didn't? Or was it rather an act of nature? Colours always match in nature.

Her stripes manifested themselves with exquisite subtlety — if you met her on the street you would not notice that she had them. She managed, with some effort, to mask them from most observers by colouring her hair in a pair of tones and wearing brightly striped shirts. On regular days she had maybe four of them running along her face, six if you include her neck. On more intensely neurotic or desperately emotional days, there would be more. On the day that we introduce the Lacuna Cabal,

---

8 Formally, we should clarify that we're speaking of the stripes themselves and also the spaces between the stripes. We leave it to the reader to determine which was which.

March 18th, 2003, there were plenty, but they were noticeable only to Romy.

So there. We have told of a body changed into a shape of a different kind. And we get to keep Emmy in our story. This does present a bit of an aesthetic challenge for us, since, as we stated in our portrait of Priya, we are interested in the written word to the ascetic exclusion of all other art forms, including all those that are rendered in colour. But we'll do the best we can.

We might as well cut to the chase, let the cat out of the bag and say the thing that was obvious to everybody except Romy herself and perhaps Emmy as well: Romy loved Emmy. She would have loved her even without her stripes, but, as she was from Bingotown, Romy's eye was involuntarily drawn to colour as something it had rarely seen. So Romy saw Emmy, and what she saw she loved, no matter how sullen was the object of her love. What's more, despite the fact that her love was unrequited, Romy remembers it with wistful fondness and has offered her diary to be used for its edifying instances of self-loathing. We have, however, for the moment anyway, declined.

Emmy sat next to

Aline Irwin.

Aline was the most controversial member of the Lacuna Cabal Montreal Young Women's Book Club, for the simple reason that she was not a young woman at all. Not that she was old, or that we would not have been able to make some kind of exemption for elderly applicants, but we're not entirely sure that we should have made an exemption for Aline Irwin, no matter what Missy might have wished.

Still, Aline was there at Missy's invitation and Missy's insistence, and there were certain matters in which no one would ever dare to cross Missy.

Priya, who was new to the group, recalled once having seen Aline, sometime in the previous year, surrounded by friends (presumably including Missy, who did everything she could to protect Aline from the world) in a breakfast café on Parc Avenue. It was something Priya recalled easily for the simple reason that she had never before seen a person who looked so miserable as Aline did that morning, especially in contrast with her crowding compatriots. It was clear that her friends appreciated Aline, indulged her, allowed her to stay the way she was: sitting with her head down and peering through her makeup at the black dress, the stockings, the shoes. They accepted her without complaint and were heroically unaffected by his moods. The way you might sit with a sick friend when it's many of you who have come to visit and not just one.

But even in this recollection we've managed already to make the error of referring to Aline in the masculine. We can't even prop up the desired illusion of femininity in our own account.

Because it was clear to all of us, including Aline herself, if that permanently alienated expression was any indication, that Aline was a boy. A boy in a dress, as distinguished from a spectacular androgyne, like Prince, or like Johnny Depp in *Pirates of the Caribbean*. Probably not even a fully grown boy, since he was working so hard to mentally suppress his hormones.

Yes, she was a he, dressed as a she, and no matter how much makeup and sympathy were ladled onto her, this remained a permanent, irreversible fact. She was never going to make the cover of *Xtra*. Where the makeup was concerned, you could always more than make out a five-o'clock shadow — a misnomer in this case, since he shaved sometimes three times a day, so it might as well have been a 10 a.m. shadow. His skin reacted badly to the foundation and sprouted abscesses with deep reservoirs. No matter how loosely fitting her drop-waist dresses, you could always perceive the blockiness of her body, the flatness of her chest, the leggings emphasizing the power of her thighs, the knobbiness of her knees.

It was appalling.

Missy (we suspect) invited Aline into the Cabal so that she might have the opportunity to meet and get to know 'other women' and have them rub some of their womanness off on her. Among other things, she wanted her to experience 'the reinvention of the self through literature' and 'a bit of a haven from boys.'

Since there were no boys allowed in the Lacuna Cabal Montreal Young Women's Book Club. Not then. Not ever. No exceptions ...

Neil Coghill was an exception. Because he was ten and alone in the world except for Runner. And he was not really a member, but, rather, merely present to the membership. Otherwise, no exceptions.

The one who was fierce in her loyalty to Aline, who sat next to her, protected her, displayed in the manner of all guardians that most profound test of loyalty — the commitment to a lie — was none other than

Missy Bean,

founder and president of the Lacuna Cabal, of whom we have already spoken. How could we not have already spoken of her? She touched and enriched each of our lives in myriad ways. She gave us books and she gave us one another, and she was lonely and she was from Westmount. She was our captain and our king. If we were the seven sages who laid the foundation, Missy alone was the engineer of human souls!

Which is not to say she could not be barbaric (or, if you prefer, particularly considering the aforementioned allusion to a quote from Stalin: which is to say she could be barbaric). She had the instinct for power and the will to find it. She left no question in anyone's mind that politics is something pursued for the love of power and the craving of attention. Government is essentially barbaric — 'barbaric in its origins and forever susceptible to barbaric actions and aims.'[9] It can't civilize itself. But it

9 Jane Jacobs: *Systems of Survival*

can certainly civilize the rest of us, depending on what book it elects to have us read and plunder.

And we would have followed Missy to the ends of the earth. As it turns out, Missy did indeed go there, to the ends of the earth, before this story came to its conclusion, and we — the two of us — did not follow her there. So this book is our attempt to fulfill the tenets of our oath some years after the fact.

Missy was a little older than the rest of us — a fact that she managed to conceal fairly easily, mostly by refraining from any discussion of her past. Truth be told, she'd had some experiences of her own, had travelled a bit and was, we've come to learn, listening very closely to the ticking of her biological clock. She kept this fact well concealed, however, allowing us to think of her as a latter-day Sappho, indifferent to the world of men, when in truth she was more like Cleopatra. And she had a rich father who kept her in furs and memberships, and provided the credit card that purchased the heater, in the glow of whose blue flame she now sat next to

Me.

The other I of the two of we: Danielle, at the other extreme end, the other one of the two of us about whom the less said the better, though I suppose we should say something:

We were brought into the club by Missy, essentially as loyalists — sort of Rosencrantz and Guildenstern to her Claudius, with the twins, Runner and Ruby, cast as Hamlet. We were there from the beginning. Missy knew that it would take an effort to control the will of the twins, though she felt that the Cabal was better off with them than without them, since perhaps without them meant against them, and that would have been no good at all.

Though we pretended fealty and friendship to everyone, essentially we represented two extra votes in Missy's favour. That was the private condition from the beginning, to be overturned only if we felt that, for some reason, Missy was committing a destructive act, against herself or against the integrity of the club. The only reason this caveat was ever discussed at all was that we, including Missy, shared a very high sense of drama, occasionally indulging in fantasies about going mad and that sort of thing.

But why should Missy not have three guaranteed votes? She'd built the cabal with her own bare hands. Whatever it was that a maverick such as Runner Coghill brought to the table, she was no leader, and she could not have begun to build such an institution on her own. Mercury burns its path, cuts a swath: it's a destroyer, not a builder. Missy built the Cabal alone.

So, yes, we were her lackeys, meant to counterbalance the influence of the twins, Runner and Ruby, and their essentially wacky ideas. Which means, we suppose, that the two of us were the anti-twins.

And that completes the call of the role for the Lacuna Cabal, March 18th, 2003, 7:06 p.m. Here we are, in all our individualized glory, with our conflicts and our quirks.

Though in many other ways — many essential ways — we were, together, a single thing. Like a unit of the army in battle, like the chorus in an old Greek tragedy, like the Scooby-Doo gang. We were then, and always will be, the Lacuna Cabal Montreal Young Women's Book Club.

Chapter Three
The Beginning of Everything

How do you describe the cave you lived in before you walked out of it? What did Hell look like before the angels were hurled into it? Was there anyone who felt bigger than life in sixteenth-century London before Shakespeare stepped onto the stage? Did the Meccans have any idea of the power their language contained before Muhammad walked down the hill?

The truth is, the two of us have had enough schooling that we no longer believe in these before-and-after visions of history. History is the history of marketing and publicity; which is the smaller way of saying it's written by the victors.

And it was certainly not all glory and roses after Runner's entrance, either.

We said earlier that Du and Anna and Runner were climbing the stairs to a bygone era. But not yet, because the Lacuna Cabal had not yet completed their latest book. Out with the old and in with the new then. Or, more to the point, out with the new and in with the old.

The book we were completing was *Fall on Your Knees* by Ann-Marie MacDonald. It was the only book we had tackled all winter, and it had borne the burden of having to distract us from daily life after the death of Ruby Coghill. Grief and loss were emotions that none of us had really experienced before, and we didn't know what to make of them.

On the day in question, that is, March 18th, 2003, just after 7 p.m., we initiated our farewell to this book with a standard ritual we called the Final Indulgence. Aline, with help from a reluctant Emmy, began to read a passage that was agreed to be beloved to everyone. It was about two women who were lovers who pledged to never leave one another, and it contained descriptions of the sea and of November. Everybody cried for some reason at the mention of the word 'November,' especially Romy, who cried out loud. We cried too, though we don't know why; we're crying now, even though we can't think of anything bad that has happened in November, other than it is only two months later than September. The truth is, we would have wept at the name of any month at all, the names of months being heavily weighted with the passage of time away from September and toward a sad and heavy future.

Emmy was weeping on the shoulder of Romy, quietly despairing that she didn't have someone like that, someone to love who could love her like that. Nobody was noticing this except for Romy herself, naturally, and her heart was both melting and bursting. Emmy worried quietly to Romy that she was becoming repellent and unclean, that she gave off a scent that said to men, 'Don't come near me.' She felt it went right down to her genes. She also proclaimed herself one of the last of the old-time nihilists, who would think nothing of throwing herself onto a scrum of sailors à la *Last Exit to Brooklyn*. Though she was also, she said, so fucking tired of her life experiences being governed by stories in books.

Romy wanted nothing more than to counter Emmy's nihilism by paying homage to her stripes, which were, to Romy, the most beautiful things she had ever seen, and which seemed to pulse with her heartbeat in a way that could be discerned only by a person sitting as close as Romy was now. But she knew that Emmy did not want to speak of such things, so instead she breathlessly protested that no single man, not even a bevy of wild-eyed sailors, could possibly affect Emmy's perfect genes and declared, perhaps a little too emphatically, that Emmy was as beautiful as she had ever been.

This was overheard.

There had been, thus far in the room, some unspoken tension, because the women of the Lacuna Cabal Montreal Young Women's Book Club were not comfortable with giving themselves over entirely without criticism to a work of fiction, no matter how important or established it was. We tried to maintain a critical distance, so that only the most sublime portions of a given work would stick. But there had been something about this book that had gotten to us, and so we found ourselves, on this evening, ushering the author of *Fall on Your Knees* into the pantheon of the greats without so much as a whisper of protest regarding length or anachronism or political relevance or anything. And so there was a creeping feeling of embarrassment that perhaps the Lacuna Cabal was losing its edge. Still, though criticism was desired as an outlet, it had to be well-spoken and deserved, and woe betide the woman who let fly for the sake of venting alone. Nobody had dared on this particular evening, and so when Romy was overheard to be speaking quietly to Emmy about beauty and blue jeans, the collective Lacuna Id, in the person of founder and president Missy Bean, spotted an outlet. She turned to Romy and dressed her down for turning her attention toward issues of fashion and beauty at a time when attention had to paid to more serious matters of literary analysis, to wit: 'We are tonight attempting to recall the deepest and greatest values of this book, but Romy, it seems, would prefer to speak about,' et cetera.

To Romy, who was the perfect Lacuna Cabal member, this was a blow.

'No, Missy, we're not.'

'Oh, Romy, you're not? You're speaking of more serious things?'

'Yes we are.'

'Could you share them with the group?'

'Uh.'

'Books suck, Missy, essentially, is what I was saying. Okay? Happy?'

This from Emmy, who opted in her newfound self-destructive manner to deflect attention from Romy — possibly the only kind thing she will ever do for anyone in this story. She went on. 'Because for me they don't do what they're supposed to do when they need to do them most.'

Missy, shocked, spluttered something about how books, in fact, 'have no needs, Emmy.'

'All I know is,' Emmy continued, 'and this is what I was telling the poor embarrassed Romy, all I know is, I lie in my bed at night, by myself, trying to read some cozy little book, but I can't read them anymore, because they're too small, and they don't matter, and I have to put them down and just get on with it.'

Missy, trying to affect a sympathetic tone, began to assure Emmy that we all knew about her 'circumstances,' an irresistibly vague term that prompted Priya to lean over and ask Romy, whisperingly, what those 'circumstances' might be.

'Priya here doesn't,' corrected Emmy. 'But you were saying?'

'Emmy, if you're not available for the necessary suspension of disbelief through these tragic circumstances of — '

'Missy, I'm not saying my circumstances are tragic. God forbid thinking they're tragic. I know they're common, they're so common that, who knows, they might even happen to you one day.'

To Emmy, Missy presented the image of manless perfection.

'Can we get down to the next book?'

'Sure, shit, whatever, shit, sure.'

But it was not easy as all that. Missy had let loose the Id, and it wasn't going to be so easy to allow it to slip back into the dark crevice from whence it had come.

Priya spoke up now — lovely, sunny Priya — suggesting helpfully that Missy 'say what the book is going to be so we can get it over with.' To Missy's explosion of protest, Priya countered that,

'Aline and Jennifer and Danielle will vote for whatever you want them to, Missy … '

Missy, mining a deep-core reserve of calm, asked, 'What is this, a mutiny?'

'I'm just telling it like it is,' said Priya.

'But it's not even true,' countered Missy. 'Aline and Jennifer and Danielle can vote however they wish, and besides, it's not my fault that our resident maverick, Runner Coghill, is missing today.'

Romy said, 'Runner Coghill is always missing on decision days. It's because she can't stand the Final Indulgence. She thinks it's stupid.'

Missy fixed Romy with a very frank look. 'Well, I don't have any sympathy for her then.'

'Missy, she just lost her sister.'

'What does that have to do with anything? Anyway, that was six months ago!'

'It's harder when it's your twin.'

'Oh, is it now?'

'Yes!'

'That's just a crutch.'

Missy did say those words: 'That's just a crutch.' It is recorded in the Book of Days. But she only said them because she didn't want to lose control of the argument, and that depended entirely on her belittling Runner's intentions. Romy was shocked and silenced by the monstrous assertion, and Missy's work was done.[10]

And so there followed a moment or two when it seemed like the dark cloud of the Lacuna Id had passed. Until Romy, moving on, suggested they take up *The White Bone*, by Barbara Gowdy, a book about elephants.

---

10 Also, for the record, a vote by Runner with Romy, Priya and Emmy against Missy, Aline, Jennifer and Danielle would bring about a tie. Since the deciding vote in a tie goes to the executive and Missy was the executive, the power came in the end right back around to her. This she knew, perfectly well.

This was unfortunate. Not only was Missy against reading a book about elephants or any other animals, but she was also, for the moment at least, against Romy. So in her argument against 'the elephant book,' she matter-of-factly revealed some private information about how Romy had become distraught over the deaths of some rabbits in *Watership Down*, a book she'd read outside the auspices of the club. The deaths in this elephant book, she pointed out, were much worse than the rabbit deaths: they were harrowing, terrible, horrible deaths, and the entire, like, herd was always aware of it. 'It's a really depressing book.'

'Wow, dead elephants,' said Romy, mortified by Missy's public revelations. Her eyes brimmed with tears and she wished that something would occur that might annihilate the memory of her previous suggestion.

And then something did. Miraculously, from the other end of the floor there came a most welcome interruption: a voice, high, piercing and clear: 'Either I'm delirious or the essence of my vulva is filling the warehouse!'

(!)

(Well, that's what she said!)

Runner would not have minded what we have written here. In fact she would have approved of our informing the reader that she had a great interest in gynecological terminology, specifically those words relating to the menstrual cycle. She was obsessed with the idea of the streamlined cycle among women who worked together in groups for any length of time. Her enthusiasm over such matters was embarrassing but also understandable, since her frailty was such that there was probably nothing much going on down there. She had told Romy once that she hadn't had any real activity since well before Ruby had died,[11] and even then there had never been much. More of a trickle than a torrent. For her, PMS meant paltry month's supply.

In other words, the scent of Runner's vulva was most assuredly not filling the warehouse, though the scent of her language surely was. Before we had a chance to turn around, she had already moved on to the dreaded question.

'How many have gotten their periods today?'

But then we saw. With Runner there was a man. A grown man. Neil was there too, but Neil was always there, by his sister's side. No one, not even Missy, would have invoked the no-boys rule against Neil. But this was different. There was a grown man, and he was holding Runner in his arms, as if he were a combat soldier. Either Runner was engaged in some kind of elaborate practical joke that would take the rest of the evening to unfold, or she was seriously hurt. The man had a kind of half-embarrassed, half-apologetic look on his face, which would have been a very satisfying expression to observe if we weren't all so totally freaked.

Beside the man there stood a chubby little rosy-cheeked girl who didn't look too interesting or too bright.[12] Except that she was carrying several slabs of stone, which looked to be interesting and so, arguably, endowed her with a veneer of the interesting. Although, on the other hand, they didn't appear to belong to her. She was carrying them cavalierly, like she wanted to drop them and have a cigarette.

Still, during the conflict that followed, this girl, with the self-consciousness of someone who was not accustomed to negotiating fragility, managed to lower the stack to the floor and allow the stones to slide away into a harmless little heap. We'd have expected her to let them drop and break into pieces. She looked the type. But there was some deep current of delicacy in this girl that we hadn't seen.

11 A lie. (Neil's note.)

12 Sorry, Anna.

'Ladies and ladies,' said Runner, now that the arms of the man had given her our undivided attention. 'I've come to propose a book.'

'You're late,' said Missy.

'That's a great leadership skill, Missy: you can tell the time.'

'That's how I know you're late.'

'But it doesn't matter because I'm hijacking the agenda. Neil, show them your rifle.'

Neil's eyes widened as he looked at Runner, and a very familiar she's-crazy expression flashed across his face. He didn't have a rifle. Still, Runner continued as if Neil had flourished a semi-automatic and sent a hail of bullets over our heads.[13]

'Now, there's no need to panic; if we keep our heads when all around us — '

'But you must know, Runner, darling,' interrupted Missy sweetly, 'that boys are not permitted to attend these meetings.'

'He can if he's got a rifle.' (Runner's baby poker face.)

'Runner, darling?' (Emmy, incredulous, her eyes stuck up inside her head.)

'I'm not talking about that boy.' (Missy, indicating the obvious and Neil.) 'I'm talking about that boy.' (Missy, indicating the boy in whose military arms Runner reclined.)

'This boy?' asked Runner, as if she were noticing him for the first time.

'Yes, that boy.'

Runner looked at the boy again. And then, as if she had only just recalled it, as if it were all slowly coming back to her, she explained that, had it not been (or, rather, had it NOT BEEN) for the assistance of this boy (i.e., THIS BOY), she would still be

13 The following was written in the Book of Days immediately under today's date: 'Salam Pax has not posted today regarding the situation in Baghdad. Why not? We can't help but fear the worst for this courageous bear of a man.' The authors of this account did not recognize the handwriting, but it has turned out to be from Aline, who managed to keep his obsession with the Iraq war and specifically the Baghdad Blogger a secret from everyone else in the Cabal.

lying in a pile of refuse on the first floor, having fallen through the ceiling, indicating the possibility that she had perhaps finally become too heavy for this world.

At the mention of Runner's surfeit of heaviness, Missy placed the tips of her thumb and forefinger on either side of the bridge of her nose, pressing hard in a believable display of martyrdom. Runner continued.

'He carried me here, and I have yet to hold up my end of the bargain, since I promised to blow him if he got me up all those stairs.'

Now we all had our faces in our hands. Even Priya. The boy, we think, would also have had his face in his hands, but for the matter that he had his hands full of Runner, so he had to content himself with casting a suffering look toward the chubby-cheeked girl who stood beside him.

The girl beside him, it should be noted, did not have her face in her hands either. She was looking almost amused behind her fulsome mug.

'Still,' Runner continued fearlessly, 'the boys aren't nearly as effective a hijacking tool as the Girl. Ladies and ladies, I present to you: the Girl.' And then, sotto voce, to the girl, 'I didn't get your name.'

The chubby[14] girl flashed a flicker of a smile, which passed as swiftly as a sparrow round a street corner, and replied too quietly for us to hear.

Runner continued. 'Anna. First order of business, and necessary for the historic tie-break between the two distinct factions of the Lacuna Cabal, is: Anna here must be received as a new member.'

After a pause, Missy inquired whether Runner had gone out of her mind. Runner ruminated on the question for a moment or two before Missy just said, 'No.' Runner asked if we could vote on it. 'No,' said Missy.

---

14 Sorry … sorry …

'Well, as it turns out, Missy,' said Runner, 'Anna owns the building we're standing in. So if this were the Notre Dame Cathedral — and Missy, I'm not suggesting that if this were the Notre Dame Cathedral you'd be the Hunchback of Notre Dame Cathedral — but if this were Notre Dame Cathedral, Anna here would be the bishop, not to mention a devoted supporter of my book proposal.'

Missy was looking flagrantly at her watch and not panicking.

'It's seven-thirty anyway. We can adjourn for now and meet somewhere else tomorrow. I will not tolerate this kind of mutinous — '

'Missy, I'm in the process of proposing a book.'

'You're in the process of conducting a MUTINY!'

'Outrageous!' said Runner with delight, as Missy continued.

'Proposing a book, any book, using threats, using coercion that undermines the sanctity of and that stamps and spits and trammels our constitution — you're … the Pony Palimpsest!

Now Runner was overjoyed. 'Don't you call me a Pony Palimpsest.'

The reader, like Priya, might turn to Romy and ask, 'What does it mean?' and be as unsatisfied as Priya by Romy's response: 'It means the gloves are coming off.'[15]

Missy continued to berate Runner in a manner that might require more footnotes.

'But I'm not sure you'll accept the book any other way!' protested Runner.

'I will not accept any book this way.'

'But you have to accept it whatever way will work!'

'What's the book?'

---

15 A palimpsest of course is a document that has been written over a pre-existing document, a holdover from the days before printers, when paper was precious and writing took a long time. So the image of a Pony Palimpsest, in the mind's eye of the members of the Lacuna Cabal, is a skittish young horse mucking up a pre-existing document, preferably printed on beautiful medieval parchment inscribed by monks. 'You are the Destroyer' would be a synonymous statement.

'That's the book!'

And Runner pointed to the heap of stones at Anna's feet.

What did we see? We saw a pile of stones covered with small notches, some kind of writing. If there was a palimpsest there, it was literature written over archaeology. Any pony prints in that hard clay would have been left thousands of years before it was ever dug up, baked and written on.

Still, impressive as the individual stones might have looked from an archaeological standpoint, there was nothing to suggest we were looking at a book.

Runner had anticipated our ambivalence.

'I assure you: it might appear cumbersome, but it's a real book.'

'Um,' said Missy, who never said 'um.' 'What's it called, Runner?'

Runner bit her lip. 'That's a matter of opinion.'

'Runner, I'm not going to choose a book that looks like that and has a title that is "a matter of opinion."'

'*He Who Saw Everything.* That's what it's called. It's Mesopotamian. It's pretty much the first book ever written. And if we are to hold on to our status as the premium book club, then we should be interested in reading the first book.'

There was a pause. And a sigh.

'I was going to propose *Possession.*'

'That book is fifteen years old!'

'Your book isn't even a book. It's a bunch of rocks.'

'And I'm willing to bet we've all read *Possession* already! Every single one of us!'

'Not as part of the group.'

(Aline and Romy agreed quietly that *Possession* was an amazing book.)

Runner shifted in Du's arms. 'I can't argue right now. I'm in pain.'

'Well, suffer,' said Missy and immediately regretted it, since it had become clear in that moment, to her as well as the rest of us, that Runner's leg was hanging strangely off the soldier boy's forearm. The truth was, Missy didn't want Runner to suffer anything but defeat, but it suddenly didn't sound like that. She was, for this rare moment, tongue-tied.

We were all looking at the leg. Aline finally ventured what she considered to be a reasonable argument, expressed in a tone of compromise: 'Runner, I'm just not sure the Lacuna Cabal should be reading, like, unpublished material — '

Unfortunately for Aline, this was the argument Runner had most hoped to receive. 'Just fuck off, Aline, okay? Why should the Lacuna Cabal be a carbon copy of other book clubs, reading only material that has been copied ad infinitum? I just want to try this book, okay? It's my most favourite book in the whole world and just because it's carved in stone and it's written in an ancient language and there's — '

An ancient language?

'— only one copy and it looks funny or weird or whatever, doesn't mean it sucks, Aline, okay? I bring the true experience of the prehistoric reader straight to your door. But if it sucks, we'll switch, okay? We'll just switch if it sucks we'll switch, okay? Okay?'

Aline had switched her attention entirely to her sneakers, which had both suddenly come untied, and she was carefully rethreading the laces so they would all be of equal length. Runner watched for a moment, fascinated by the totality of Aline's absorption in something so meaningless, and then she laid down her ace.

'You'll love it, I swear, on the grave of my sister who's added her weight to my own.'

This maxed everyone out. Suddenly the pressure was unbearable and we were all desperately in need of escape. Runner sensed it. She paused and let out some of the steam. A beat. A breath. Then she offered to read a bit — just the beginning, just the beginning of the story. *He Who Saw Everything*. Literature as escape. It was deftly done.

'Just let me read a bit. Just a little bit. A little bit of the first words that anyone ever thought to write. Just let me read a few of the first words of the first book. And then we can see if I'm crippled for life.'

We accepted it. It was allowed, though Missy was the only one who said, 'Okay.' There was no vote. Runner looked to Neil.

'Neil, put down your gun.'

Neil looked at Runner.

'Now get me the first stone.'

He did as he was told, as his sister spoke a brief editorial preface: 'There is, incidentally and for your information, Missy, a goddess at the top of the heap in this book who might sound familiar to you.'

Neil poked around the heap and finally pulled out one of the irregularly shaped stones. What indicated its status as first among the slabs was by no means apparent, though it was certainly believable that these stones were old. We could see that there was writing, if you could call it that, on both sides, and also that there were small patches of blank space, roughly textured, as if the text had been eroded. We, or some of us, found ourselves wondering how Runner would make the leap over these gaps, these … and the word occurred to Missy alone: these lacunae. With a sense of dread as pronounced as anything she felt about her own womb, Missy caught a flickering moment of import, as if something here were being fulfilled — a prophesy, like Herod first hearing of the baby Jesus.

What's more, Missy realized, whatever was to come, whatever this prophesied, she herself had been the inadvertent origin of it, the namer of it. She wished she knew what it would be, this gap that held the future. This perfectly obscure lacuna.

Had she named the Cabal for this?

Neil handed the stone up to Runner, who sat up a little in Du's arms and slowly began to translate the alleged first words of this alleged first book:

*In the very old days, back when years were long, like the first
year of a child's life, only this is the way things felt to adults
and children alike, because it was the beginning of the world,
the future was full of everything and there was nothing in the
past —*

'I wish I could feel that way,' murmured Emmy.

*— there was a time when everyone was happy in the beauti-
ful city of Uruk, with its strong walls and its proud goddess
Inanna —*

Neil interjected, as if on cue, 'Who was like Missy?'

*A lot like Missy: always ready to leave if she didn't get her
way, march straight out of the universe ...
    But like rabbits in the warrens of Watership Down —*

Romy forgot Emmy, for a moment.

— for a thousand years the people were happy.

And Runner paused and looked down at everyone from the
arms where she wanted to spend the rest of her life.

*Look at the walls of the city. They surround you. They were
built for you, to protect you from the rain. These walls were
built by one man, and he made them well, although in other
ways, all other ways, he was a tyrant, with a stride as long
as a league and eyes the rarest, rarest shade of ...*

She paused and paused some more. She would have paused
forever and Missy would have let her, quietly praying for everyone to remain silent. But Romy, with her weakness for colour,
took the bait.
    'Of what?'
    Runner smiled, as sweetly as anything Missy might venture.
    'Can we vote on this?'

Romy could not believe it. She had been manipulated once again into taking the rap for the whole group, only this time it was at the hands of someone she trusted probably more than anyone in the world: 'Runner Coghill!'

'I'm sorry, Romy. I do what I have to. Can we vote on this?'

Missy sat stoically with eyes downcast. Calmly demurred. 'I'm not ready to.'

Runner's turn to panic: 'I have to get to the hospital!'

'So we'll take you to the hospital.'

Romy demanded to know what was the colour of the tyrant's eyes, but Runner kept her focus on the Missy stop-gap.

'But you're interested.'

'Whatever.'

'You are!'

She was. It was obvious from the hesitation that followed. This proved enough for Romy, who was holding the Book of Days and so was entrusted with proclaiming the calls to vote. She shouted the motion as Neil quietly bent over his notebook and wrote, *On this very day …*

'The proposal is to do Runner's stone book and also to accept the new member Anna so we can keep coming back to this building. And also learn the colour of the tyrant's eyes. All in favour?'

Romy, Priya and Emmy all raised their hands with Runner, who almost broke her bearer's nose. Aline raised her hand, tipping the scales in Runner's favour. But then Missy raised her hand too, taking our breath (the breath of the two of us) away. And as our hands (the hands of the two of us) shot up as one, faster than the speed of thought (because it was true: we were curious too), Romy shouted in tones of joy, 'The motion carries us!'

And Missy, standing and pulling her fists to her hips in that exquisitely Wonder Woman pose: 'Carries. The motion carries, Romy.' Then, turning the full weight of her attention toward

Runner and her injury, she managed to take her into her arms without acknowledging the presence of the boy.

'Let's get you to the hospital, you stupid crazy girl.'

And she swept across the floor to the stairs, the rest of us following, like all her little dogs.

✛

Dumuzi would have been relieved to be alone again with Anna, were it not for the anxious revelation that Anna did not wish to be alone with Du. She was following the crowd and he couldn't shake the thought that it was mostly to get away from him.

In a flurry of semi-words that came out in an improbable series of W's and B's, he tried to inquire politely where she was going. He had longed for nothing more than to be alone with her again. Instead he got this: Anna, always moving on, always heading toward some future that did not include him, leaving him with his anxiety spikes. It was amazing how swiftly they came on. Just amazing.

'I just want to see her to the hospital,' said Anna, annoyed.

'But you don't even know her.'

'I don't know. She reminds me of … somebody.'

'Who?'

'Somebody.' And then she flushed with her subtle anger, wounding him, as Priya might say, with the lash of an eye: 'I don't know who. That's why I want to go. So that I can figure it out, you know?'

Dumuzi felt there was only one way now. 'But I thought you wanted to, uh.'

A glint came into Anna's eye, transforming all of Du's anxiety in an instant to basic, focused arousal. 'I thought you didn't.'

His flurry of B's and W's again.

Anna put him out of his misery. 'Meet me here tomorrow — next floor up.'

'When?'

'Same time.'

'Okay.'

'You sure?'

From Du a single W, half a B, and then a gesture of assent, and then Anna was gone. This was much more pleasant. An uncertain road, rife with even bigger spikes, land mines even. But for the moment everything was great. Sex. The feeling of possession. He tried to stop thinking, blowing out from puffed cheeks, blowing out again, waiting, allowing Anna to get far enough ahead of him that he couldn't catch up and tell her he'd changed his mind or have her tell him the same. Then he followed.

✝

And then Priya appeared briefly from the shadows. She came out and practiced a song she was working on. Lately, we're told, she was in the habit of imagining a small, modest audience for herself — far from a capacity crowd, but one that served as a buffer between the world and her fragile ego.

Priya gave a lot of thought to her audience. She considered that she should strive always to earn its loyalty, behave as if she were the hero of her own movie, acting selflessly and morally as events demanded. It's hard for us to take this idea seriously as we write about it. But don't we all walk around with private movies unspooling in our heads? Even we lovers of literature? Could we not go so far as to say such an imaginary scenario has, in truth, replaced the idea of God in the minds of most people? Or the gods? The Pantheon?

Perhaps this imaginary audience can even be credited with Priya's decision, made on this very evening (before she stopped playing and ran to catch up with the others), to start coming up with better songs — better than the shit she suddenly felt she'd been writing.

Chapter Four
Royal Vic

The Royal Victoria Hospital was, as always, Runner's destination of choice, despite or, we suppose, because of the stories of mould in the walls of the surgery rooms that got into the bodies of patients and killed them. Runner loved the Royal Vic because it was flagrantly, royally Scottish, designed in the Scottish Baronial style, which reminded her that she was herself Scottish, or at least part Scottish, that her surname came from a Scottish word for a Danish word for someone who wore hoods regularly, a practice she was planning to take up very soon. Perhaps, she thought, she would take up the wearing of hoods when the day came that her eyes got too big for her head, perhaps in this very hospital.

Runner loved the Royal Vic because it was nestled into the side of the mountain, perched in solitude on the slopes. The main building, she would explain to you, had been conceived and constructed as a fortress for the sick and injured among the city's poor, and so she loved too the fact that, since no one dared to use the main building for the low purpose of privately treating the wealthy, the Ross Pavilion had had to be built up and behind, shamefully sequestered. If the private patients wanted a building, she imagined some nineteenth-century hospital president saying, they could go and chip it out of solid rock.

There were, she felt, no new political arguments under the sun.

She loved the fact that nurses used to live in the attics. She wished she could have lived there with them, dressing up in their uniforms and shrieking with delight after hours, scaring the patients in the upper wards. She loved the fact that the Emergency was located in the back of the building, up the hill, and required a running start. And she loved that in winter some of the emergency exits led out into twenty-foot snowbanks on the side of the mountain. She wondered whether anyone had ever been buried in an avalanche because some jittery kitchen worker had pulled the fire alarm.

She liked the balconies a lot. She used to go out onto the balconies and wait for Neil, who liked the cafeteria on the third floor. And she would count the entrances and exits (seven main, plus a hundred and five extra) while he played with his food and looked at the people and wrote in his notebook.

She had spent a lot of time here. And so had Neil, to keep her company. Neil had taken up the writing of notebooks in this very hospital. He had purchased his very first notebook here in the gift shop. The only family he had ever known was his big sisters Runner and Ruby. And now there was only Runner.

And now, on March 18th, 2003, 10:14 p.m., he sat by the door to Runner's hospital room and ignored Runner's condition as best he could, filling his notebook, as he did most of the time, with disparate, irrelevant thoughts.

He wrote: *I like to do my homework in the dark with a headlamp behind the couch.*

Well, who wouldn't?

He wrote: *I like to roll change with a headlamp in the dark too.*

He wrote: *I've been making wallets and change purses out of duct tape.*

He wrote: *I've been studying origami.*

He wrote with an absorbed concentration that he knew could be shattered in a moment by Runner's voice, speaking up eventually from her bed when the parade of girls had passed and they were finally alone.

'So, Neil, we got them.'

'Yes.'

'We got them on our side. We get to read all ten tablets. Isn't that great?'

Neil put away his pen and nodded vigorously.

'It's a special, unique book,' she said, sighing happily and lying back into the pillow that was big for her head if not her eyes. 'We just have to do it in our special, unique way.'

Neil was full of ideas for how the Lacuna Cabal could do the book in a unique way, but before they could be expressed they were interrupted by the entrance of the new girl, Anna, bearing a glass of water.

Runner, he could tell, was thrilled that Anna had stuck around. Romy had wept and Priya, arriving late, had been spooked by the look of the place. Missy would have stayed but she said she had to go home and water her plants. Missy's father had purchased for her a greenhouse and filled it up with bonsai as something they could cultivate together. But really, she explained, it takes only one person to cultivate a greenhouse full of bonsai. It had seemed like an unnecessarily elaborate explanation. And then she had said how sorry she was about the broken leg and left.

Anna had hung back. Some spidey sense had prompted her to stay. She handed over the glass.

Runner said, 'You're left-handed.'

Anna said, 'Yes I am,' and blushed.

'How very interesting.'

'Why, um?'

'Some people say that all left-handed people are one of a pair of twins.'

'Oh, I'm not a — '

'They mean at the beginning, before you were born. So you might not know.'

'Oh.'

Runner said, 'So maybe you pine for a long-lost sister,' flirting. 'Other signs are crooked teeth and funny birthmarks.'

Anna's hand went instinctively up to her mouth, even as she smiled a little. 'I do have crooked teeth.'

Runner smiled back, sharing the secret, delighted. 'Yes, I know.'

Anna, covered her whole mouth now. 'My parents wouldn't let me get braces.'

'Oh no, don't worry,' said Runner. 'It's like a mole on the cheek: the flaw that accentuates beauty.'

Anna tried to think what else to say and then she said she had to go. She did like this girl, though. This girl was a crazy chick, but she was smart. She was smart with an open heart, and that made her do stupid things. Anna never did stupid things. Not deliberately, anyway. She was too careful for that.

'Will we see you tomorrow?' asked Runner, hopeful, failing always to keep her cards close to her chest. She meant for the book club. Anna had to remind herself. It wasn't her habit to hang around so much with women, preferring the company of men, but maybe now she'd take it up, maybe it would be good for her, like eating beets.

'Yeah, sure, yeah. It's fun,' she said, and realized it was true.

'Nice to meet you.'

'Nice to meet you too.'

Anna hesitated. She didn't know how you were supposed to address injured people. She ventured, 'I hope you feel better.'

Runner beamed. Anna backed out of the room, nearly tripping over Neil, and then was gone.

In a moment, Runner was sulking, taking pills she hated. Moments she enjoyed went by far too fleetingly, she thought, wishing she could find some way to stop time, instead of gulping pills like she was doing now.

Neil sat quietly for a while, distracting himself by folding a sheet of paper. Finally he spoke up. 'You scared her.'

'No I didn't,' said Runner, who felt like maybe she had, but it was okay. 'Not really.'

'You want her to be a twin too. Why?'

'No I don't, Neil! We were just talking.'

Neil crumpled up the half-formed origami. He was in a bad mood now. And jealous. 'How did you get osteoporosis and, and accident-proneness all of a sudden, anyway? You were the healthy one.'

That was true. Though Ruby had been plagued all her life by brittle bones and an overactive thyroid, Runner was athletic. It was often said that she chose the solo pursuit of track and field in order to spare Ruby the sight of her on the field as part of a close-knit scrum of girls. Later, the Lacuna Cabal was a team they could join together.

And Runner loved to swim, even as Ruby hated to put one single toe in the water. Runner had a swimmer's milky complexion — both healthy and ethereal — whereas Ruby's was merely ethereal. Of course, to say 'merely ethereal' is akin to saying 'merely angelic' or 'merely brilliant.' It is 'merely' the condition one aspires to before all others. That's what Runner must have believed. She must have idealized her sister's condition. Not 'healthy body/healthy mind,' but 'brittle body/aerial mind.'

It had been impressed upon Runner from an early age that, for her, a healthy lifestyle and diet would easily keep bone brittleness and other thyroid-related problems at bay. The only way she could ever develop such problems as plagued her twin would be by becoming full-blown self-destructive.

Which brings us back to Neil's persistent questioning.

'How come you fell through that floor?'

'You'll have to take that up with the floor.'

Neil paused to consider the option of becoming a structural engineer, rejecting it. He wasn't about to spend the rest of his life trying to protect Runner from harming herself. He might as well go in for mass-producing throw pillows; he might as well start telling jokes.

'We shouldn't call you Runner anymore — we should call you Hobbler or Limper or something.'

'Don't make fun of a cripple.'

'A fake cripple.'

To which her response was disappointingly mild. 'How dare you.'

'You were the healthy one.' Pleading a little.

Runner closed her eyes, which was, for Neil, the worst. Like a city blacking out. Like a fin whale heading for the beach. But he had to bear it. As she spoke, a familiar-sounding fatigue crept into her voice. But hadn't she slept for ten hours last night? This was not fair.

'Don't worry, Neil, it's nothing. It's just hard for twins to be separated, that's all.'

Here he was concerned for her very survival and she was bringing up the ineffable.

'I know,' a cappella. 'I know, I know, I know.' And then, after a brief pause: 'I know.'

'But don't worry. We're doing the book now. It's going to be fun and it has a happy ending.'

'But it's just a book.'

The desired effect. Runner's eyes snapped open. The room filled again with light, though Neil was going to have to pay a whopping bill.

'It is not just a book and you know it. How can you even say that? Anyway, people who live in glass houses should not throw stones.'

'What do you mean?'

'Well, don't you think maybe it's time to drop the bookish-kid act?'

'What?'

'The act. It's limiting for you. I mean, you know, Harry Potter is just a boy in a book. You're a real person. You should be Neil Coghill the Real McCoghill.'

He didn't have the slightest idea what she was talking about. If she wasn't aware that he had repudiated the entire genre of nine-to-twelve literature, then he wasn't about to tell her now. He'd let her figure it out on her own.

'Who gives a shit about Harry Potter?'

There was a brief pause.

'Well, why do you wear those empty frames?'

Oh. The empty frames. Did Harry Potter wear empty frames? Surely Harry Potter didn't have the imagination for that. Surely Harry Potter's glasses would be regular prescription glasses. But Runner suddenly lacked the discernment to credit such a distinction. Oh, she was sick all right.

'I've been wearing these since before Harry Potter.'

'Really?'

'Yes.' As witheringly as could be conveyed in a single syllable.

'Oh.'

Runner abruptly changed the subject. She decided to affect putting on makeup, something that annoyed Neil. Digging around inside the chaos of her shapeless purse: 'Well, anyway, we can talk about it tomorrow. You should get home.'

'I want to stay here.' This despite everything, despite the inevitability of Runner's closed eyes, despite the necessity for him to hide and sleep underneath her bed in order to escape the notice of the night nurses. But Runner would know it was cold under that bed without a blanket, since she desperately needed hers. And she would have thought that lying on hard floors under hospital beds for hours on end, even if he'd already done it hundreds of times before, would cause him to develop the weaknesses that had so disappointed Ruby (and her) as they grew. This could not happen to Neil. So she pulled out the next tools of alienation: mascara, blush.

'You can't stay here, it's a hospital; you should go home.'

'I want to stay here.'

(It's true, the mascara was difficult to endure, but 'Go home because it's a hospital'? How lame.)

What she really needed, if she was going to make up like she meant it, was a hand mirror. She dove into her purse again.

'No, you can't stay here. Really. You should go home.'

'I want to stay here.'

She found the hand mirror.

'No, you've got to go home.'

'I want to stay here.'

She looked into the hand mirror.

'You've got to go home, Neil.'

And then she saw Ruby. Her face. In the hand mirror. So close to her own. Pale. Lonely. Like she was at the bottom of a crevice, or in a bungalow on the other side of the city, forever. Like she had been left in a room somewhere hanging from a nail, where nobody would ever find her, her mouth open, dry, cracked. Ruby. She looked very weak. And her pupils moved strangely, like flies crawling on the surface of the mirror. How Runner had longed to see her again and now here she was and it was scary. Runner wondered what might be below the edge of the mirror's frame, whether Ruby was holding a book, whether she was opening it and closing it, endlessly, displaying pages of words to Runner that Runner could not read.

And Runner spoke too. Although she didn't know it, she said, 'That isn't really you,' and Neil had written that line in his notebook without any further comment. Now he was looking at his sister with two parts fear and one part accusation.

'What's with you?'

'Nothing, it's a — '

'A twin thing.'

'Yeah.'

Runner looked into Neil's living eyes and saw that he too was scared. She realized, not for the first time, why repressed people were heroic. Because they sought to spare such deadly emotions in others as wracked their own trembling frames. They shut down the bad feelings before they could spread, even if it cost them. She wished she had learned. But there had been no way of knowing, as one of a pair of twins, together the fifth and sixth of nine children, of which Neil was ninth and youngest, that she would come to be his sole guardian, looking at him like this from a hospital bed and trying to shut down her fear. There'd been no early training for her in the withholding of emotion. She had always considered it a virtue to let rip, and it was too late to stop now. The effort would kill her. There had to be some other way.

'Actually, Neil, you know what?'

'What?'

'I think I want to go home too.'

She was ready with a reason — she wanted to go over her notes for the next bit of the first tablet — but Neil didn't need a reason. He needed no excuse to transform a horror story into the story of a great adventure. Because he had sized up the task ahead and he knew they weren't just going to walk out of that hospital like normal people. Oh no. Runner was supposed to be sequestered for the night. Snug in. Battened down. No, they were going to make an escape. And if Neil could only get his hands on a wheelchair and a porter's uniform, then he would be the master of their escape. He would be the operator. The bus driver. The taxi man. The angel of endless stairwells. A crazy carpet over the cold reflecting ice sheet of death. The living saviour. Life itself.

Chapter Five
Ius Primae Noctis

'So I guess you're not in the track and field club anymore, Runner.'

Missy had lost no time. Late in the afternoon of the next day, while all was still quiet in Baghdad,[16] on the fifth floor of the Jacob Lighter Building, where it was minus five degrees Celsius and the only heat came from the blast of the blue flame-thrower, Missy was taking full advantage of Runner's patched-up, less dramatic state to reassert her authority over the group. Like everyone else, she had been relieved (greatly relieved) that Runner was okay, but, given that she was okay, there was no need to dwell on it any longer. Fresh tragedy had been averted. We could move on. For her part, Runner was attempting to augment the dramatic effects of the leg cast by eschewing crutches and limping around like a marionette.[17] She felt some anxiety about not having come up with a special way to tell the story, but remained confident, with her usual flung faith in serendipity, that an idea would present itself.

---

16 Even quieter, since everyone had purchased earplugs. According to the Baghdad Blogger (faithfully, if secretly, followed by our own Aline Irwin).

17 Did we mention she already had a cast on her right wrist? She broke it trying to break a fall and has consequently opted to just give into the fall when it happens, even if it turns out to be a drop of several feet as, for example, between the second and first floors of the Jacob Lighter Building. Apparently, she conducted mental exercises to ensure that, if she felt herself starting to go, she would close her eyes and fold her arms lightly across her chest. At least according to what she wrote in her diary.

Runner said, 'What makes everyone think they can be mean to a cripple just because that cripple is me?' and, 'Track and field doesn't interest me anymore.'

For the call of the role, taken by Romy, present were Romy, Priya, Runner (and Neil), Missy, Jennifer (ahem), Danielle (ahem), Aline and Emmy. All of us suitably bundled and sitting close to the heater, crisp on one side, cold on the other. Anna was, conspicuously if inevitably, absent. This was not surprising to anyone, though Missy sure pretended. 'Why isn't the bishop joining us?'

Runner (who, correction, was indeed surprised, and wounded) said, 'She said she would come.'

'She's late. Romy, could you mark that down, please.'

Romy was anxious to finally discover the colour of the tyrant's eyes. She started to ask but was interrupted by Missy.

'Did you mark it down?'

Romy marked it down. 'Are we starting?'

Missy said, 'Yes!' and then more gently, 'Yes.' It was occurring to her that she'd been horrible to Romy the day before, regarding the elephants and the rabbits. She cast an involuntary glance toward Neil, feeling like a bad example.

Aline put up his hand. 'I move that if we embrace the past then we must also embrace the future. I move that if we accept books of stone then we should be able to propose blogs. I'd like to propose a blog for our next book.'

Priya said, 'What's a blog?'

Missy said, 'Not now, Aline.'

Aline looked down at her shoes. She said, 'But it's a relevant blog.'

Priya said, 'What's a blog?!'

Missy said, 'Not now, Priya!'

And there was a swift flurry of whispering between Priya and Emmy, who, we presume, knew what a blog was.

Romy said, 'What colour were his eyes, Runner?'

Runner, who didn't know what a blog was either, looked genuinely confused for a moment, and then she understood. And then she seemed to grow two inches.

Cedar.

She gestured subtly to Neil, who brought her the first stone. And the room felt warmer. All discussion of blogs and the future was hushed. Those tablets emanated heat: they were clay, and had been written while still wet and then fired in a kiln to fix the words, and they release the heat again only when the words are lifted from them by the act of reading. This was a good book for winter. Even if our winter was almost through.

The king's eyes were the colour of lumber in the Forest of Cedar, uncut trees as plentiful as the stars. His eyes kept that colour to remind him to keep them fixed on this forest and the future.
But he was focused only on power's pleasure.

She looked around. Everyone was listening. Even Missy. She continued.

So let us not idolize him, for he was a tyrant.

Priya said, 'What was his name?'
Runner said, 'I'll get to that.'
Priya said, 'You're not going to give us a name?'
'You should assume he lived so long ago that names hadn't been invented yet.'
'Then why did you say you'd get to it?'
A time before names. It would have been easier to accept if we could have shaken the notion that Runner was hiding something. We knew it was well within storytellers' rights to withhold information — it's not supposed to turn them into suspicious characters. You can't arrest a storyteller for withholding information. Well, maybe in America.

✝

Anna had kept her promise, though not in a way that she knew. She was in the building. Up on the sixth floor. By the edge of the wall, near a window facing south, where the setting sun was still coming in. Up on a clean wide ledge. She'd remembered that it was insulated up there and so it was warmer than the fifth. She'd left a message for Du on his cell. She was reclining in her jeans and a big charcoal Colombian sweater that went practically to her knees, waiting for Du, wishing she'd thought to wear a bunch of skirts and heavy leggings instead of jeans. Near where she was, unseen in the shadows, was a big jagged hole in the floor[18] that opened through the ceiling across the room from where we Cabal girls were sitting. Perhaps someone had fallen through it at some point and that's why it was there, but nobody was going to fall through it today. Nothing would pass through it today but a gaze.

When Dumuzi finally appeared, late, he was exhausted and tried to explain that he'd been up all night, due to troubles with his roommate and best friend, Coby. By any standard other than Anna's, he'd been heroic. He'd even thought to bring a heavy-duty sleeping bag, all rolled up in a bundle, under his arm.

'Hey, uh, sorry I'm late. Coby — '

Anna said, 'You ready?'

Dumuzi said, 'I'm ready.'

Anna said, 'You sure?'

Dumuzi said, 'I'm sure.'

Anna said, 'You sure you're sure?'

Dumuzi, handing her money, said, 'I'm sure I'm sure I'm sure.'

Anna said, 'Okay, whatever.'

The jeans-over-the-hips manoeuvre is always difficult, and finishing the job is even harder when you're wearing thick socks.

---

18 Really, that building should have been condemned.

We know. We've all done this. It's difficult to be graceful, especially when it's so cold, though there's something in that lack of grace that's very satisfying to everyone involved. We can't speak for Anna on this, but we're pretty sure she would agree with us. Her feelings of regret with regard to the jeans had been, perhaps, too hasty. And the oversized charcoal sweater helped. A lot.

✝

We would like to affirm at this point, on behalf of all former members of the Lacuna Cabal Montreal Young Women's Book Club, that we are none of us voyeurs. We defy anyone to look away from what we saw.

That said, we can move on.

Runner was telling us the story of the beginning of the stone book. It concerned the particular manner in which the king expressed his tyranny. In those days there was no escaping the city, which was surrounded by farmland surrounded by wild land surrounded by mountains — semicircles of terrain moving out from the centre like rings in the water, as if some god had thrown a stone into the desert and watched the ripples of civilization form.

So the people, to be safe, were stuck in the city, Uruk, and the tyrant prevented them from living happily.

Behold the king, who thought because he shielded his people, he should reserve the right to be a bully and a rapist; for he had declared the Ius Primae Noctis, *his right to sleep with every bride before her husband on their wedding night.*

Aline shifted uncomfortably, unsure she wanted to participate in a story about a rapist. She looked at her shoes — a pair of Pro-Ked sneakers whose primary function was to moor her firmly in neutral territory between the sexes.

The people of Uruk knew they needed to find a hero to defy their king. A man of equal strength —

'Another man?'

It's the last man, I assure you.

'Yeah, right.'

'Aline, don't worry. They needed the second man to straighten out the first man. Without the second man, the king would have run rampant forever. Anyway, it's the last man of any substance to step into this story. May I continue, please?'

Runner waited for a moment to see if there would be any more argument, and then paused for another to translate the next phrase.

And that's when she heard a small cry from across the room and above, drawing her attention like a *deus ex machina*, gliding her across the room like someone not wearing an enormous cast, like someone about to get the answer to a question she didn't know she was asking. She was followed first by our eyes and then by ourselves, until we were all standing in the shadows at the far end of the room, silent as ghosts, looking up through the jagged break between the floors.

Runner, hushed and breathless: 'Now, what's going on up there is clearly consensual, but let's think of it as the illustrated version.'

The long heap of green sleeping bag had rolled over on the ledge and we could see quite clearly that it was Anna and the boy. Missy gasped like some other girl, and then blushed and growled at Runner: 'We're spying!'

'You'd have to agree it's more exciting than our *tableaux vivants*.'

It's true. The previous August, when everything was still good, we had tried to depict the futuristic three-way sex scene in *The Handmaid's Tale*, but it was so hilarious that nobody could pull it off for even five seconds without laughing. Aline, who was new then, kept firing the trios until she'd gone through the whole group and had to give up and draw a picture. We've tried to find the picture, to exhibit it in this account, but it has been suppressed or otherwise gone missing.

Now we were witnessing a real sex scene, and it wasn't funny at all. We were all flushed and quiet, and no one was laughing. This was drama. Runner was getting ideas. She attacked the narrative with renewed enthusiasm. She thrust a finger toward the gap, like a windsock, and whispered her shout:

There he is! The tyrant with the bride! His cheeks are stub-bled, like the bark of a tree. The hair on his head grows thick as laundry. He is tall! He is magnificent! He is terrible! He scours her body like a Brillo pad! With his zabb he digs from her most shadowy slopes —

'Zabb?' asked Missy, disgusted.
'It's from *The Arabian Nights*. Look it up.'
'Zabb,' confirmed Aline, also disgusted.

With his zabb he digs the well from which a mighty race will spring!

And then, after a great gulp of breath:

It is clear that the tyrant should be stopped! But will any one of us step forward?
    I think not.

Above us in the half-light, the bag was squirming. Missy looked like she had suddenly developed a migraine. She was, we found out recently, unpleasantly reminded of her own activities from the previous evening. After watering the bonsai, presumably.

Runner continued.

Here we are, the wedding guests, still standing around with wineglasses in our hands, and the king strides right in and deflowers the bride in front of everyone. No one can stop him. This is how our story begins: with a serial rapist king-ass bastard. And the city beholden to the gods to send a man of equal strength who will put an end to the tyranny of this king!

Though Romy had kept her hands clapped over Neil's eyes through the entire ordeal, he still somehow managed to write the following in his book: *Run, Runner, run.*

There was sound from above. Priya said, 'I think they're almost done.'

There was a big long sound from above. Romy said, 'I think they're done.'

They were done. A king's sexual proclivities had been amply displayed. Runner sat down on the floor, satisfied and spent. This was way better than their *tableaux vivants*, their re-enactments, their efforts to live within books. This was a book as the world. This was the world. It was like she was shooting a documentary for the exclusive viewing pleasure of the Lacuna Cabal. Like they were already descending the stairs into a bygone era, where a trap door in the floor would take them deeper still, into the Sumerian underworld.

Priya whispered, 'He's saying something. What's he saying?'

We struggled to listen, but all any of us could hear was the blow and the flame of the heater behind us. Missy managed to hold a disapproving expression steady on her face as she moved over and shut it off. And then rushed back.

He seemed to be worked up. Priya had the best ears, and translated for us.

' ... a friend of his ... he's saying ... naked ... he'd fallen. It was his fault, he's saying ... it's his fault ... Mud everywhere ... slippery ... uh, the floor ... his friend slipped and ... concussion ... hospital.'

It sounded to Runner like a broken stone of cuneiform. She whispered, 'Are you saying his friend was naked or he was naked?'

Priya said, 'I think he said his friend was naked.'

Runner said, 'Are you sure?'

Priya said, 'Maybe I didn't hear it right.'

Aline said, 'Sounds like he's crazy.'

Priya said, 'No, he was panicked or something. The guy up there said it was his fault.'

Runner was getting excited. 'Where is this naked falling man?'

Priya said, 'Hospital.'

Runner said, 'I have an idea.'

✢

MARCH 18TH (i.e., 'the night before'), 11:13 P.M.
Coby, Du's roommate, was a student with the Centre for Intelligent Machines at McGill University, where he was developing a project, under the supervision of both the Haptics Lab and the Ambulatory Robotics Department, to design and create little robots that become intelligent through exploration and a sense of touch.

Co-operation between the two departments was allowing Coby to create a little thing, programmed initially to seek cover and comfort in the shadows and avoid other ambulatory creatures (including humans). Technically it was known as a hexapod, but he called it the fitzbot.

Apparently, if you were to visit Du and Coby in their apartment during these days, you would be forgiven for assuming that they kept a budgie that roamed freely through their little rooms. There was a sign on the bathroom door that said 'Please Keep Closed' and another on the toilet that read 'Please Keep Lid Down.'

The truth, however, was that Coby had been working on a subroutine in the fitzbot's haptic system that would equip it with the ability to test the surface onto which it was about to step; if it was water, the fitzbot would discern it as a surface it should avoid. It could crawl across many different kinds of surfaces, but its circuitry would certainly be fried if it plunged into the water. Because Coby wasn't sure he had mastered this new subroutine, and because he considered the inside of the toilet to be a relatively dark place, and therefore much too attractive to the fitzbot, the seat, until further notice, was to be kept down — a challenge to which, by all reports, Dumuzi was not always equal.

Coby was possessed of a halting, unpleasant manner of speaking, like an overgrown four-year-old, which, along with his AI obsession, made him seem barely human. Or perhaps all too human. Among his colleagues, many of whom felt he behaved like a child in a playground of high-tech toys, there were those who claimed that he would notice a woman only if she had green skin and pointy ears. Come to think of it, he sounded like Captain Kirk, a fact he might have claimed was no coincidence, since they both hailed from the same neighbourhood in Montreal.[19]

Du and Coby lived together in an ugly old U-shaped, five-storey apartment building with a courtyard which, though it was barely there, glamourized the whole living experience for both of them. It was not the kind of Montreal apartment we adore, but the laundry lines that swept their laundry from window across to facing window, high above a courtyard, presented as exotic an image as Du and Coby had ever encountered, and they never stopped appreciating it. It allayed their constant disappointment in linoleum floors painted grey and ongoing battles with cockroaches.

The previous night, in the apartment, the toilet seat was up, although it would be hard to say who left it that way, and a fair portion of the grey linoleum in their living room was covered with mud and lumps of clay, as if someone had taken up sculpting. Coby was asleep among the lumps, sitting up, a look of pure

19 NDG.

sadness on his face, like he had nodded off after realizing how bad a sculptor he was. He was covered with mud. And he was naked. As if newly created by the gods.

Do you remember when we mentioned the backpack that Neil found back in Chapter One, left on the ground floor of the Lighter Building by Dumuzi, who, admittedly, was under a lot of pressure? Well, it might be important to mention at this point that the backpack contained the fitzbot, borrowed by Du, without Coby's permission, early that morning while Coby was still asleep, because he wanted to show it to Anna. At least this was what Du was now telling her in their post-coital moment on the sixth floor of the Lighter Building. By the time Du entered the apartment, there had been thirteen or fourteen hours of straight despair for Coby, who thought his intrepid creation had up and walked away.

It should also be mentioned here that Du had, over the course of an eventful day involving an encounter with the Lacuna Cabal Montreal Young Woman's Book Club, forgotten all about his borrowing. So when he entered the apartment late last night, he was presented with a bit of a shock.

'Coby?'

Nothing. Du thought for a moment that he should wade over to his room and close the door. But he'd have to take off his shoes first.

'Hey, Coby. Psst.'

Coby awoke.

'Huh?'

He didn't know where he was or how he looked.

'Coby, you fell asleep.'

'Oh. Yeah. Wow. Sleep. What a miracle. What time is it?'

'I don't know. I just got in. Coby, what's this mess?'

Coby looked but did not quite see. 'Ohhh,' he said. 'You see a mess? Did I make a mess?'

'Yes, Coby.'

'That's a shame really,' said Coby, struggling to keep his head on top of things. 'So you don't see ... you know ... even a little bit ... the ... the primordial sludge from which all life ... you know ... embarked in their little bobbing boats?'

'No, Coby, I don't.'

'No, huh?'

'No, Coby.'

'Oh.'

'Why?'

'Well, uh, because ... '

And then Coby began to weep. Something else Dumuzi had never seen before in this day full of firsts. Tears both lent grandeur to Coby and took it away.

'Oh, I think I've had too many behaviour-therapy classes. I think I've had too many artificial-intelligence classes. I think the whole Bottom-Up AI Race, the Intelligent Machines race is, uh, starting to get me down.'

Dumuzi wondered what the 'Bottom-Up AI Race' was.

'I miss my home, you know?' Coby went on. 'I miss my mum and dad.'

Dumuzi had never heard Coby mention his mum and dad.

'Coby, I've never even heard you mention your m— '

'No, I'm fucked up, Du. I mean, somebody stole my fitzbot.'

Suddenly comprehending everything, Du went straight into defensive-asshole mode, desperately but privately trying to determine what had become of his backpack. 'Is that what this is about?'

'No. I'm just saying, somebody stole the fitzbot sometime in the last twenty-four hours. It's worth one hundred percent of the practicum mark ... and I ... you know ... don't care!'

Coby was making an effort to change his own feelings in the matter, a tactic Du was familiar with from his relations with Anna. He was still trying to retrace his steps to locate the backpack. He asked Coby why he was covered in mud.

'Oh yeah,' said Coby, embarrassed. 'I tried to make a human the old-fashioned way, like, with a little bit of spit and some dirt, like, the way they did it in the Bible, you know? I knew it wouldn't work. I just thought it might be good for me to fail. Because we're not failing at these things anymore, we're really not. Over in the department? We're really not. But that doesn't mean we're gods!'

Coby had become impassioned, hell-bent on expounding on his proof that we are not gods: that he could not breathe life into his little golem. But Dumuzi wasn't paying attention. He'd been struck by a vision — so clear it turned his head — of a bulky back-pack, sitting on the ground in the middle of the room on the fifth floor of the Jacob Lighter Building. Just sitting there, all by itself. This would have been a great relief except it was also the moment when Coby rose up to declaim against the gods. The mud slid over the linoleum and out from under him, his feet went up in the air and he fell and hit his head on the corner of the coffee table, causing a concussion and a deep cut that released an impressive amount of blood.

It was not, as some have reported, a suicide attempt. Though it sure looked like one. As Du gathered him into his arms, digging for his cell, Coby spoke with sudden clarity.

'I'm sorry, Du.'

'Aw Jesus, Coby.'

'I'm such a fuck-up.'

The cell was out of power. Dumuzi tried to keep Coby's head up and covered as he dragged him over to the land line. 'Coby. I mean, good God, Coby.'

'I have to change my priorities.' Coby's voice was starting to slur. The phone was all the way over in Coby's room, on the bed. Du managed to get to it and punch the three buttons.

'Emergency, could I get an ambulance over to 5468 Avenue du Parc, apartment number 203, it's the second floor, the door's open, just come in. No, just come in. Just — please, he's, uh … he's hit his head and I … I don't, uh … I don't … Thank you.'

The sound of a dial tone. Du dropped the phone without turning it off, more than a little shaken. This was the second freak accident of the day.

'Okay, they're on their way, you'll be fine, you stupid, fucking … Why didn't you go for a run or … get some exercise, or … man, you're going to be okay, but … Coby, you've got to know: you don't have to change your priorities, because I took your fitzbot, I took your stupid … fitzbot to impress Anna. But I didn't even … take it out of my … fucking backpack, and truth be told, I forgot about it. But I know where it is. It hasn't flushed itself down any toilets and it hasn't even been turned on. I know exactly where it is but I forgot all about it because Anna started talking this line about selling her body to old men on Saint-Laurent for money and … and to me, even. And then we got interrupted by a whole bunch of girls and … and … with an intense little book club.'

Coby, woozy, forgiving: 'How can a book club be intense?'

'This one is, Coby.'

'Oh yeah?'

'Yeah.'

Du could hear the siren. Coby sounded like he was drifting off to sleep.

'Jesus, Du, you sound like you've had quite the day.'

'Yeah.'

'You're right, though. I should get more exercise.'

✛

And that's what happened to Du the night before, granting little sleep for his encounter with Anna. One wonders whether he and Coby passed Runner and Neil as they fled the hospital. Did Runner see the boy? Did the boy see Runner?

One wonders, too, whether their ambulance came anywhere near the dark alley where Missy was, we've recently learned, hiking up her skirt and silently praying to all the goddesses that the crackhead who was doing his business might incontrovertibly knock her up.

But they were coming from the north and Missy did all her prowling downtown. Apparently.

Back in the present, and the Lighter Building, Anna and Du were still post-coital and the sun had set, leaving the Lacuna Cabal standing below them in the dark. Runner explained to the others, but quietly, quietly, how we were going to use the man upstairs and his naked, wounded friend to do our *tableaux vivants* one better.

Missy said, 'But that boy isn't really our king.'

Runner said, 'Nobody was complaining a minute ago. We could do the whole book this way.'

Missy said, 'You mean spying?'

Emmy spoke up: 'At least spying is witnessing real life unmitigated by the pointless filter of fiction.'

Romy's mouth fell open.

Priya said, 'Wow.'

Missy said, 'The pointless — '

Emmy said, 'And with a little bit of life experience, maybe one of us will be able to write a book of our own one day.'

'Even if you're a nihilist?' asked Missy.

It was another deadlock. But then Fate played a hand in Runner's favour: there was a decisive movement from the bodies on the floor above. We looked. The boy had pulled himself naked out of the sleeping bag and stood up.

'You see?' said Runner. 'My point exactly. Totally unpredictable.'

And then he began to walk across the floor above, in the direction of the stairwell.

The Lacuna Cabal Montreal Young Women's Book Club, it must be said, panicked. And scattered. Even Romy, who had taken responsibility for covering the eyes of Neil. It wasn't easy, but she was a hefty girl, so she managed to lug him along safely as she went. It was thrilling and hilarious to all of us, even to Missy, who flushed almost orange.

Swiftly down the stairwell we went, all the way down, to the quiet anonymity of the third, second and first floors, and then out into the giddy freedom of the freezing Saint-Laurent night, just as the boy stepped through the door.

✝

Du appeared, wearing pants now, holding his clothes in a bunch in his arms. He was shivering from the cold but in too much of a hurry to dress properly, until he came to the forgotten backpack lying halfway across the fifth floor, where Neil had left it.

He picked it up and turned to show it to Anna, who was following close behind, annoyed that he'd roused her. She was carrying her clothes too, practically hopping, having opted to stay inside the bag, and had nearly tripped on the stairs. She was pissed. But Dumuzi didn't notice. He'd found his backpack and was happy.

'See?' he said. 'Here it is.' And he started to unzip it.

'Don't,' she said. 'I don't want to see that creepy thing.'

'Suit yourself. But this is the thing I was talking about. The fitzbot. This is where all the trouble started.'

But Anna wasn't listening.

'Oh shit.'

Dumuzi felt a familiar spike.

'Oh sorry, oh shit, I just remembered, there's a meeting of that ... '

'What?'

' ... that book club, and ... '

'Oh, that.' Du was relieved. He'd thought it was something important. Still, he watched amazed as Anna checked her watch. He'd never seen her look at her watch before. He didn't even know she had a watch.

'Ah shit,' she said, 'it was supposed to be a half an hour ago. Well, fuck. I don't care. They can just ... '

Du had often seen her talk herself out of being excited about something new. This time, despite himself, it made him sad. 'Where is it?' he asked.

'I am *such* a loser. Oh, she was such a nice kid. Oh fuck. Oh fuck. I don't care. I don't care.'

This was her mantra and he hated it.

'Well, where is it supposed to be? We could, uh, get you there in a — '

'Oh, I don't know. I don't know.'

She stopped suddenly. Realized.

'Right here.'

'Uh.'

'It was supposed to be right here.'

'Really?'

Anna looked around, confused. 'This is the fifth floor, right?'

Du looked around. 'Yeah.'

He was getting an unpleasant feeling. On the plus side, it wasn't spiky. It was the sense that he was being watched. He looked around again, and then again, continuing until he had practically done a pirouette. Anna was regarding him evenly.

'Du, obviously they're not here.'

'Yeah,' he said, spotting a jagged hole in the ceiling, with an unpleasant sensation. 'Yeah, I just ... I ... yeah. I thought they were for a second.'

Naked Anna or no, he wanted to get out of here. Anyway, it was freezing, his skin was turning blue. He jumped into his boots, his clothes, cast one last look about the room, avoided Anna's eye, and scooped up the backpack that had been lying at his feet.

'Right. I've got to get this to the — '

Chapter Six
Emmy's Skin

Back inside the Royal Victoria Hospital, Du was pleading with a nurse. 'Yes, I'm aware I can't see him right now, but I can't stress enough how important it is that he get this bag. Very, very important. It'll speed up his recovery by quantum — '

And the nurse said, 'It can wait until tomorrow.'

Then she was gone and Du was turning on his frustrated heels, when who should appear before him but the girl with the broken leg and the straw hair. Right there in front of him, half his height in the hallway. Meeting his eyes with that unnerving buggy gaze. He remembered the first time (just yesterday) he had to contend with that gaze, and the hair on the back of his neck stood as he recalled earlier in the evening, in the warehouse, when he felt like he was being watched, wondering whether it was this girl who was doing the watching.

'Hi,' she said.

'Oh,' said Dumuzi. 'Hi.'

'I got it,' she said, indicating her cast.

'Yeah.'

'The floors are solid here. It's safe.'

This made him even more nervous. She was engaging him.

'For what?'

'Not falling through.'

'Oh.' Oh.

Then she referred to the backpack and the disappeared nurse. 'She's a bitch. I know. That guy a friend of yours?'

'What guy?'

'With the bandaged head.'

'Yeah,' he said, wondering if he was giving anything away.

'Good friend?'

'What's it to you?'

'Why is he here?'

'Uh, he thinks too much.'

'Really. And therefore he is too much, he thinks?'

Uh. Duh. 'I guess so.'

'A ambulataster.'

'What's that.'

'"—aster" is a suffix that denotes poor quality. He walks, he falls down.'

'Yeah well,' he said, surprised by the suddenness of his rage. 'He's not a poor-quality kind of guy. I would prefer if you ... '

'He looks like a good guy.' The tone would be soothing if it didn't squeak.

'Sure,' said Dumuzi.

'What's his name?' she asked, coy.

'How come you want to know?'

'The world is a cold and lonely place.'

'Pl— uh.' This was not like any answer Du would expect in a million years. 'Uh. Coby.'

'Oh.'

She broke her gaze and turned to go. What a relief. Except, against his better judgment, he wasn't finished with her yet.

'Look, I don't even know if — I just don't want you to say those things to me anymore.'

'What things?' Her smile was appalling.

'You know ... the sex things. I don't know if you're joking or not. I don't care. I just ... They make me uncomfortable. I think I'm a different sort of person than you.'

'Okay.'

'Thank you.'

'No problem.'

That was a relief. He figured he should put in a plug for Anna. 'Uh … Did you, uh … By the way, did you guys have a meeting, like, this aftern— ?'

Her words came out like gibberish and it took a moment for him to decipher them: 'You mean when you were doing the dirty with Anna?'

He knew it. 'I knew it!'

And there was nothing to do but go, which he did, as fast as he could, Runner calling after him, gleeful, triumphant. 'You're a fine facsimile of our king! Though I don't even know your name!'

Runner, 2. Dumuzi, 0.

✛

And thus we leave Dumuzi, feeling violated and paranoid, to wander the streets of downtown Montreal, and stick with Runner in the nighttime hallways of the hospital. She shouldn't have been here, but she'd developed an expertise, through years of honing, in becoming invisible in this place. Emmy, of all the people to use for a secret weapon of feminine wiles, came out of a nearby ladies', where she'd been waiting with Neil while Runner gathered her information. Romy should have been with them, but she wasn't. No time to solve that puzzle. There were discussions to be had, there was information to be conveyed.

Emmy's skin was flushed to a dark crimson on the one hand and a blackish blue on the other. Red is a conspicuous colour in the daytime, but not so after dark. This is called the Purkinje shift phenomenon and explains why Runner couldn't tell how equal Emmy was to the task she was about to give her. Here in the shadows, her face was burning for only the darkness to see.

'His name is Coby,' said Runner, hoisting the first stone from her handbag.

'Okay,' said Emmy, who'd been apprised of her task and clutched the small scribbled square of paper that Runner had given her.

'Don't be so glum about it,' said Runner, still not perceiving the chemical explosions taking place across Emmy's skin. 'You're going into battle.'

'I'm all right,' said Emmy.

Runner was not convinced. 'You know, you don't have to do it if you don't want to.'

'No, no, I want to,' said Emmy, still tonelessly. 'It's, like, "Why not," I volunteered. "It's bigger than a book," et cetera.'

'If you're going to tame a wild man, you might find you need a little enthusiasm.'

"Oh, I don't know.'

'Emmy,' said Runner, 'you've got to forget that guy.'

The red brightened on Emmy's face for a moment, so that Runner almost saw the change. 'I'm not going to forget that guy, Runner. Nobody should be telling me to forget that guy.'

We have to say at this point that we don't give a shit about 'that guy' — his name or anything else about him. He contributes nothing to this story, other than the state in which he left Emmy, without which and without whom ... Emmy's feelings for him, on the other hand — with those we could have filled volumes, at least until they faded. Still, since this is sometimes a book about ghosts, we will briefly salute 'that guy,' wherever he may be, and stand with Emmy as she admonishes Runner for dissing him.

'Okay, okay,' said Runner, hating to be wrong.

'What's his name again?'

'Coby.'

'Oh God. Oh well. I'm numb anyway. That's why I agreed to do this.'

'I thought it was because you were a nihilist.'

'It is because I'm a nihilist.'

'Okay,' said Runner. 'But you might try out existentialism from time to time, to combat the nihilism. Like, we shall defend our island; we shall never give up! We shall never surrender! Know what I mean?'

Emmy was getting tired of this conversation. 'I'm not into existentialism, Runner.'

'Okay, it was just a suggestion.'

'Strictly nihilism,' she said as she opened the door to the dark room and slipped inside.

'Good for you.' Runner stood by the door listening for a moment, with Neil beside her. Then began to wonder what had become of Romy. She looked up the hall, as Neil followed her eyes. And then she looked down the hall, walked, listened at a door, walked a little further, listened again and opened up to Romy in a broom closet, listening the other way.

'Did I miss anything?' asked Romy, clearly hoping she hadn't, though she had.

Runner had no choice but to give her the straight goods: 'First sighting of our wild man,' she said, 'our man of mud, running through fields on the edge of the tilled land near Uruk, actually found in a hospital bed, convalescing with a bandaged head.'

'Oh,' said Romy. 'Has Emmy gone in?'

'She has,' said Runner solemnly.

Romy's face fell. 'I miss everything.'

Runner pulled out the stone again. She was getting tired and hungry — she could almost taste the Ichiban she'd share at home with Neil. But there was one more thing to do. Everyone was waiting at Hurley's Pub, listening to a poetry reading, waiting for the news of this adventure. There'd been some discussion as to whether they should come, but you can't cram a book club into a broom closet, so the compromise involved the scouts reporting back to Hurley's. Still, Runner didn't want to go there. She pulled out a notepad and a stub of a pencil and held them out to Romy.

'Will you remember to tell the others?'

Romy's eyes widened. She nodded and, hands shaking, took the implements.

'Word for word exactly?'

The pencil was poised, like a hummingbird. Romy could do no more than this. The runner becoming the race, the scribe becoming the scrawl.

'Plug your ears, Neil,' said Runner. 'This is dirty.'

Neil rolled his eyes and put his fingers into his ears. Runner began to translate the rest of the first stone for Romy:

A god touches down briefly and leaves a man behind when he goes, a man like we have never seen.

'Oh,' said Romy.

'Write it down quick.'

A man who runs with the deer and has never felt the weight of a single thought. He's strong, though. Strong as the king. Stronger maybe.

Now, I am a wise man. Do we agree on that?

'Yes,' said Romy, who did.

A wise man has sent a trapper to set a trap to catch the wild man down at the watering hole. A prostitute named … uh …

Runner couldn't remember. 'Shamhat,' said Neil, fingers still firmly in his ears.

'Shamhat,' Romy confirmed, and wrote it down.

Shamhat is a temple priestess, not our modern-style run-of-the-mill prostitute. Hers is a sacred task. Tonight she has been instructed to, uh …

'Do not recoil but take in his scent,' quoted Neil gravely, and Romy wrote it down.

'Isn't that disgusting?' said Runner, joyed and appalled. 'But what I want to know really is whether a woman's touch can really save a man or not. Speaking scientifically, I mean.'

Romy's pencil was hovering, a quavery look in her eye. 'Uh,' she said.

'What?'

'Emmy is the prostitute with the man?'

'The temple priestess.'

'Emmy is the temple priestess with the man?'

'Have you got a problem with that?'

'No.' (Lying.)

'Okay.' (Knows she's lying.)

'Can I be the trapper?'

Runner was doubtful. 'What would you do?'

'I'd wait by the door,' said Romy, decisively.

Runner was still not sure.

'It's a good task,' begged Romy.

It was.

'It's noble.' Romy was nothing if not noble.

'You won't forget to tell the others?'

'I won't.'

'Then go,' said Runner, and Romy went.

Runner stood with Neil in the dark hallway, suspended for a moment, and then she let out a breath. 'Let's go home,' she said. 'This story can hum along on its own for a while.'

✝

In the room it was dark but for a stripey glow near the window by which Emmy could discern a bed with a pair of knees bent up to make a tent under a blanket. From the other side of the room she could hear the snoring of an older man. The snoring was dreadful but it comforted her and she hoped it wouldn't fade during the task she was about to undertake. She hoped, too, that she'd be able to read the little slip of paper Runner had given her.

As she approached the bed, she wondered if she would see the boy's face, but the cones in her eyes sparked and gave her a splash of colour that blocked her view. For a moment she could see nothing and so stood still. If the snoring man were to have woken at that moment, he would have seen a tall wraith, poised and luminescent in the winter room.

Coby later wrote in his diary[20] that he experienced a documented phenomenon when Emmy climbed on top of him and he opened his near-sighted eyes. It is called Aubert's phenomenon, an optical illusion in which a bright vertical line in a dark room tilts to one side when an observer tilts his head to the opposite side.

In darkness, some surfaces produce shimmering effects, like mother of pearl. E's surface was one of those surfaces. She was bioluminescent: her skin produced its own light. This surprised me because most bioluminescent organisms live more than 1,200 metres below the surface of the ocean, where no light ever penetrates — similar to E's childhood, or the inside of her bedroom at night.

I was also surprised that Emmy was there at all, but that's another matter, and more private.

(Too private for his own diary?)

Coby didn't know what was happening to him in his hospital room. But we do. Emmy had crawled onto the bed and on top of Coby in the dark. She was tall in the glow of the blinds, and she woke him up by saying, 'Hello.'

'Hello,' he said, dreaming. In the dream there was a long, stripey, bioluminescent woman, with long hands and bendy fingers that get places, and a long body covered in a fitted stripey

---

20 Used with permission: Coby believes his story is of the cautionary variety and hopes our telling it might prevent something similar happening to you.

shirt, made from some cotton-lycra blend, that descended forever in the darkness below him, where he saw it coil away, and her long hands were sliding everywhere with their bendy fingers, along his body. He looked down and saw her mouth rise, and now his penis was painted like a barber's pole, unmistakable even in the shadows from the blinds, and he worried that he would never be able to change it back, as she slid up his body and placed herself there, her long face as high above him as a god's, and her mouth open.

'Oh, wait,' he said. 'I thought I was — '

'I get it,' she said, and slipped him inside her. They moved. He was barely aware of what was happening to him.

(Technically, he was being raped.)

(Technically …)

He said, 'Are you a therapist or something?'

'No, are you?'

'No. Are you a nurse?'

'No,' she said. 'You?'

'Oh no, I'm not a … So, are you a doctor?'

'No.'

'You don't think I'm a doctor.'

'No.'

'But you're another patient.'

The snoring still rose from the other bed. 'No,' she said.

'Oh,' he said. 'Uh. I give up.'

'Good,' she said. 'Don't look at me like that.'

'Like what?'

'Like you're circling the drain. You're not going to die.'

'I'm not?'

'To tell you the truth,' she said, moving skilfully, 'I'm here to make you whole.'

'Holy shit.'

'A god touches down and leaves a man as he goes,' she said. 'That's you.'

'Okay.'

Now she was reading out loud from a slip of paper, but he didn't care.

I have a crown, a throne, the truth, the loosening and binding of the hair, the quiver, the art of sex, the art of the hero, the art of power, the art of the craftsman, the art of war, morality, mortality and a pair of tired arms. Lots of other things too. I give them all to you. But there's a price.

'What's the price?' he asked.

The beasts you run with will flee when you come.

'I can live with that,' he said. 'I was never much of an outdoorsy — '

Oh yes you were. And they'll fear you. Since you have gained the civilized mind of a woman.

'Okay,' he said.

You're strong.
You're a cowboy in the city;
You'll do what I say.
You're handy.

'I'm handy.'

You don't think too much.

'That,' he said, 'will be a relief.'

☩

When these two rolled out of the hospital very early in the morning, they would disappear for just over a week and get to know one another in the unhurried if claustrophobic environment of Emmy's bare-walled box of a bachelor apartment, where they'd practically starve to death. She would have a lot of time to convince Coby through various entertaining and persuasive methods that Dumuzi was a tyrant and a serial rapist, that he preyed upon just-married women, citing an ancient, misogynist code called the *Ius Primae Noctis*, that it was Coby's responsibility to go after him, talk to him, fight him, stop him. It's amazing what a boy will come to believe when his head is full of sex and his heart is filled with Emmy. She would civilize him. This was the practical task Emmy had to accomplish in the coming week. Not that it was a small task by any means, but everything else was gravy. For her, it was shaping up to be what one might call a classic rebound. For Coby, it would be sex like he'd never felt it — that is, with someone other than a computer. For Coby, it would be a good measure of brainwashing.

But right now we're still in the darkness of the hospital room, with the light and the dark of the striping blinds. Coby's hair was slick with sweat. Emmy slid her hands into it and drew her face down, from on high, close to his. Imprinting.

And somewhere else in the city, Runner was laughing with Neil. They were on their way to listen to CDs and fall asleep. Over at Hurley's Pub, the rest of the girls were laughing too, though Missy was looking at her watch and thinking she had places to be. But it was the middle of the night. Who needs to be anywhere in the middle of the night?

And outside Coby's door, almost forgotten, Romy stood guard as the trapper in the story, listening. She'd forgotten to ask Runner how long this scene was supposed to go on. Later, on the door of the pub, the rest of us — sans Missy, gone to her errand — found a note in Romy's hand, fixed there with a piece of tape:

> *A prostitute waited for the wild man by the river. They went at it for seven days. I waited in the hallway. When the wild man tried to return to his friends? The wild beasts after that? They all ran away. Elephants, rabbits, everyone.*

Chapter Seven
Coby in Love

For the next six days there were no meetings of the Lacuna Cabal Book Club. Time had to be allowed for Emmy to do her work.

· Your two faithful narrators spent the week doing nothing worth mentioning. Neither did Romy. Runner reread *Don Quixote* in a new translation that hadn't been published yet. She got her hands on an advance copy by calling the publishers and telling them she only had six weeks to live and couldn't wait till November.

Neil spent his days after school trying to get access to the university's new x-660 laser cutter, so he might better score sheets of paper for origami. Being a ten-year-old in elementary school meant that he didn't get very far.

Priya spent the week at home, babysitting in the evenings and making some extra cash. One afternoon she went for a walk into Chinatown and saw a big crowd of people marching with signs down René Lévesque. Something about a war she'd heard a bit about on the radio.

Aline, from his flat near the Beaudry Metro (and we don't want to pretend we knew about this because we didn't have the first clue), followed the postings of the Baghdad Blogger, who seemed to be up at all hours. For a few days anyway. And then all postings from Baghdad suddenly stopped.

Missy (we didn't know about this either) woke up the first morning, alone and hungover, in a hotel room, the pleats of her skirt tacky and stained. Bastard had pulled out at the last minute. She wondered for a moment whether she should have volunteered to be the prostitute for the man in the hospital. But that would have represented a serious incursion of the Cabal into her private life. Anyway, what kind of world is this, she wondered, when you can't rely on a man to take advantage of a woman when she's drunk?

✛

In the hospital, Emmy had pre-empted Coby's worst fear about his first time. It had been engendered by a story he'd read when he was fifteen by a boozy Toronto author named Barry Callaghan, in which the male protagonist, unable to perform, had been thrown out of his paramour's apartment. And so, burdened by perpetual performance anxiety, Coby had come to curse books of a fictional or otherwise personal nature. He did not read them or even look at them; he did not want to have to deal with any new problems they might inspire in him. He banished them from his room. Only technical manuals graced his shelves. He had chosen Du as a roommate on the condition that Du had no books and would bring no books into the space they shared. Du had agreed and, as far as Coby knew, had never broken this rule.

But now everything had changed. Emmy had done away with all this fiction-hating angst by taking Coby's virginity while he was half asleep, in the dark, in a hospital bed, while he was recovering from a serious head wound. Not something Coby would have seen coming, and it certainly had never been depicted by Barry Callaghan.

Close up to Emmy, under a blanket, Coby thought the yellow and purple he saw in her skin were from bad acne. He didn't mind it, the acne. It endeared her to him. Who would be surprised by this? Love was something he'd never felt before. His parents had protected him from it, so that he'd get his work done and not squander his youth. All that meant was he postponed it till his twenties. But that's like getting the mumps as an adult. Bad mistake. Big disaster. It becomes a problem, not least because you remember it for the rest of your life.

Love is light. The sun sits there in the sky, like a balloon, though in reality it weighs more than anything else in our experience. Emmy's heaviness made Coby's love more substantial, made it sink down deeper, past his heart and even past his gut. The two of them laughed hysterically at cookies and they watched Bruce Lee movies. Coby had never seen a Bruce Lee movie. This was part of his training. In the deepest darkness of the night, Emmy would tell him she wanted him to own her, and he would puzzle over that as he lay awake beside her while she slept.[21] Is this what it was like to be a cowboy in the city? He did not think once about his fitzbot, which was best, since as far as he was concerned it was still lost. Dumuzi had taken to carrying it around with him, in the backpack, in case he spotted Coby, or Coby's ghost, wandering along the top of a park, monastery or prison wall, or a path on the mountain or through the Jean Talon Market, or down Saint-Laurent. Coby didn't care anymore whether the fitzbot was lost or found, for real this time. He felt freedom in occupying the role that had been tailored for him. Cowboy in the city. Not too bright but handy. Man of few words. Didn't think too much. Handy. Bit of a problem, that handy bit, but he'd get to it. He just had to buy some books. Some handbooks. Or handy-books, as the case may be. He had a plan to improve himself.

Somewhere in here, Coby noticed the strange shimmer of Emmy's skin in his peripheral vision and did not know what it was. Once he scratched her. 'Sorry,' he said. 'Don't say sorry,' she said firmly. 'But.' 'Don't say sorry.' Later she nicked him with her IUD. Vagina dentata. Blood everywhere. She said sorry a lot. He forgave her every time.

It's difficult to see the person you love, even when you think you're looking all the time. This is what Coby concluded when it occurred to him, three days after it had happened, that when he had scratched Emmy her blood had come out blue.

---

21 Or pretended to sleep, since she claimed she never slept in those days.

There was nothing to do except, when he had a private moment, look it up. The only explanation he could find was that it contained a copper atom, apparently, instead of the iron atom that usually makes blood red.

And so he asked himself, 'Is she human?'

(Six days, almost seven, and he still hadn't noticed the stripes.)

All he knew was that he loved her. And apparently he was going to have to prove it by picking a fight in a doorway with his only friend, Dumuzi.

✝

We might consider Du's position: Coby had disappeared from the hospital days earlier. Anna was not returning his phone calls. He was subsisting somewhere between limbo and hell, spike-points registering off the scale, so he took a lot of walks. Montreal can be a cold city, but it holds you tenderly in its embrace even as you move through it, and it provides you with company when you don't have any other.

Dumuzi did not read, but for one remarkable exception. When he was ten years old he had found, in a cardboard box at the end of a driveway, a purple hardback edition of a book of three thousand years of Chinese poetry, old, with an iffy spine and a worn-away gold-leaf title stamp. He had kept this book secret from everyone in his life, so there was no problem complying with Coby's stringent flat-mate conditions. He'd always kept it in an underwear drawer; he'd often considered abandoning it but never could.

He pulled it out when he was alone, and on rainy days, and mostly he would just open it up and look at its pages without reading. But this past winter it had held no solace for him, as the edge of Anna kept him burning from something that was not lit or even love. Only porn would give him comfort, though he hated it. It was, he felt, hurting him. Destroying his spine, leading him to wonder whether a grown man was just a head full of jizz.

But during the week of worrying about Coby, he found he couldn't do that either. Though Anna's lack of interest still tormented him, it didn't entirely remove his concern for the welfare of others. Well, certain others. Well, Coby. In these periods, he felt like Montreal could burn and he would wander through it without seeing, perhaps breathing in the pulverized dust of commuters without so much as a cough. And he did wander. Runner would attest to that. It was her responsibility to keep an eye on him, even if it was difficult for her to remain inconspicuous. He would wander and then return to his grey linoleum apartment and find himself reading the purple Chinese book again. Not just looking at it either, but really reading it. He read some poems in there by a woman from the ninth century who had been a prostitute and then a nun, and then a prostitute and a nun, all the while remaining a poet. This blew his mind, since he tended to think of writing, when he thought of it at all, as a profession that people took up and then gave up if it didn't work out for them. Her name was Yu Xuanji and she had died at twenty-five, younger than Du, after having been framed for the beating death of somebody else's servant. For several days Dumuzi was enthralled with her story. He wished he could show it to Anna.

She wrote, *in meeting and parting I lament the unsettled clouds.* She wrote, *Love and affection should learn from the river in flowing on and on.*[22] He didn't know what the first statement meant, but he sure agreed with the second.

---

22 Both quoted passages translated by Jan W. Walls, currently an SFU professor, who writes: 'My PhD dissertation was *The Poetry of Yu Xuanji*: a translation, annotation, commentary and critique, in which I translated all fifty of her extant poems. I never did get around to publishing them, but have had that in the back of my mind for over thirty years now. I can retire next summer, so maybe I'll have time to revisit her then. Right now I feel like I was just another in a string of unfaithful men in her life who took advantage of her, then abandoned her for their own career.'

Once, Yu Xuanji wrote a poem about a student, recently graduated, who had come to her while grieving the death of his young wife. The young man tells the courtesan that his wife's fragrance is still in the curtains of their home, that her words still pour out of her old pet parrot. He has left his home in teeth-grinding despair and come to bend the willow of Yu Xuanji. Yu Xuanji consoles the student by telling him his wife is an immortal who cannot stay long in the world of men. Coloured clouds, she says, are rare, and quickly pass. (Har har, thought Dumuzi, I wonder if Anna's saying something like that to some tearful man right now, even as she offers up her ass ...[23])

But the thought was fleeting. Du couldn't believe that he cared about Yu Xuanji, but he did. In the spikes-off-the-scale absence of Anna, he cared about Coby and a woman from ninth-century China.

(And he cared about Anna.)

And so he got hooked on old books. And eventually he started wondering about the one we were doing in the Lacuna Cabal. That's how it happened. He decided to look it up. Hadn't Anna been interested in that girls' club? Maybe he could find the book for her and help her get a leg up.

But what was he looking for? That girl with the broken leg and buggy eyes had called that book the oldest book — she had called it a stone book, or a book carved in stone. Surely, he thought, there had to be a translation. It wasn't just the new stuff that got worked over. Wait a minute. She'd even had a name for it. She'd called it something. What was it? *He Who Saw Everything.*

---

23 Sorry, Du.

PART TWO

Chapter Eight
The Epic of Gilgamesh

There's a gap at the beginning of Tablet Two, perhaps to allow for a little privacy for the lovers. Seven days' worth. But then 'the harlot,' as she is sometimes called, takes the wild man by the hand and leads him to the shepherd's camp. There she gives him some of her own clothes to wear, since he is naked, and then she leads him to Uruk, where, she says, he will find a place for himself among all those men and women of the city. Her tales of the king's abuses have offended his wild idealism. The next time the king tries to stride through the door of a bridal bedchamber, the wild man is there, blocking his path.

March 27th, 11:29 a.m., on the pedestrian walkway of Prince Arthur, just off Saint-Laurent. Specifically between Hôtel-de-Ville and Laval. Runner had wanted Anna to be there to make everything perfect, but there was no way of getting hold of her, and, besides, she was not reliably punctual. As it happened, through some miracle (Runner credited the goddess Inanna and a ghost that lived in her hand mirror), Anna did appear and fulfilled her role, all-unknowing, as if she had been scripted and directed.

And Emmy and Coby were there. Having emerged from seven days of carnal and caressive, if not connubial, bliss. Emmy had conspired to get them into the vicinity, under the auspices of 'going for breakfast.' Runner had promised that Dumuzi would run into them, coming around the corner of Hôtel-de-Ville, on his way back to Saint-Laurent and the half-hour walk home. She said he'd been tramping the same morning beat for days.

It was a sunny day, around four or five degrees. Still spring. The wind was coming from the southwest at about ten knots. Perhaps the reader is wondering how we could possibly know that. For the record, it was also the last time a meeting of the Lacuna Cabal would include the narrators of this account. For reasons that will soon become clear. So, if we have details that we wish to convey because we saw them with our own eyes or felt them with our own skin or measured them with our own instruments, well, that's our business. We were there. We, Jennifer and Danielle, were there, and anyone who thinks we're depicting the day with too much detail can just fuck off. After this, we'll be piecing things together entirely from the accounts of others. Maybe then we'll allow things to get a bit sketchy.

So.

Dumuzi was walking southwest on Prince Arthur. Anna was heading northeast, toward Saint-Denis. She says she was heading toward the Sherbrooke Metro to get to school after having an early lunch on Saint-Laurent. There was an anthropology class she was planning to attend and she didn't like to take the bus.

And we were there too, as we have said: the Lacuna Cabal Montreal Young Women's Book Club. Loitering on the cobblestones. The call of the role was made with everyone present, albeit in the background, out of the way, local colour. We'd been informed that the wild man was on the move.

Through the mysterious alchemy that allows people to perceive and shun desperate affection, Anna was not happy to see Dumuzi. Dumuzi, for his part, pretended this was not true, that he was simply misinterpreting the expression on her face a half a block away.

'Anna! Anna!'

She stopped — some might say froze — as he ran toward her.

(Runner, quietly, gave Priya a high five.)

'Hey, Du.'

'Hey.'

'What do you want?'

Du took it on the chin. Promptly ignored it. 'You know, that was great the other ... last week... I mean, I'm sorry you missed your meeting, and I'm sorry, too, if I was a little distracted ... or ... But it was great ... And ... um ...

Her face failing to brighten, he cut to the chase. 'I guess. I guess I just want to know ... '

'What.'

'Have you been out yet? Did you go out last night?'

They both understood what he meant by this, though their auditors had no idea. Anna hesitated, clearly contemplating the mind-your-own-business option.

'No, Du.'

'Oh.'

'Soon, though, so you've got to stop asking.'

Hopeful. 'What's stopping you?'

Brutal. 'I've still got money.'

Helpful. 'Why don't you sell that building? If you're going to need money?'

It was clear that Du had rehearsed this conversation. Selling the building, as far as he was concerned, was a very good option. Property values were finally starting to go up in Montreal. That's what he'd heard anyway. It was one of the reasons he and Coby were living in such a shitty apartment. Nice flats weren't as cheap to rent as they'd once been.

But Anna had agreed as a condition of inheritance to refrain from selling it until 2010, when, her shrewd grandfather had reasoned, prices would be so high that Anna would make enough off it to maintain a certain level of independence for the rest of her life. In the meantime there was a trust fund to pay the property taxes.

This was, however, nobody's business but hers. So when he asked her, she shrugged and said she didn't want to.

But Du was spiralling and getting dizzy. 'It makes me a little, uh, crazy.'

'You should think about something else.'

'I'm spending ... I spend my days looking for Coby, all over the place; he's been missing for a week now. And look ... ' He shrugged off the backpack. 'I've still got his science project, in case I run into him. And then at night I'm alone in my apartment. It's bad.'

Anna was looking for an opening in the crowd. Her eyes, he could not fail to notice, were devoid of all expression, her bee-stung lips unattractively askew, the lower one getting badly chewed. 'Don't think about it.'

'I try not to think about it.' He didn't tell her about the Chinese poetry. 'I keep thinking they're going to find him in the river.'

Fear of death was surely a subject that would capture her attention. It did. Anna said, 'Du.' She would have put her hand on his arm if she felt she could make such gestures to men without provoking a declaration. Still, Du spotted her weakness and was in there.

'But you really haven't tried anything yet?'

'No.'

(Blurting.) 'It's all I can do not to come around and, like, look in your window.'

This is the worst. The stalking boy. Anna had dealt with it before. 'Dumuzi,' she said, like she was talking to a patient.

'Just to see if you're alone.'

'You haven't done that.'

He paused. He had her full attention and wished he didn't ever have to respond, so she would remain forever in anticipation, even with that disapproving look.

'No.'

'You haven't done that, Dumuzi.'

'No, I haven't.'

'Because if you did, if you do, I swear to God ... '

'I got to the end of the block once.' And as her eyes widened bigger than the window behind her, 'My block, not ... *My* block.'

'God.'

Tears. 'It's just hard.'

And then came the miracle. At least as far as Du was concerned. Anna rummaged through her bag. 'I'll give you some Valium.'

There are those who, no matter how hard they try, simply cannot understand why Dumuzi could be so deeply moved by Anna's offer of Valium to help him deal with the anxiety and heartbreak of her rejection. To do so, one must embrace the mindset of a desperately unrequited lover.

'You do care about me,' he said.

Anna continued to rummage. Tears filled his eyes. She let the tone slip a little. 'Course I do.'

She'd found them. Two loose pills. She held out her hand, her lissome wrist sliding out from beneath her sweater. He reached out, past the pills in the palm, and took hold of her wrist. He was gentle. She tried to pull away and his grip tightened instinctively. He had not meant to do that. So much behaviour is instinct.

'Anna,' he said. And that was all he had time to say, since Coby chose that moment to spring.

✛

And this was also when we stopped being wallflowers. The sitting (standing, walking) session of the Lacuna Cabal was underway.

We noticed that Coby had the starting advantage over Du, having, 1. basically appeared out of nowhere, and, 2. been the subject of great concern for Dumuzi, who could not easily transform relief at finding a living Coby into a defensive posture.

'Leave the girl alone!' Coby shouted as they tumbled to the cobblestones.

Du's shock was such that he didn't fight back for several seconds. 'What are you doing?' he shouted as he fell onto his hands.

Coby called back, 'Getting some exercise,' keeping an attitude of levity and a fixed smile for Du and the passersby (who quickened their step). The truth is, he looked terrified. But he had promised Emmy he would do battle with his friend.

We have no way of knowing whether Emmy felt any pleasure in seeing her instructions carried out. As we've said before, she is not co-operating with this account and is apparently quite hostile toward it. She has her own account, a theatrical one (languishing unproduced), in which, for the scenic equivalent of this event, her character does not speak. Here, now, in our own account, she simply stands on the sidelines, mute and strangely burnished. You can't get beneath the surface of someone who won't be gotten beneath.

But back to the boys on the ground.

'Get off me!' Du shouted.

'Stay away from the girl.'

'What?'

'Leave her alone.'

'Coby, this is Anna. Anna. You remember Anna, she's an old — '

But Anna was mostly interested in saving her designer Valium, which had fallen in the scuffle.

Coby continued. 'Leave her alone.'

'Don't tell me what to do!'

Priya wanted to know why they were fighting. Romy tried to explain that it was the challenge to the *Ius Primae Noctis*, but she couldn't pronounce the words.

Missy asked, 'So this is Chapter Two?'

'Tablet Two,' corrected Runner.

Missy maintained her disapproving stance. 'Do these boys know they're advancing the story?'

'Not exactly,' said Runner.

'What do you mean, not exactly?'

'Well, not at all, really.'

Aline cut in. 'You managed to manipulate them.'

'Boys will be boys, I guess.' (Runner, pointedly, to Aline.)

Meaning boys want to be manipulated, thought Aline. Meaning these boys are still close enough to the age when men are fully grown but still impressionable enough that they'll do anything to avoid shame in the eyes of those around them.

We stood silently and watched the fight for a moment. Somebody asked whether we shouldn't be having a discussion. No one realized that Aline was already having one, all alone in her head. We noticed that Coby wasn't so much a fighter as a flailer. Dumuzi was starting to get the upper hand. Finally Missy stepped forward, concerned, taking charge.

'Okay, that's enough of that.'

Her tone was such that the boys stopped and looked up at her. Then Coby scrabbled away to find Emmy. Dumuzi looked around, wild-eyed. If there'd been any doubt about his awareness of our presence, it was now dispelled. He was seeing us for the first time. He looked like a trapped animal. 'What are all these girls doing here?'

Scandalously, Missy pointed to Runner. 'Ask her.'

Missy and the two of us stepped away from Runner, while Romy and Priya (and Neil) stepped in to block her from the boy. Aline was of two minds about it.

Dumuzi's eyes focused and he saw her. Runner Coghill. We believe he still did not know her name at this point. 'You,' he said, wrathfully. 'What are you doing here again?'

And then spluttered a little more before gesturing toward Coby. 'What did you tell him?'

Runner chose to say nothing. Neil, meanwhile, pulled out his book and spoke his own tablet translation as he wrote:

In the street a crowd had gathered. The wild man had blocked the door with his foot.

Du looked at the kid, uncomprehending. And then: 'Oh man, I just want to talk to Anna.'

Anna, hanging at the periphery, was trying to cut her losses and leave. She turned toward Runner in her halting, low alto.

'Hi. Sorry I ... missed the last meeting.'

Runner countered cheerfully. 'We're having another one.'

'Oh.' Anna was caught off-guard. 'When?'

'Right now.'

'Oh, I ... I have class.' She turned to Dumuzi. 'Du, I have to get to class.'

But Du wasn't listening. He was having his eureka moment.

'Oh. So. So this is your next meeting. This,' he repeated, wide-eyed, gesturing significantly around the scrum of girls, 'this is your next meeting. And you know what?' He was now addressing Runner: 'You're a crazy fucking girl, you know that?'

Missy had stopped feeling smug and was starting to worry for Runner's safety. But Runner didn't look worried at all. She met Dumuzi's gaze with an equal and opposing ferocity, intoning.

The virgin bride wiped his dirty mouth with the hem of her dress.

It was an unmistakably dirty-minded remark. 'I asked you not to do that.'

'I'm just quoting.'

Dumuzi knew. She was quoting from that book.

'Oh. Oh yeah,' he said. 'Oh yeah, you're quoting. You're quoting your crazy fucking book. You know, I know your book. I asked around about your book. Because I had to distract myself, you know, because my best friend had disappeared after he had a nervous breakdown and nearly died, and my girlfriend is off doing some kind of psychological preparation for prostitution.'

'I'm not your girlfriend, Du.' Anna interjecting (harshly).

But he continued, one might even say heroically. 'Not to mention that the Delta Dawn Society here has been following me. So I asked around — how hard can it be? What's an old book, I ask. Carved in stone, I ask. Maybe known as *He Who Saw Everything*. They tell me. Turns out it's got another name. It's called ... '

Runner, with growing horror, had seen where this was leading. 'Don't say it,' she said. 'You'll ruin it.'

'I don't care,' said Du, and he didn't. Runner was feeling truly sorry she had ever involved him. She watched as all her great works were tumbling around her. 'Look at me,' she cried desperately. 'I'm not trying to seduce you anymore.'

But Du was ascendant. Finally, something to distract him from Anna. Finally a situation where he could take control.

'Because you know, you all should know, it exists as a book, and she knows it, too, and there's nothing special about it because it's not just carved in stone anymore, it's even out in paperback for fuck's sake, in a Penguin edition, and there's another version translated by an American professor in a leather jacket who died in a motorcycle accident.[24] And another one by a guy who believes the pyramids in Egypt were built by amphibians from another planet.[25] There's even a version that includes the gaps from the broken stones, with a dot-dot-dot here and a dot-dot-dot there, and it's called ... '

Runner's final half-sentence attempt: 'I'm not trying to embarrass —'

'*The Epic of Fucking Gilgamesh.*'

'YOU ARE NO FUN!'

Now that the damage was done, Runner could switch from supplication to anger, a state with which she was far more comfortable.

---

24 John Gardner.

25 Robert Temple, whose version is titled *He Who Saw Everything*.

And yes, the damage was done. We were all trying to determine whether we'd heard that right. Romy first. 'Runner, *The Epic of Gilgamesh*?'

The fact is we all knew this book. It wasn't perfectly clear yet to most of us, due to the swirl of events, but we knew the book. And not through Runner's stone-book obfuscation of it either. We knew it through another book, a famous book, a favourite book. A fact that, it would seem, Runner did not wish for us to know.

She was smacking Dumuzi in the chest now. 'Ugh! Now they're going to be seduced by a ... ' Du didn't even seem to care. He was happy. He'd screwed things up for the Cabal and he felt happier than he had in months.

'Runner!' Romy protested again. Why didn't you tell us we — ?'

Runner continued to smack and to speak. 'They'll be seduced by a substitute when I — '

'Why didn't you say we were reading *The Epic of Gilgamesh*?'

' — seduced by a substitute when I hold the real thing in my arms!'

Romy was explaining it all now to the rest of us. 'That's the book with the line from the book by — '

Aline said, 'The line from what book?'

Romy corrected. 'No, it's the title of a book.'

Missy demanded, 'What book what book?'

Romy: '*In the Skin of a Lion*, by ... '

And we all gasped. All of us. Laugh if you like — consider this to be the satiric chapter of the book. Things will get serious again later. We all gasped.

Runner gestured to us mildly, contemptuously. 'See?' she said to Dumuzi. 'Do you see what you've done?' As the wind started to rise and a cloud covered up the sun.

The author of *In the Skin of a Lion* had been our begetter. Three years before, he had come and given an exclusive, spontaneous reading of new material, hurriedly arranged through a professor of Missy's who was a colleague of his. Missy had rounded up a few of her friends, including the two of us, and then rushed down to the coffee shop at Parc and Milton — the one where they don't play music so that serious people can work — and said to the three girls (Emmy Jones, Romy Childerhose and Ruby Coghill) who happened to be sitting at the big central table, 'Who wants to come hear a private reading by ... ?'

She didn't even know them. She just needed bodies. They didn't even know each other. But that's how the Lacuna Cabal was born. That reading, in a house around the corner from Open Da Night, from a novel that hasn't been published yet,[26] elevated us, even in our inception, from the echelons of the everyday, Oprah-style book club, and established us as a cabal. A secret society. Nobody could bring up this man's works within our ranks without causing some commotion, without his works taking precedence over any other works, even the oldest work in the world.

Aline said, 'Really? So that quote? That beautiful quote at the front of his book?'

Missy completed the thought: '... is from the stone book?'

Romy said, 'Totally.'

Priya said, 'You are fucking kidding me.'

We were all getting excited about our new book now. Runner rolled her eyes and protested: 'No, that quote is from a seriously out-of-date paperback translation by N. K. Sandars, in which she glossed over all the gaps and wouldn't allow — '

But we were trying to remember how the quote went. The quote that served as the epigraph.

Romy started: *And when you have gone to the earth ...*

Missy: *I will let my hair grow long for your sake ...*

Romy: *I will wander through the wilderness ...*

Jennifer and Danielle (!): *In the skin of a lion!*

Romy said, 'Runner, why didn't you say something?'

---

26 Correction: We're thrilled to report it's being published at the same time as this true history.

'Ugh!' said Runner. 'Because I was hoping that an ancient and noble book might succeed on its own merits rather than ... '

And then she switched her indignation to Dumuzi. The first writer of the first book in the history of human culture had just been upstaged by a contemporary Canadian author whose early novels had been written in short poetic fragments that, as far as she was concerned, barely held together, without the excuse of having been composed on crumbling stone, and who, she could never forget, had in his more recent work glamorized the life of a Second World War traitor. Runner was incensed and disgusted.

'Do you see what you've done?'

But Du was having none of it. 'What I've done?'

Runner chose a more dramatic word. 'What you've wrought?'

But Du was on a roll again. 'What I've done? You're ... You ... You're just ... psychotic. I should call the police and charge you with ... charge you with ... '

'What?' said Runner.

'Spying.'

'I didn't really spy.'

'Then what are all these girls doing here, huh? Peeping Tomboys, wrecking my life!'

Aline said, 'We're not tomboys.'

Romy, comforting: 'He's just being clever.'

Runner said, 'I didn't wreck your life.'

'Whatever,' said Du, who was only getting started. 'I've been reading this book. Yeah, I haven't come to the big famous quote but I've been reading it and it's a funny coincidence because here the wild man comes in from the cold and blocks Gilgamesh the king from coming to fuck some bride, and he — he — ' Here he went and grabbed Coby, who let him, and then let him go. 'Here's my old friend Coby who's been gone for a week, suddenly here. Here he is. I'm not stupid. They fight but their fight ends up in a draw and the two men all make friends. Gilgamesh and Enkidu.

What friends they become. Marching off on their big adventures because the king is all virtuous now. I'll tell you, though, we were already friends, this one and me. But we're not friends anymore. So if I'm right in thinking that this is your weird little retelling of the book of Gilga-fucking-mess — well, it isn't perfectly pristinely, like, accurate.'

Runner retorted somewhat weakly, 'You're not reading the correct version.'

Dumuzi turned to Anna and said, 'Come on, let's go.'

'No, Du,' said Anna.

'What?'

'I don't want you to come with me.'

'Anna, I just want to talk to you.'

'I have class.'

Du started to melt, giving Anna a moment to address Runner. 'I'm sorry,' she said. 'I'll come to the next one, I promise.'

'I just think you'd like it,' said Runner.

Anna turned back to Dumuzi. 'I have to go. You stay here. Be a king or something.'

That was very funny. This girl, we both thought (yes, us), could be very funny in her dry, expressionless way.

Du did not think it was funny. 'Be a king?'

'I'll pay you something,' she said.

'Very funny,' he said as she was leaving. 'I don't want to be a king.' And then, as she kept walking, west, he shouted after her, almost crying, 'I don't want to be a pimp!'

We really didn't get that one at all, but he was kind of crying now, so maybe it didn't matter.

'What's your name?' asked Runner, gently.

'Why should I tell you my fucking name?' asked Dumuzi, weeping.

'Because we know each other, sort of,' said Runner.

Du cursed under his breath for several more seconds, and then he said his name.

'Dumuzi,' said Runner, 'I don't want to embarrass you. I mean, God, men are so sensitive! But really, don't you want to know what it feels like to be a hero for a bunch of girls?'

'Yeah, right, I know what it feels like to be a dupe to a bunch of fucking girls.'

'So now you're in the loop. You know the story. You can tell it. You can be king. You can lead!'

Missy's ears twitched like a donkey's. 'Wait a minute.' Runner had anticipated and tried to deal with her succinctly. 'Missy, don't worry, it's not going to compromise your status as a ... '

Dumuzi was saying something like 'Why don't you act like a normal girl?' but Runner was giving her full attention to the Missy crisis now.

Missy said, 'You're not allowing him in.'

Runner said, 'Please, Missy, not now. I'll talk to you about it, but first I have to — '

'No boys,' Missy said evenly. 'No boys.'

'Pony Palimpsest!' shouted Runner.

'No, it's the bottom line! No boys! It's that simple!'

The wind was really blowing now. And the sun hadn't returned. For one chill moment it felt like the winter was returning. Runner started to plead: 'We don't have to make them full members ... '

Missy exploded. 'No! No boys! I don't want to hear bullshit. These boys are boys! We allow no boys!'

'We'll make them five-eighths members — they won't have a vote. We need them.'

To this day, we (Jennifer and Danielle) still do not quite understand why we needed them. Why we couldn't have done the book without them. But Missy did not argue. She just told Runner to suffer.

'What's the big deal anyway?' asked Runner.

'Boys make everything that much more serious,' said Missy.

118

'It takes both men and women to make the world,' countered Runner.

'This isn't the world!' shouted Missy. 'It's the Lacuna Cabal Montreal Young Women's Book Club!'

'Yeah, well,' said Runner, pulling out the not-so-secret weapon, 'maybe we have a man in the club already, eh, Missy?'

'What is that supposed to mean?' said Missy, shooting daggers.

'Oh, come on. You know what I'm talking about.'

Aline had already begun to drift self-consciously away from the scrum, but Romy grabbed her in a full-body, practically vaginal bear hug. Coby and Emmy had been hanging back, sitting on the curb; she'd been touching his face and closing her eyes and kissing him like they were somewhere else. But Coby now extricated himself and stepped forward, taking advantage of the silent power struggle that was playing out between Missy and Runner. Addressing Missy, he said, 'Ma'am. I just want to spend my days with Emmy R. Jones.'

Missy was taken aback, but not enough to stop being curious about the R. 'What's your middle name?' she asked Emmy.

'Rosalind,' said Emmy, which is true in both this fiction and the real world.

Missy was visibly impressed. She turned to Coby and, in her kindest tone, commanded, 'Don't call me ma'am.'

Coby continued undeterred. 'I just want to be … I don't want … ' (Coby was not accustomed to speaking in public, in front of strangers, in front of women, and he was certainly not accustomed to speaking about matters of his heart, which he had only recently discovered.) 'Yeah,' he said, confirming his thought before he made it, 'I want to be involved in something that's human, you know? I want to be a real boy, et cetera.'

'Okay, Pinocchio. Is this who I'm dealing with here?'

Missy had tried not to laugh even though she found this hilarious. But it stopped being funny a moment later when Coby dropped to his knees before her. Missy felt this gesture from the tips of her toes to the top of her head. To be a queen. Why not? Runner was thrilled. The fact is she never had any desire to thwart Missy's power. She sought only to manipulate it from the wings, like Machiavelli or Karl Rove. She turned and whispered to Romy that she had not expected this. Romy wanted to know whether it was part of the book. Runner said she would have to check.

Coby continued to articulate his position (or try). 'What it is,' he said, 'is this is the best thing that ever happened to me. Emmy and her … instructions.'

Missy was now at a loss for words.

'Essentially,' concluded Coby, 'I'm her slave.'

'Oh, please!' Dumuzi erupted.

But Missy had found herself overwhelmed with pity, and she still had command of the floor. 'His head is bandaged,' she said, with a sob in her voice.

'He's an ambulataster,' said Runner.

'What does that mean?' Missy asked.

'"—aster" is a suffix that denotes poor quality.'

If Du had heard, he would have objected. Coby didn't care. Missy glanced once more to the supplicant on the ground and turned back to Runner. 'You want to make him an honorary member?'

Runner had been speaking of Dumuzi, not Coby, but she considered this a minor detail. 'Half a member.'

Dumuzi crept up to Coby, trying to lead him away, but Coby wasn't going anywhere. The two of them were crouched there on the ground before us.

'Coby,' he said, trying not to look at anyone but his friend, 'you don't need this.'

'It's a new thing, Dumuzi.' Coby was anxious to explain himself. 'It's a richness. The spiral staircases have extra spirals these days. I see fresh snow, even when there's no snow, you know?'

'No, Coby, I don't, but … Do you have to be her slave?'

'I'm not really a slave.'

'You told her you're a slave.'

'No, I'm not really a slave. I mean, I've got free will, and … '

'Coby, what are you on?'

'Nothing. Nothing, Dumuzi. I just think this girl is going to save my life.'

'You remember you tried to make a little mud man a week ago, Coby. You remember you weren't wearing any clothes. You're not yourself.'

'I was trying to make a point.'

'You were trying to pass your course.'

'No, Du, I was — '

'You are so full of shit,' said Dumuzi, who was weeping now, feeling the full weight of responsibility for Coby's breakdown. We had to give this to him. He seemed to be in touch with his emotions. 'You were trying to make a point. What was your point? That we're not gods. But these girls aren't gods either … '

'I have to work on the little things that make me human. I was a skinny, geeky nerd before, and I didn't know anything about real life, Du.'

'You are still a skinny, geeky nerd, Coby!'

'I just want to live in my skin.'

Priya leaned over to Emmy and whispered, 'He loves you, hey?'

And Emmy the nihilist whispered back, 'Yeah, I know. We have to talk about that sometime.'

Both boys were weeping now and it came off very touching, down on the cobblestones like that. Runner crept up to Missy's elbow and said, 'Look at that, Missy. You've got the men on their knees. What are you going to do about it?'

And then Missy did something that rendered the Lacuna Cabal forever divided. The flaw of the tyrant lies in her feelings, or, more accurately, her sentiments. If you want to win an argument with Missy the tyrant, bring real tears to the table. It will work every time.

Missy pronounced, 'All in favour of allowing these two boys to be honorary members of the Lacuna Cabal, though only half-members and sharing a single vote between them, raise your hands.'

Du whispered to Coby, 'This is just so I can keep an eye on you.'

Missy had her hand raised. Runner joined her immediately. Priya raised her damned subversive hand too, no doubt wishing she'd been first (that anarchist). Aline, the fence-sitter, kept her arms crossed. Romy was not sure, but she eventually raised her hand too. Emmy, when she saw it was safe, raised her hand. And Aline finally, with an expression of defiance, offered a small gesture of assent. There were only two members of the Cabal who still held their hands resolutely at their sides, balled into fists. Jennifer and Danielle. Us. Me and Jennifer. Danielle and I. Looking at the two of us, Missy said, 'Opposed?' And then our hands went up. Oh yes they did. It was both our proudest and most shameful moment. The Lacuna Cabal Montreal Young Women's Book Club Shall Accept No Boys.

We would have followed Missy to the ends of the earth. And we know now that she did go there. To the ends of the earth. Don't say we didn't warn you. *The Epic of Gilgamesh* starts out as an adventure story about a hero and his friend, but then some-body dies and everything changes, and the hero goes on a long journey, in search of wisdom and the secret of eternal life. And the Lacuna Cabal Montreal Young Women's Book Club is noth-ing if not thorough. And Missy was its leader. She was its captain and its king. She gave us books and she gave us one another, and she was lonely and she was from Westmount. She could tap into the untold wealth of her father and bring the girls of the Lacuna Cabal wherever they wanted to go.

But not with us.

And don't say we didn't warn you.

We would have followed Missy. This book is our attempt to fulfill the tenets of our oath of loyalty, some years after the fact. We, her lackeys, meant to counterbalance the influence of the twins. We were the anti-twins, and so perhaps our time was in the past. It is said that the copiers of the Gilgamesh epic for the library of the great king of Nineveh, Ashurbanipal, were prisoners, who conducted most of their elegant work in chains. Perhaps we will achieve some elegance too.

Missy stamped her foot, or we thought she did anyway, though it might have been a car starting in the next street, and our hands jumped out of the air. But we had raised them. The motion had passed but we had voted against Missy, who had herself, in our opinion, voted against the integrity of the club. We were sacrificing ourselves for the honour and purity of the Lacuna Cabal.

Missy said, 'The motion carries.'

Priya corrected her, using Romy's finer phrase, 'The motion carries us.'

Neil pulled out his pen and wrote in his little book: *A feat that never was done in the land.*

And so, at noon on March 27th, 2003, Jennifer and Danielle took a one-week leave of absence from the Lacuna Cabal, due to strong feelings about the inclusion of boys.

(One single solitary week.)

(One measly week.)

(And so they missed Everything.)

(We missed everything.)

(And we mean Everything.)

Chapter Nine
The History of the Coghill Tablets

In our capacity as scriveners and narrators, archivists and engravers, we find we cannot tell the history of the Coghill Tablets without telling also the history of the Coghills themselves, their flaws and their virtues. The two stories are linked, sliding down the tree from where Neil perches at the top, past the brittle branches of Runner and Ruby and all their brothers and sisters, to pause at the sturdy limb that is the paterfamilias.

Runner and Ruby's father was, as you might imagine, bigger than life. Also, as you might imagine, he thought nothing of spinning tall tales, a fancy that did not always do no harm.

To motivate his children to do better in school, Harry Coghill amiably informed them that they all had a debilitating genetically transmitted aging disease that was incurable.

As a result of this, he told them, they were in more of a hurry than most of their peers to get educated, because once the brain's capacity began to diminish, there could be no more learning. What's more, he said, an active brain that made a go of it, cramming itself to the rafters with stimulation and information, stood a better chance of sticking it out and leading a normal life.

This, in any event, is what we've been told. It explains a lot.

In fact, it explains more. Harry Coghill's fictional diagnosis, designed to inspire and stimulate his children, became a self-fulfilling prophesy, with anxiety levels gunning Runner's and Ruby's already overactive thyroid glands into hyperdrive. It wasn't till later that it turned into full-blown Graves' Disease, with its symptoms of rabid heartbeat, muscle and bone weakness, tremors, blurred vision, high anxiety, fatigue, decrease in sex drive (which we can hardly believe — honestly, was Runner having us on the whole time?) and, finally, osteoporosis, emotional disorders and a weakening heart muscle leading to its failure. For the first sixteen years of their lives, the twins simply had undiagnosed hyperthyroidism. But then tragedy struck, which had a negative effect on their nervous systems.

He was an engineer, their father. When a builder wanted to build underneath a pre-existing structure, Harry Coghill was part of the team in charge of the stilts. He threaded the existing foundations with concrete beams, which themselves somehow got perched upon pillars that descended into the pit. Basically, he was a real-life Italo Calvino, travelling the world to build real-life invisible cities out of the air beneath buildings. That's the kind of father he was too, at least when he wasn't terrorizing his children with motivational tales of brain-atrophying diseases.

He worked with a group of intrepid stilt-building engineers called Quinn Dressel Associates until he gained enough mastery of the craft to leave the company and found a family business with his brother Dirk, called Coghill & Coghill, not long before the birth of Neil.

But we're getting ahead of ourselves, leaving untold the whole life he led before that. There are some who say that these two Catholic brothers had always been far too competitive with one another to ever properly collaborate on anything. Dirk was a year older and had set a tough pace, plowing through an engineering degree in only four years and then bouncing from university into one engineering firm after another. Harry was hot on his tail, though he did have to struggle a little harder and rarely slept during his early twenties. He was also a family man, having married his sophomore sweetheart and sired children at a pace that caused Presbyterians to blush when they observed the pack of them walking in the park. Harry found that even the mention of multiple offspring presented unpleasant sexual implications in traditional Ontario, so his family eventually pulled up their roots and moved to Montreal, that den of Catholic iniquity.

Despite all the dramatics, Harry kept pace with his elder brother. The two of them made every major purchase in their lives always within days of each other: first used car, first new car, first condo, first house, first bigger house. By the time Runner and Ruby were born, numbers seven and eight of what would be nine children, their uncle Dirk was living all alone in a house as big as theirs, in Toronto no less, with more space than he knew what to do with. And Harry had gotten the job with Quinn Dressel.

As a result of his family's size, however, cash flow was a bit of a problem for Harry. Despite his successes, he could afford few toys for his children. So when he happened upon the cuneiform stones on the job in Montreal in 1987, he must have quietly slipped them into his bag and brought them home to the seven-year-old twins.

So he was a thief, out of an impulse of fatherly love. No one came after him, it seems, for his thievery. He was home free. As it happens, the twins couldn't make heads or tails of the stones, but they kept them under their beds for nine years.

The job in Montreal in 1987 was the retention system that allowed for the integration of Montreal's 127-year-old Christ Church Cathedral into a major downtown 'redevelopment scheme.' Ahem. The task was to build a two-storey shopping mall and parking lot underneath the church without disturbing prayer services. Quinn Dressel Associates managed to put the whole neo-Gothic structure up on stilts that descended several hundred feet into the earth while leaving the regular church floor in place and confining all construction work to the basement and below.

The twins had never seen anything as deep as that pit below the church. Perhaps that's what originally gave them the idea that you could climb down to the underworld.

Pater Coghill must have found the ten cuneiform tablets somewhere in the lowest cellar of the cathedral, where much preliminary work had to be done to prepare for the underpinning and the pillars. Runner never did learn the full story, neither how her father had got his hands on them nor where they had originally come from. We have ourselves, therefore, taken the liberty of conducting some research and come up with the following timeline and scenario:

Ancient tablets like these were first discovered at a dig in Nineveh in 1852. The Christ Church Cathedral was built in Montreal in 1859. In 1872, an archaeologist named George Smith deciphered from them a story very much like the Biblical account of the flood and, after tearing off all his clothes with excitement while reading the account, presented his findings to the British Society of Biblical Archaeology . So our theory goes like this: an intrepid archaeological enthusiast who happened to also be the dean of the Christ Church Cathedral, having learned that physical evidence has been found to corroborate the Biblical story of the flood, travels to Baghdad and purchases ten beautiful tablets from an independent dealer who probably dug them up himself.

In developing this scenario, we've had help from Professor Bruce Kuklick of the University of Pennsylvania. He tells us this is the most likely scenario: 'It's less likely for them to have been transported by Western explorers, since there were so few of those and they were all well-known. But there were many travellers to the Orient at that time,' he writes, 'and a multitude of dealers there.'

We might as well include the professor's entire message. He knows more about this then we do.

Tablets of various kinds show up all over the U.S. university world by the early twentieth century. We have no idea how they got there, except to say collectors bought them from some dealer, or some enthusiast got them for his school. (The dealers got them from locals who just picked the stuff up from the sites and sold them off.) It is always possible, especially if you know the character of certain tablets, to say that they must ultimately have been dug up, say, at Nineveh (although saying when would be going too far), and made their way by various means to the church, in your case. The exquisite condition is not necessary for their importance or readability. They are remarkably durable in any event. Certainly, however, it would have been easy for someone on a dig to smuggle out some on his own. Does this help?

Yes, Professor, it most certainly does.

We wrote him back to ask how it was possible that so many of these stones lasted so long. 'Oh,' he replied, 'they are rarely pristine or whole, but they are lasting.'

When we read that, we took a deep breath. It seems that anyone who devotes her life to handling these artifacts is blessed. Even Runner, despite her tragedies. Even Runner's father. Even Anna. Even us.

The ten tablets, by the way, are each about seven inches high and six and a half inches wide. They contain six columns, three on each side, averaging about 265 lines of text for each stone.

✝

Runner's father, as we have seen, had somewhat of a flawed character. A great character, but a flawed character. Among his other qualities, there existed a penchant for boastfulness. It ran in the family. Runner had it too, in case the reader has failed to notice. Even Neil has it, a little bit. Tears spring to our eyes whenever he exhibits it, because we don't know whether, in the bosom of his large and living family, it was a quality that would have burgeoned or shrunk away. As it stands, his penchant represents the ghosts of the Coghills in the machine of Neil.

Uncle Dirk had it too. When Harry and Dirk joined forces in 1990 to form Coghill & Coghill Associates, they continued to put buildings up on stilts and create imaginary cities in the sky, reinforcing concrete and one another's brilliance. One might add that they reinforced one another's failings too, because they continued to boast of their achievements. Anything in the general vicinity of the Saint Lawrence River and the Golden Horseshoe was fair game to cajole family members, immediate and extended, to tour and to toast their pillared feat.

The guard dog for a lumber company, a family business, in Brantford, Ontario, had died of old age. After the family had finished their grieving, they used the death of the dog as incentive to move the storage for the lumber company from a fenced-in area behind the building to a large area directly underneath the offices, the size of a city block. This so they would not have to purchase another guard dog and grieve its passing when it, too, died.

It was a particularly complex engineering feat, the underpinning, due to the questionable stability of the building's foundation, so both brothers were involved equally in the installation and excavation. Both of them felt the job was notable mostly because the building they were preserving was, as far as they were concerned, a piece of clapboard trash, and the pillars, the caissons and the beams were themselves more valuable than the structure they were holding up. Still, they completed the job and, before the bulldozers moved in to begin construction beneath, they invited a whole collection of uncles and aunts and cousins and grandparents and brothers and sisters and nieces and nephews and children to survey their work, to experience this unique display of the underside of life, a building from below.

When the feat suddenly displayed its flaw.

The reader does not know any of these people, except the father, and so we will not dwell on the details of this tragedy. We didn't know any of them either. On the day in question, it had been decided that Runner and Ruby would not be taken out of school, back home in Montreal, due to the scheduling of a test in their Modern History course, specifically about Churchill and the Second World War, a subject particularly beloved of the twins. Neil, who did not relish car rides, had been left with a babysitter. They were the youngest in a family of nine children, covering an eighteen-year spread. By the middle of the day all the rest were gone.

Included among the dead were six children we have not mentioned anywhere in this account. We trust Neil will forgive us for not telling their stories, but there is only so much investment we can allow ourselves in the lives of those we never knew.

We know, we know. It's terrible and tragic and colourful. It's a freak show. But it's also true.

It's also too bad that lumber-business family couldn't have just gotten another dog.

✛

Runner and Ruby were sixteen years old when their family died. Neil was three. All they had to recall their parents and siblings was the life insurance, two cars they couldn't drive and a house in a suburban neighbourhood they had already begun to despise. And the ten stones in cuneiform under their beds, which had been ignored in the nine years they'd had them. The secret gift from their father.

And so they set out to learn how to read them.

Runner dropped out of school and started signing her name Runner Ruby Coghill, while Ruby stayed in school and started signing her name Ruby Runner Coghill. Each had chosen the other's first name at confirmation, despite the fact that there were no saints named for either of them. Still, they were allowed, and so, in signing one another's names, they weren't doing anything illegal. Just confusing.

They began to attend school on alternate days, as the same person, while the other stayed home to look after Neil. They got all the way through high school and university this way. University was much easier, since they were known from the start as a single individual and weren't always bearing the celebrity weight of an exotic tragedy.

Runner eventually began to wonder whether the strategy hadn't been another Coghillian self-fulfilling prophesy.

But that's later. We're still revelling in the home they made. They sold their house in the suburbs and purchased a flat in Old Montreal. Money didn't always flow freely, due to prescription costs. So a time came when the twins opted to drop the medicated aspect of things. Runner, who, as Neil has previously mentioned in this account, was the healthier one, began to attend appointments for both of them, and soon the doctors stopped demanding visits altogether.

And they learned cuneiform. They read the stories from the Coghill Tablets to one another until every one of its adventures and notches and grooves were written on their tongues, and even then they did not stop. They wondered how a piece of text written six thousand years ago could speak so eloquently to them about their own loss and grief, until eventually they stopped wondering and accepted that it was so.

It was also through the Coghill Tablets that Neil received the bulk of his education, learning about math, astronomy, friendship, sex, the features of the earth's crust, the vastness of the ocean, injustice, the responsibilities of leadership, the love of his sisters, and the fear, and the overcoming of the fear, of death. Runner and Ruby assured him that he must not think it contained lessons in the differences between the characters of men and women, since that was something, they said, that had changed a lot in modern times. This aspect of the epic, with its prostitute-priestesses, its violent and lascivious goddesses, was something that should be viewed by Neil with skepticism, at least until some later date when he'd be mature enough to be entertained by it.

Runner and Ruby found other stories in the library — most notably a story of the great goddess Inanna travelling to the underworld and living to see another day. Hers was the earliest-known story of death and resurrection. But we'll get to it in due time. Suffice it to say, it was a secondary story the twins kept to themselves and did not share with Neil. The story from the tablets was the one they all learned together.

Neil, it must be said, lived the most enviable of lives through this period. Under the tutelage of his sisters, he led the life of someone who must be shown all that he has to gain before he has a chance to realize everything he's lost. Can you imagine your entire life consisting of two identical twin sisters, thirteen years your senior, revolving like satellites around you and your pleasure? He barely remembered his parents and did not care to. He wandered his young days over the cobblestones of Old Montreal and the waterfront, and spent so much time observing the ships in the docks that he devised secret means of boarding them. He became a creature of the river. For a long time his life was the greatest. But then Ruby died, and the story of Inanna's descent to the underworld became, in the mind of his surviving sister, ascendant.

Chapter Ten
Notre-Dame-des-Neiges

Out of the shadows again, this time on a grassy bit of the long northern slope of the mountain, half an hour early for the next session of the Lacuna Cabal, on a day that didn't require much more than a light wool sweater, came Priya Underhay, in a big coat, addressing her imaginary audience — itself comprised of a pantheon of characters from across the cultural spectrum of her own aimless reading: there was the Norse goddess Freya, standing by a tombstone with her falcon coat; there were two or three roadside Ganeshes, bundled up with sticks and rags, conjured from several postcard photographs sent graciously in response to Priya's fan mail by a favourite author; there was Anne Carson's Geryon, shy and red and not really like a monster at all but more of a person. And, lumbering in the background, appropriately embarrassed, was Marian Engel's flea-bitten bear, which had followed Priya around like a ghost since she read the book at sixteen and it instigated a combined but hardly discussable sexual/literary awakening. Any time Priya wondered aloud how she could have found herself part of a young woman's book club, she remembered the bear with his long illiterate tongue and fell silent.

Our uninspired songwriter had come early to play an uninspired song or two and also to ask her outdoor audience if they could see the future. If they were gods, she reasoned, then they could see the future; but if they were merely an audience, then, like any other audience, they didn't know anything, no more than Priya herself. Even the reader of this book, sitting quietly by, has an advantage over Priya's imaginary pantheon of an audience: the reader can always flip ahead. Time is represented only by the numbers at the bottom of the pages. Priya's pantheon, on the other hand, divine or no, is stuck following Priya, all the way through the story, from start to finish. So it seems we can all agree the reader is better off than an imaginary audience.

But here we are speaking to our very own pantheon, when we're supposed to be depicting Priya's. And it's too late for such talk, since the others had begun to show up. Suffice it to say Priya was wondering about the future because she'd had a premonition, like the witch she was, that something bad was going to happen.

✝

MARCH 29TH, 1:06 P.M. Thomas D'Arcy McGee Mausoleum, Notre-Dame-des-Neiges Cemetery.

We would like to think that the Lacuna Cabal chose to hold the next sitting session here because they were in mourning for the loss of certain members.

Since, by the way, we two humble narrators are no longer present for any of the events to be depicted, it should be noted that everything must be put together through interview and reconstruction. Rather than peppering our narrative with phrases like 'by all reports' and 'it was alleged' and 'Priya told us later what went through her head as follows,' we have opted instead to adopt the omniscient voice. It's really the only thing we have going for us at this point.

The Cabal was congregating on the hillside on top of D'Arcy McGee not because he was a father of Confederation who was later assassinated by one of his former fellow Fenians for turning coat, allegedly, but rather because there was a large patch of grass up there, unobstructed by tombstones.

At the entrance to the cemetery, on this warm spring day, Du caught the scent of curry in the air. He walked up the hill, past the empty field with its lone tree, past the new stones and the blank stones, past the big mausoleum. He wondered whether Coby would be there, since he'd still not been home in the two days since they'd cried together on the cobblestones of Prince Arthur.

It was a warm day, but colder in the cemetery. Du walked past the chapel, past a stone that displayed the names of a number of Chapdelaines, none of which was Maria, past a stone called 'Parent' and a stone called 'Forget,' past a sixty-something man in a fine camel's-hair overcoat who was down on his knees, digging with his bare hands in front of a stone. He had gotten about four inches down.

Du walked past a mottled white stone for Maggie, died aged twenty years on the nineteenth of September 1871, and arrived at the grave of Thomas D'Arcy McGee, represented by a metal door fixed into the side of a hill, with a little chimney on top poking out of the grass. It emitted no smoke and perhaps was meant to let a bit of air in there. Gathered around it were the female forces of Du's newfound torment, and Coby. Backhoes had been foraging in the area, spring-cleaning the cemetery. Runner had already picked through one of the many nearby piles of dirt and was employing a yellowing tibia as a walking stick. 'It's in much better shape than either of mine,' she said.

Du was greeted with a paper hat. Priya had made them for both boys in order to reflect their remedial status as inaugural male members. An admittedly mild hazing, but it served.

The hats looked like this:

for Coby, and this:

for Du, and they wimpled in the slight breeze but stayed on their heads.

Coby was embarrassed to wear his hat at first, but Emmy didn't seem to object, so he opted to accept it by pretending it wasn't there. She rewarded him for his indulgence by paying attention to him, going so far as to pass notes back and forth, even though he sat separately in the grass with Du. To prevent her notes from blowing away, she wrapped them around little pebbles and threw them at his head.

Despite appearances, it was no paradise between Coby and Emmy. She had already had a dream in which the two of them were locked into a dungeon together and were waiting for someone to come and torture them. Coby, doomful optimist that he was, had been touched by the dream because he'd been right down there with her.

Also, Coby had finally started to notice the stripes, and if we know Emmy, then we know that this would have indicated to her that he was getting too close. For the previous couple of days, Emmy had been blue, both colours equally blue, and she didn't have the clothing schemes to offset such a monotone effect. She felt vulnerable and would have preferred to be alone, but it's not so easy to get rid of the guy you've spent the last 216 hours with. She found herself longing wistfully for her former days of bitter heartbreak and loneliness. Still, for the time being, no matter what she might have thought, there was nothing to be done: her flesh still sought that contact.

Emmy had been infected, it turned out, by an iridovirus, which had formed crystalline structures inside the tissue of her skin, allowing it to glow blue and blue alone. She didn't seem to think there was anything wrong, despite her hypochondriac tendencies, and it took much scanning and scheming and, finally, searching the Net (Google search: 'Blue') to lead Coby to the conclusion that Emmy had been infected with a condition that normally appeared only in wood lice — that killed wood lice — and this condition, if left untreated, would cause her to expire in a matter of days. When he told her this, calling in his firmest voice from the computer, he noticed in very short order that the room had become suffused with a strong ammonia smell. He turned and saw Emmy crumpled on the floor in a dead faint.

It turned out he just had to sprinkle her with salt, and everything was back to normal in a few hours.

Still, it was no paradise.

But you couldn't have said that to Romy. For Romy, the whole situation between E and C had become intolerable. It had been bad enough to endure the scene behind the door in the hospital, followed by the solid week of rumours. Now they were all expected to sit together on top of D'Arcy McGee's tomb and be part of the same club.

Not that Romy was gay. She wasn't. God, no.[27]

But this chapter isn't supposed to be about a love triangle. (Neither is this book, alas.)

Present at this Saturday-afternoon cemetery sitting session were Priya, aforementioned; Runner, who cannot be summarized; Neil, who sat close to the boys; Missy, who was probably as powerful as ever despite the absence of lackeys; Romy, bearing both the Book of Days and life in general; and Aline, whose suffering in the presence of boys is not something we should neglect to mention.

And then there were the two boys themselves, the newest members, or half-members, in their impressive paper hats, creasing in the breeze.

---

27 Sorry, Romy.

Runner had once again expected the appearance of a healthy and resplendent Anna. She heaved over to the gable of the mausoleum and searched down the hill, visibly agitated. Neil told us recently that, in Runner's mind, the absence of Anna meant the presence of Ruby, in all her silken glory. It had begun to develop into a hard equation: chubby, reckless girl equals Life, dead sister equals — well, we've spelled it out, haven't we?

So, Ruby was present too, apparently. And Runner's lack of focus translated into lack of focus for the group, wicking away increments of afternoon like so many smooth stones, at least until Priya finally cleared her throat, pronouncing those five most exciting words in the Lacuna Cabal lexicon: 'I've been to the library.'

'You have?' asked Runner, snapping back to attention as Ruby faded to five points per billion in the sunny spring air. Priya nodded with mock gravitas and gestured for everyone to gather in a tight circle around the mausoleum chimney, accomplished despite a deluge of intimacy issues. And then she began.

'Ladies and gentlemen,' she said, swishing her big coat, 'behold the topography of the world.'

And then she walked in a close circle around them, her feet not quite touching the ground. 'Okay,' she said, indicating what she'd just done, 'so this is us. This is the city. Uruk, right?'

'Uruk,' affirmed Runner, beaming.

'Located in the part of the world now known as Iraq.'

And then she performed a little two-step: 'Iraq, Uruk; Uruk, Iraq. Gilgamesh was the twelfth king of Uruk, of which there were 120 altogether. The first was said to have reigned for thirty thousand years. So they thought their city was pretty old and their leaders saw themselves as well-nigh immortal, Gilgamesh being no exception.'

Aline spoke up. 'Excuse me, but,' a phrase she had picked up from the Baghdad Blogger. 'Excuse me, but if it's true that this book is set in Iraq, don't you think we should maybe devote a little bit of discussion to what's going on there at present?'

Everyone looked at her. Priya said, 'Why, what's going on there at pr— ?'

Missy interrupted her. 'Aline, don't you want to hear what Priya has to say?'

Aline said, 'Yes, but … '

Missy said, 'You'll get your turn. Anyway, if I've done the math right, this story is four thousand years old. Current events aren't exactly relevant, Aline.'

Aline said, 'I'll wait my turn.'

Priya said, 'I'd love to hear what you have to say, Aline. I didn't do research about what's going on in Iraq at present.' An image flashed through her mind of a march down René Lévesque.

'I'll wait my turn,' said Aline.

Priya continued to set the Mesopotamian scene: the city of Uruk surrounded by farmland, surrounded by rough country and then the wild. She ran around the edge of the hill and up into the grass again. All eyes followed her. Neil tells us that Runner saw for a second another blur beside her. Ruby. Priya continued over the empty grass till she arrived a bit of a distance from them and had to call across.

'Out here is the Forest of Cedar, where next we go.'

Romy called back, 'It seems a long way.'

Priya called, 'The gods take walks there. It can't be just around the corner.'

Emmy, tossing a note, asked, 'Is there anything beyond that?'

Priya gestured, smacking an old stone with the back of her hand. 'Beyond that is the — ouch — is the edge of the world.'

And then she turned away from them, looked across the rest of the cemetery, toward the mountain and the trees and the Oratory. She shouted, as if to some distant hearer perched on top of the dome: 'Beyond that, a pair of twin mountains, where the sun both rises and sets. And then you get the path of the sun, the garden of jewels, and then, at the very edge of the edge of the

world, you get a bar — like, a drinking establishment, the propri-
etress a minor goddess named Shiduri … '

She hesitated. Her eyes were shining. And then she ran
suddenly back, until she was standing over them all like some
flaky prophetess. 'And, just, I'd like to express my appreciation
for this class act. It's like before you cross the waters of death, you
get to stop at a bar with a wise woman who has eschewed ambition in the rock-star realm of the gods and offers you a drink.
Hello? Can I request that when we get to the part about Shiduri
that I get to play Shiduri? I know I'm jumping the gun on this,
but can we vote on it?'

They stared at her. She had been doing so well with this presentation, and now it turned out she had a hidden agenda. Priya
wanted to choose her part.

Missy said, 'Priya wants to play a minor goddess. She does-
n't want to be a rock star. All in favour?'

Everybody put up their hands except for Emmy and Coby,
who were miming a discussion of the contents of a very small
note while Coby rubbed the side of his head.

'Opposed?'

Nobody raised a hand.

'Emmy and boy? You're abstaining?'

Coby said, 'Oh, uh.'

(Du thought, 'Uh-oh.')

'Yes, we abstain, yes,' said Emmy.

'It passes.' (Missy, annoyed.)

Priya continued. 'Be advised that the bar by the water is only
the *beginning* of the end of the world. Then you have the ocean
of death and across it you have the fabled home of the oldest man
in the world.'

'And that's it?' (Runner.)

'That's it.'

'We can go on?' asked Runner, hobbling to her feet as Neil
hoisted a stone from his bag.

'Where were we?' said Priya.

'Tablet Three,' announced Runner, and everyone turned to face her stern poetess demeanour, shining in the afternoon sun.

The brides of the city were safe. Or sad, some of them, since the days of the royal lay and sloppy seconds for the husband were over …

'Jesus Christ,' muttered Dumuzi, 'does she never … ?'

And the king cared only for Enkidu, his friend, wrestled with his friend, sought adventures with his friend. The Forest of Cedar stored a throng of timber, housed in trees tall as the sky; they breathed out when we breathed in and blocked the sun from half the world.

But they also had a guardian: a monster called Humbaba, the first tree-hugger, eco-terrorist, protector of the forest. It had its intestines on the outside, all over its face. And auras. Seven shining auras.

'Sounds pretty,' said Romy.

To the Forest of Cedar our heroes went, to catch and kill Humbaba for the good of industry, housing, male-bonding and the re-establishment of the king's virtue.

Uh-oh, Du thought. Killing. Real sex was one thing, not to mention a real fight on Prince Arthur. But real killing? Is this why they'd arranged to meet in a cemetery? How far, Du wondered, was this book club willing to go? Were they going to have a lottery? God.

He said that out loud.

'No,' said Missy, 'we are not going to have a lottery. And we're not going hunting either, just to nip that idea in the bud.'

(Missy had a hunting licence, something she had worked hard to acquire several years ago as a way of spending more time with her father. They had always planned to go on a hunting expedition together in Vermont.)

Du said, 'But our heroes have to hunt a monster.'

Missy said, 'All right, then. If you can suggest any monsters to hunt, then I'm all for it. Take off that ridiculous hat.'

Du took off his paper hat. Coby swiftly followed. Aline suggested they hunt Saddam Hussein. Nobody seemed to know who that was. She then suggested the U.S. president, eliciting little more than a shrug from all of them.

'Do you people never read the news?' Aline asked.

'I listen to the radio,' said Priya.

'I read the news,' said Emmy. 'I just don't like to brag about it.'

'Newspapers go into the trash. Literature endures.' (Missy.)

'Newspapers, yes, but not news.'

Aline took advantage of the moment to expound on a new favourite subject: the cyclical nature of respect for human life. 'Have you ever read the Bible story of Abraham and Isaac?' she asked.

'Oh God,' said Emmy, but Aline had waited her turn and was taking it.

'No, really. God told Abraham to sacrifice his son on the altar, but at the last moment he was allowed to switch the boy for a lamb.'

'Did he kill the lamb?' asked Romy, ignored.

'It was supposed to be this big moment in the history of civilization, overturning a tradition of human sacrifice that went all the way back to your Gilgamesh. But the truth isn't like that. Each generation finds some way to push the lesson of Abraham aside and start the slaughter again.'

'Why don't they just read the story again?' asked Romy.

'Because books suck,' said Emmy.

'But Humbaba wasn't a human sacrifice,' said Missy. 'He was a monster.'

'How else do we justify the killing of humans if not by calling them monsters?' asked Aline. 'That's what we're doing now. We've created a new set of monsters.'

'Humbaba wasn't a monster?' Romy was getting dizzy from the argument.

So was Du. But he had an idea. 'What about the fitzbot?' he asked.

It was as if Coby suddenly woke up. 'What about it?'

The fact is, Du was still carrying the fitzbot around with him in his backpack. He wanted to give it back, but he wasn't even sure if Coby knew it was there.

'Well,' he said, wilting a little under Coby's sudden glare, 'couldn't we hunt that? Isn't it designed to avoid you and run for the shadows?'

'It is?' asked Aline.

'Yeah,' said Du. 'It is.' Almost proudly. 'Coby did it.' Proudly for his friend. 'As proof of the bottom-up philosophy of artificial intelligence.'

Coby was colouring. Ambivalent about allying himself, cowboy-in-training that he was, with this former science project. On the other hand, the fitzbot was a spectacular creation of artificial intelligence and solar-power engineering, and he was proud of it.

He opted for the middle ground of mockery: 'Oh ... What, so you want to shoot a tiny little harmless robot in the back while it's running away?'

'It's not so tiny,' said Du, who wanted to settle once and for all the matter of its safekeeping. He pulled open the drawstring on his backpack and turned it upside down, allowing the bot to slide out and drop to the ground. It hit the grass on its back and everyone gasped as its legs started to scuttle, swift and small, in the air. Du gently flipped it with his shoe. For a moment, the robot sat on the ground, like a piece of yellow metal that had fallen off a backhoe. Then, with an unnerving triple click, it stood up on six legs, stretched to its full height, halfway up to Du's knee, and scuttled straight for Runner.

Everyone screamed. Runner emitted a nervous laugh and stepped out of the way, but the bot kept coming. She backed into the sun and poked the creature with her tibia, whereupon it changed direction and scuttled away. Coby jumped to his feet and took off after it as two old women praying in Section R stood up and looked around.

It didn't go that fast, but those six fully articulated legs moving independent of one another created the illusion of potent and disquieting speed. Coby was easily able to catch up with it, though, and scooped it up to his chest.

'Creepy,' ventured Missy.

'Gross,' said Priya.

'Why did it — ?' asked Runner.

'It didn't,' said Coby. 'It goes for the shadows. You were standing in the shadows.'

Neil told us recently that Runner believed what happened was that she was standing in Ruby's deeper shadow, that Ruby was standing next to her and the fitzbot was the proof: seeking a shadow to eclipse all other shadows.

Coby came back up the hill and asked Du to please hand over the backpack, then kept his gaze in the grass as he quietly slipped the fitzbot inside, looking vaguely humiliated. Still, the backpack stayed within his protective arms, close to his chest, skinny but shielding. Emmy, for her part, said nothing.

'It's like it's alive,' said Missy.

'But it's not,' said Coby firmly, eyes still down. 'The illusion of life is not life ... This thing doesn't ... thrill to the sun on its skin or the ... or the breezes in the air or the ... tickle of the grass, or — '

Du was getting embarrassed again at Coby's newfound flakiness. He interrupted. 'Yeah, but isn't there anyone in your department who's built another — '

'I don't want to go back there!' said Coby firmly.

News to Du, who tried to ignore it. 'Yeah, but hasn't someone built a security robot or something big that they don't need anymore, so maybe we could borrow it or offer to test it by hunting it down and, like, killing it?'

'YOU CAN'T KILL A ROBOT. We don't make robots alive.'

'Yeah, but you know what I mean.'

'No, I don't.' Coby was sounding firmer than ever. 'We're not gods,' he said, like he did before, in the apartment, only this time he wasn't naked and covered in mud. 'We don't make robots alive, so we can't kill them. And I don't want to go back to that department. That's a fate worse than death, as far as I'm concerned. You might as well kill me.'

Now, that was really embarrassing. Du could hardly refrain from rolling his eyes.

'The point is to kill something that's alive,' said Emmy helpfully (though she must have wanted to roll her eyes as well, she must have).

'Only living things die,' said Coby.

'Something powerful,' said Emmy, 'like an elk or a bear or a moose — '

'Or a monster,' said Coby.

' — or a man,' finished Emmy. 'And then we hunters look into its eyes as it dies and teach each other something.'

'We're not going hunting!' (Missy.)

Romy was sitting apart in the grass, pushing her finger through to the cold soil. 'What do we teach each other?' she asked dully.

'I don't know,' said Emmy. 'To be afraid. Or not to be afraid. Or … the value of life, or … the beauty of death, or … '

Sex and annihilation. Emmy had bought into it. Oh, brother. Coby had done nothing to erase the effects of *that guy*. In fact he had augmented them, since sex was all they had in common.

'Where are you getting this from?' Romy was trying not to yell or cry.

'I'm trying to think like a hunter,' said Emmy.

To which Romy practically shouted: 'I don't want to kill anything!'

'Nobody's asking you to,' said Emmy, starting to get annoyed.

'NOBODY'S ASKING YOU TO, EITHER. It's these boys here, right? They're the heroes.'

And then Romy stood up and addressed the group. 'I have an idea.'

Which is always exciting. But she paused a little, unsure. Then she spoke. 'I'll be the monster.'

'What?' (Emmy.)

Romy went on, gesturing to Coby and Du. 'They can kill me,' she said. 'Or not that they can kill me, but, uh, they can ... ' Romy was embarrassed, colouring, ready to die, but plowing on nonetheless. 'They can try and cut off my hair.'

This was horrifying. Romy was already beyond the edge of where she'd ever dared to even look before. And she knew there was no going back. 'I want to fight them.'

'But, Romy,' interjected Missy, 'you're a girl.'

'This is just a book. And, anyway, I can take them.'

'They're two boys,' insisted Missy.

'I can take them,' said Romy. And then, since everyone was ignoring the lion's share of her idea: 'They can try and cut off my hair and I can try and stop them. Life and death.'

Missy said, 'But your beautiful hair!'

Romy said, 'What, so I'm ugly without my hair? Is that what you're saying, Missy?'

'No!' Missy was practically weeping with concern.

Romy continued. She was standing now, and had moved to stand on higher ground, so close to the gable that even Runner thought she might fall off into the road. 'I don't want anybody to kill anything for real,' she said. 'So these two,' gesturing again to Coby and Du, still not looking at them, 'will try and cut off the hair of the Forest of Cedar. And that will be like my death. The death of Humbaba. It's a reasonable facsimile.'

Romy had always wanted to ally herself with the wilderness, even if she was only from Bingotown, and now she was getting to do that and it gave her intense satisfaction, especially since it also seemed to annoy Emmy, who was flaring shades of blue and red. Romy liked her new name too. Humbaba. Protector of the forest. She had claimed it. It was hers. Way better than Romy. She sat back down in the grass by the gable, satisfied.

Dumuzi spoke up. 'I don't want to do that,' he said.

'You have to,' said Romy, still not looking at him.

'I don't want to.'

'I don't want to, either,' ventured Coby.

Dumuzi went on. 'It's sick, it's … it's not even heroic. What kind of male-bonding exercise is that?'

'One that was invented by a woman,' said Romy.

Emmy was furious, but everyone else, especially Runner, was impressed by Romy's riposte.

Du had to shout to get their attention back. 'NO WAY,' he said. 'There are barbers for that.'

Romy looked at him, square in the face. 'Please?'

'No,' he said, looking at his shoes.

Runner, with her most coquettish perspicacity: 'Please?'

Dumuzi, like he really meant it: 'No.'

Runner, exploding: 'Must you return to the precognitive state of before? In the square? Would you rather be manipulated?'

'Oh no,' Du said uneasily. 'Nobody's going to manipulate me anymore.'

'We've granted you free will in these proceedings!'

'Yes,' said Du. 'And I'm saying no.'

'Ack!' shouted Runner, who looked like she was going to crack him over the head with her tibia. 'It's hard to show how a work flows naturally when there's a boy in the field saying no all the time!'

'I'll do it,' said Neil.

'There,' said Du, grinning with relief. 'Neil here can be your Gilgamesh.'

'He's not strong enough,' protested Runner.

'What?' Du was feigning disbelief. 'Oh, come on. I'll bet that's not even true, hey, Neil?'

Neil beamed. Du mussed his hair. It was charming. Runner asked him to kindly refrain from being so manipulative. Still, it was a palpable hit. Only it missed its intended target and thrust straight to the heart of Missy, who forgot everything else in that moment except that the young man Dumuzi was good with children. Her cheeks flushed. Her eyes dilated. Her lips surged.

'If you did this one thing,' she said, transforming into her after-hours persona right in front of everyone, 'we'd be eternally grateful.'

'What?' said Du, turning toward her. 'You?'

It was not the answer Missy expected. Suddenly she was unsure what her question had been, or whether it had been a question at all, or what they were even talking about. 'Wh— What do you — ? Why? Well, why not?' she stammered. 'Why not me?'

Du turned to look at Romy, then offered his explanation to Runner: 'I'm feeling a bit ... hemmed in.' Then he looked over at the Oratory and wondered what the hell he was doing there in that cemetery.

'All right. Okay,' he said, for no reason he could understand, except he was exhausted. 'I'll do it.'

Missy looked around and asked Priya what it was exactly she had just asked the boy to do. With some bemusement, Priya whispered back that she'd convinced Dumuzi to fight Romy and cut off her hair.

'Oh, I ... Oh,' said Missy, shocked, waking up. But it was too late. Runner was already explaining the rules of engagement: that it had to be both boys in the fight even if that didn't seem fair. It was left to Coby, of all people, to politely ask why Romy would do such a thing.

'I don't know!' said Romy. 'We want to know what it is to kill? We want to know what it is to die? Here's the best way I can think of. I don't know!'

Aline said, 'This is not what I meant.'

'But it's what I meant,' said Romy. 'We want to teach each other something? The hunter and the hunted?' She turned to Coby: 'You want to know what it's like to rely on your friend in a task like war?' She turned to Emmy: 'You want to know what it's like to wait for the man you love to come back from the war?'

Emmy, too late, tried to be gentle. She said, 'Romy ... '

'I don't know, I don't know!' continued Romy. She turned to Runner: 'Don't you want to see everything?' She turned to Aline, too clear to be crying: 'I don't want anybody to kill anything for real, but this way maybe I'll know what it's like and then maybe later, if I ever have to fight for something more precious and real than my head of hair, like my hymen or maybe a baby too, or, like, in a real war, I'll be able to do it. I don't know.'

Everybody was standing up. Nobody could stay on the grass. Aline put a hand on Romy's shoulder. 'But this is something real and pre— '

Romy interrupted. She might as well have been speaking from the tablets now:

You have to care about what you're losing if it's going to be like your life. And you have to know what you're taking if it's going to be like your life.

But I don't want anybody to take a life. And I don't want to be just the trapper in this story who waits outside the door!

Then she looked at Emmy, who had edged away a bit. 'But if Emmy tells me not to do it, I won't.'

Emmy was looking pointedly at the ground, ignoring her, embarrassed.

'I guess it's settled,' said Romy. And then, turning to Coby: 'And I want you to swear that no matter what happens — '

'Hey,' said Coby. 'This is the twenty-first century. Swearing isn't way up there on the list of sacred — '

'Swear by some horrible death sent to Emmy,' said Romy evenly.

Coby dropped the demeanour: 'Okay. I'll do it. I swear.'

'All in favour?' asked Runner, raising her hand, even as everyone was starting to drift uncomfortably down to the path. Still, they all put up their hands. Aline was hesitant, but nobody noticed. He went home after that and wrote: *Violence Violence Violence Violence Violence. The solution for a new generation.* He wrote it in his very own, very private, pov.blogspot.com, and then expanded on it and then scaled it back, as he always scaled his postings back, and then cut it altogether, and then replaced it with the line he always left at the end: *Innocent people suffer in war.*

Chapter Eleven
Humbaba

MARCH 30TH (i.e., the next day), 4 P.M.
Neil wrote:

> Up on the roof, above the sixth floor, bare of all but Romy,
> preparing to become Humbaba the monster, binding her
> hair tight and close to her head in a kerchief. (Otherwise no
> effort to look like a monster.)
>
> Below, still on the fifth floor, all the others waiting. Neil
> was there too, writing the rules in his book:
>
> 1. There would be scissors.
>
> 2. The scissors would stay on the ground until the
> monster was pinned.

And then he looked up at the others around him. Aline was
looking up at the ceiling. Runner was studying the fifth tablet.
Missy was writing furiously in her own notebook. Emmy was
looking at the floor. Priya was fiddling with the frets of her travel
guitar.

Aline mumbled, 'I always thought this was a haven from
boys,' and then, 'I don't want to leave Romy alone.'

Runner looked up from her tablet. 'We're not presenting it as
a drama, Aline. It's like real life. There can't be anyone watching.'

A sound of disgust from Aline.

'I'm sorry, Aline. You might have trouble understanding the
difference between drama and real life, but it's not like there was
anyone watching in the Forest of Cedar.'

'We're not in any fucking Forest of Cedar.'

'They were alone,' insisted Runner. 'They fought alone. Humbaba was alone. Everyone was alone.'

'Somebody stop this girl before she starts quoting Nietzsche.'

As a distraction, Priya told a story that this whole event/ ritual reminded her of. She even sang a bit of a song about it, which was very pretty and sounded like waves but was incomprehensible. The story went like this: there was a barber in the States, she said, who had discovered, while conducting experiments in his bathtub, that one can clean up oil slicks better with human hair than with any chemical means.

'Really?' said Aline.

'That's amazing,' said Runner.

Emmy was now pretending to be reading, of all things, a book.

Priya went on to say that Romy's sacrifice was comparable to the cleaning of the environment with this symbol of feminine beauty.

Missy said, 'I don't wish to be pedantic, but back when they wrote this book, it would have been right and good for the men to kill the monster and cut down the forest to use for human industry.'

Priya (who had spent the previous evening reading up on current events) said, 'Leave it to Missy to take the neo-con line.'

Missy said, 'It's not the neo-con line, Priya. So Humbaba protects the forest. Who cares? I don't like that Romy is up there losing her hair. It's backward in terms of where our sympathies should lie. I'm just saying.'

Aline said, 'I agree.'

Priya said, 'Who says she's going to lose her hair?'

Missy: 'Oh, come on, please. Can we step into the real world for a minute? Miss Hippie-Dippie? I can't believe I didn't think clearly enough to put a stop to this nonsense.'

'Miss Hippie-Dippie?' asked Priya. 'Jesus, at least my brain-cell count doesn't stoop in the presence of men.'

Missy froze. Just for a second. Then she said, 'Stoop. That's a good one. That's a hawking term. Do you dress up in your elf boots, camisole and cloak and go hawking with your hippie friends?'

Priya said, 'You forgot the Renaissance sleeves.'

Missy said, 'Guess I did.'

Priya said, 'How do you know it's a hawking term?'

Missy said, 'Maybe I hawk.'

Priya said, 'With your hippie friends?'

'I don't have hippie friends. Maybe I hawk alone.'

'Best way to do it.'

Runner couldn't believe it. 'Are you being serious? You two hawk?'

Priya said, 'We just know a word.'

And then they heard — or thought they heard — a thump from up above that silenced everyone.

Neil was still writing in his notebook.

At once the scissors were …

And then he crossed that out and started again.

At once the shears, pulled from the scabbard, were put to work. Held in front of the hunters as they stole their way either to the Forest of Cedar or up to the sixth floor. And then up to the roof.

They stopped there. They placed their scissors down on the copper.

In fact, Neil had never been up to the roof of the Jacob Lighter Building. He didn't know whether it was copper up there. It could have been sheet metal, he says now. It could have been plain old tar.

Humbaba was up there, on the roof bare of all but a view of Van Horne. It was cold but above zero. The trees are conif- erous, good for palace-building, ship timber, pitch, tar, resin for cough medicines, salves, ointments for export to Egypt, embalming mummies …

Coby and Du spent last night talking through the unpleasant task facing them. In the Lacuna Cabal Montreal Young Women's Book Club, they are the men in a universe full of goddesses. They simply have to endure the tasks that are chosen for them and try to imbue them with common decency and compassion. So, they've decided that they will tackle Romy between them, up on the roof, with the skinnier Coby on top and Dumuzi below, breaking her fall so she won't get hurt.

Today, faced with Romy right there, wide-eyed and heart-rent, it all goes according to plan except that the fall, the thump against the roof, hurts Du a lot more than he expected it to. For a moment he sees red, but not enough to inflict damage. For a moment he sees Anna in his mind, walking through the city with him, heading downtown into Chinatown that afternoon last week. Today she would be almost dressed for spring. Her legs. Her eyes. He finds himself imagining her pregnant,[28] with a full round belly, his child inside, her wildness put to rest by biological necessity.

But once the three are down, it goes a lot more smoothly, though not without its hitches. Coby tries to imagine that he is a cowboy and this is a rodeo, and the sweaty T-shirted, pulsing pink sobbing body below him a steer or a sow or … It's not working.

The boys have somehow thus far permitted themselves to believe they will be applauded for what they're doing. But now they know it cannot be true.

And that is as much of their point of view as we can stand.

Romy is pinned on her chest, the roof pressing her breasts in against her heart, hands holding her head down to the tar and the cold of the blade expected at any moment against the back of

---

28 Du's note: He most certainly did not imagine her pregnant. That's just outrageous. And a very poor male point of view, I might add.

her neck, though she knows they're trying to keep it away from her skin. Everyone's granted that they're playing by the rules, the compassionate approach to conflict, the best interests of their quarry at heart.

Be brave, Romy.
This is not the end.
You'll see.

Romy grits her teeth. Here it comes. That feeling. That man's hand is in her hair, he's pulling her head back, like a scalping. The scissoring blades are coming in and then she feels the shear. One clump is gone. She heaves and the scissors clatter to the roof a few feet away. One man's going to have to get them while the other struggles against her back.

A small voice inside her head is saying, 'Romy's being raped.' She's imagining it, absurdly, as a matter-of-fact conversation between Runner and Missy in a library, and Emmy, reading a magazine beneath a beautiful lamp, looks up and says, 'Sh.'

She feels the shears again. Another clump gone. Shit. The problem with this kind of haircut is that once the first piece is taken, the damage is done. One small gap devalues the whole head. Like slashing a fancy dress or spitting in a drink of water. Still, she'll make them fight for every last lock. She thinks she has one advantage over a rape victim: she knows she is complicit in her humiliation. She has asked for this. She's asking for it. When these boys say they were just following orders, she'll know that the orders they were following were hers. Even if this is what annihilation feels like. Well, anyway, it's done now. Almost. There's always that small comfort in knowing a part of one's mind can't be touched. It's detached. The trick, though, is not to allow the detached mind to take over for good, nor to let it take over so much that you won't struggle.

As, for example, when she finds herself thinking about that mouse in the goldfish bowl, jumping, struggling to cling to the lip at the top. Snip. Another piece gone. And then another. She thinks, Oh yeah, for sure, it will all be over soon if I just stop struggling.

But instead she twists over onto her back, chin jutting and eyes like daggers, right breast pinching on the way around. Her body is more exposed this way, but not her hair. They're not trying to get anything from her but her hair; they want to be back there, so she's here, and her hands are free to slap and poke and grab. Her feet are free to push and kick. She might even get a bit of man hair between her own fingers.

If she really were Humbaba in the Forest of Cedar, perhaps she would be looking up now at the view of the sun and the sky up through plentiful green. But the truth is, Romy doesn't think of cedar trees and leaves, not even once. She thinks only of her own life.

There was a kid once, many years back, a counsellor at a summer camp. Maybe he was nineteen. Romy was ten or something. He had come to work at the camp with his girlfriend, but over the summer the girl split with him and took up with someone else. He had been devastated and yet still every day he worked with her and the others, her new guy included.

One afternoon, a very hot day, he went to his cabin, doused himself with gasoline and lit a match. The burning cut a swath as he ran through the woods toward the cookshack, looking for a way out of that bad decision. Some of the kids saw him. They saw that he had changed his mind. Yeah, thought Romy, I'm changing my mind too. There's one kind of pain and then there's another. There's the anxious grating pain of being rejected by a lover, along with everything it includes, but it comes from within, like a mouse in a fishbowl, scrabbling, sliding and gnawing. And then there's the pain that is externally inflicted. Gasoline and burning flesh.

Still, she thinks, what that boy did was selfish. There were children in the area. He was traumatizing them. He might have started a forest fire. It was a dry season. Romy has never thought of that particular wrinkle before: *It was a dry season.*

And now Romy remembers that there are children here too. *Neil.* What is Neil going to think about this? What is he thinking now? So much violence can't be good, even if it's only meant to convey an ancient death that isn't even real.

And so she tries in this moment to put a stop to it. She even cries out. Hollers, in fact, leaving a permanent ringing sensation in one of Coby's ears. But it's too late.

✝

Raven and brown and red and golden
Four hundred loads of fresh-cut hair
From the girls who live along the coast
Four hundred trucks to the ocean there.
The ocean's as black as the east
From oil as black as a tree
And a bald girl along for the ride looking north,
Who's given her hair for the health of the sea.
   — from 'The Oil Men' by Priya Underhay (2003)

Coby appeared first, asking for Emmy, going to her arms. He said, 'That was awful.'

Then Dumuzi came. Looking grim. Priya said gently, 'Home from the wars.' But he was looking bitterly upon them.

'There,' he said. 'Everybody happy now? Huh?' And continued to mumble something about how if it had been a task invented by a woman, then why the fuck did the woman get the short end of the stick.

And then Romy came. Appeared in the doorway. Darkened it, really, if we may be so …

Romy.

Priya was still speaking gently, asserting her empathy, risking words. 'How does it feel, Romy?'

Romy's eyes and cheeks were red, and so was what hair she had, which was not much.

'It feels awful,' she said. 'I lost my hair.'

'Oh, Romy.' (Missy, weeping.)

'I've got no hair, my beautiful hair. I look like an egg or a cancer patient or … '

'Your beautiful hair.' (Missy, still.)

Missy drew Romy to her in an embrace that obliterated every mean thing she'd ever said to her. But why had she said mean things to her? If she wanted to protect her? If she loved her so much?

Everyone was weeping — really, really weeping — except Priya, Du and Emmy. And Aline, who was crouched on the floor, smouldering like a firepit.

And Priya was behaving as if no one were weeping. If you discounted the fact that she had just produced seven water bottles out of a plastic bag at her side and started handing them out, you'd think she was coldly proceeding as if there weren't any tears at all.

'Don't worry, Romy,' she said, still gently. 'You look pretty cool, I think.'

'I don't look human,' sobbed Romy.

'But what was it like?' she persisted, earning an approving look from Runner. 'What was it like to be the monster Humbaba?'

'Stop pestering her.' (Missy.)

'But we have to talk about it, Missy. Otherwise it's a waste of time. To the victors go the spoils, but the victims get the visions, and people should hear about it.'

'What people? What visions?' asked Missy.

'Us people,' said Priya. 'Our visions.'

'I want to go home,' said Romy.

'I'll take you home,' said Missy.

'No, you should stay here and talk about it.'

'I don't want to talk about it.'

'I don't want you to go with me.'

'But I want to!'

'No!' said Romy, and this echoed through the building. 'You're so beautiful,' she continued, trying to explain so Missy wouldn't be hurt. 'Your hair too. It's so beautiful. I don't want to see it shining in the sun.'

'Oh, Romy!'

'I know, I'm sorry!'

'Would everyone please stop crying!' yelled Dumuzi.

'I'm not crying,' said Priya.

'I'm not crying,' said Neil, who had stopped as soon as Dumuzi asked.

'I'm only sort of crying,' assured Runner. 'My rational mind is intact.'

(Emmy was not crying, but she did not mention it.)

'Look on the bright side!' said Du, still with more volume than necessary. 'She's a monster! She's, you know, vanquished!'

'I wish I'd never done it,' breathed Romy, fulfilling Dumuzi's greatest fear.

'But you didn't die,' he pleaded. 'Nobody died.'

Aline spoke quietly from the floor. 'I can think of many cases,' she said with preternatural cool, 'where nobody died but the trauma was lifelong.'

'Trauma?' (Du.) 'Oh great, trauma. For a little bit of play-acting, we get trauma.'

'Play-acting?' countered Aline. 'My opinion is that you should be a little more sensitive.'

'Your opinion? Me more sensitive? Me? I'm the one who … '

But Aline was suddenly up and moving in. Du spotted the attitude. 'What?' he said, but didn't have time to say more. Aline's fist shot out and connected with his jaw. The jaw was a clear target and made what a foley artist would consider to be a satisfying pop. Dumuzi's knees dropped below him and in less than a second he was out cold on the ground.

There was a moment of silence. Even Romy stopped crying and turned to look at the sprawled Dumuzi.

'Oh my god,' she said. 'Is that in the book?'

'Last time I checked,' said Runner, 'nobody ко'd Gilgamesh in the book.'

Missy leapt to tend to the fallen man, employing first-aid training she'd acquired for all the adventures she was going to undertake with her father.

Priya was looking at Aline, her own jaw practically on the floor. 'I thought you said he made you nervous,' she said.

'You think I wanted to do that?' asked Aline, looking at his hands, clearly upset.

'Nervous isn't the same as being a wilting flower,' said Runner. 'Especially for men.'

Aline blushed redder than he already was.

'You have a violent streak,' said Priya.

'I am trying to change.'

Aline slumped back to the floor, troubled and penitent. Priya wondered for a moment if that was why Aline wore a dress. Therapy for a violent streak. Whatever the answer, she wasn't going to learn it today.

'I'd better go,' Romy said. 'Please don't adjourn. I just want to be alone for a while. I just … I don't know why I let them do that.'

Emmy quietly spoke up, 'You didn't want to kill anything for real.'

'No,' countered Romy. 'I guess I wanted someone to kill me instead.'

Which brought Emmy, finally and to her own great relief, to tears. 'Romy,' she said and started to move.

'Don't,' said Romy. 'I'll be fine. Don't worry. I'll be fine. Really. Just comfort the men who killed me, really, it's fine.'

Missy, tending Du, caught the jibe, though she was not its target. 'Romy,' she pleaded, 'he might be seriously hurt.'

'Look,' said Coby, anxious as a defendant, 'I didn't want to do that.'

Romy looked at him. 'I did, though,' she said. 'I did. It's not your fault. I absolve you. Since I'm dead I can do that, right? I can absolve you.'

And then she looked around. Realized she was done here. There was no possibility for return. She would go out through that door and never come back. Her eyes, already shining, teared up again.

She was free.

'Since I'm dead,' she said, 'I can finally admit that I read all kinds of shit, like even the crappy magazines that I pretend to despise. I read bad, pulpy books, too, and books that scare me, though not so bad as when the rabbits died in *Watership Down*. I read all kinds of shit, I might as well admit it since I'm dead. And I'd be a hypocrite to mind you comforting the traumatized and fallen heroes, the men, since I wish the women could comfort me too. I do. I really do. I might as well admit it since I'm dead ... '

She couldn't quite believe she was speaking out loud like this.

'Emmy could hold me to her soft breast too, and I would feel her breathing and slow down my breathing to the level of her breathing too. That's comfort. That's what comfort is. And people get comfort when they win, not when they lose. Do you see why I want to be alone for a bit? I'll see you tomorrow, 'kay?'

And then she was gone. Disappeared into the stairwell. Slipped down through the floors and out into the darkening streets as a god.

Chapter Twelve
Runner's Fall (ii)

Anna was listening at the fourth-floor stairwell. Someone had just passed en route to the ground floor. There didn't seem to be anyone following, but still she found herself stalling, already annoyed with the nervous man hanging back in the shadows. If he was so nervous, why did he want to sleep with strangers? Anna strove to keep her stomach in order and her best neutral face. Maybe this was a bad idea. No, it was a good idea, it was a good idea.

'They don't sound like they're going anywhere for a while,' she said, matter-of-factly unbuttoning her blouse. 'And don't worry, it's just a stupid book club. They go for hours. It's incredible.'

Anna tended to be subtle and silent in all sexual matters, due to a stint in early days living below a particularly expressive woman. It occasionally made her partners self-conscious, slowing down the process, particularly in cases of low self-esteem.

This was, not surprisingly, the case with the john, who fumbled and fumbled and fumbled, until Anna began, with no small feeling of dread, to consider emitting a bleatlet or two. A bona fide sigh was out of the question, since she feared it would come out impatient, exasperated even. The sound had to have some pleasurable connotation for her, so that it would come across. She considered, as he fumbled, what such a sound might be, and immediately recalled, for the first time in a long while, the horse-riding lessons she had taken as a child. Dressage.

She thought of the smart outfit, which she loved, and her accessories for grooming, which she carried with her always up to the stables in a leather pouch. Currycomb, hoof pick, rasp. The john continued to fumble. More than any other object, however, she loved the saddle, that beautiful simple 'U' of her English saddle — no phallic horns or swells, no roughhouse fenders (fumble).

Uh-oh (fumble), *better be careful, or else in no time at all you're going to be thinking of —*

Tilly. That was the name of her horse. A small brown gelding named Tilly, who had not lived long at the stables in Carignan, but long enough to be established primarily as Anna's horse. She was twelve years old when she started riding Tilly and trained with him for two whole years. Two years of loyal service on the part of Tilly and the deepest devotion from Anna.

I wonder if this guy will go for tears? (fumble, fumble) *Guess not.*

And then she had lost interest. For years after that she'd had no interest at all, hadn't even wanted to speak of it — more interest in boys than in horses, really, other than the dull feeling occasionally in her gut that she was allowing something to slip away. Until the shock set in that she'd been away from Tilly for twice as long as they'd spent together. Was this what growing up was? Allowing the years to distance you from everything you've really loved?

Then life (fumble) *should be short, and everyone should die at fifteen.*

Even now, beneath the farty strivings of ho-boy, she felt it was already too late for her. Too late to die. She might as well live.

But she had to stop thinking of this right now. Get to the sounds. Tilly had made certain sounds. Pleasure sounds. She had to find one that was utterable by a human, and utter it.

There were only four that she could think of: the whinny, definitely out of the question; the nicker, a sound she loved but it would come out like she was trying to get the guy to giddyup, which was true, but still; then there was the snort, the thought of which in this context nearly made her laugh out loud. And then the blow. The blow was pretty good, and it was a sound that people made: if it was cold you made it to say you were cold but all right. If it was hot you made it to say you might be in need of a cold drink of water. Yup, the blow. A perfect sound, under the circumstances. Though, considering the circumstances, the thought occurred that perhaps she wasn't really cut out for this job. Not that she cared, really. (Fumble.) She really didn't care.

✛

Upstairs, Emmy noticed that everyone was looking away from her. She could see an exact profile of each of their faces. Statistically speaking, it could not have been a coincidence. She opted for a joke.

'I didn't realize we were going to do *The Epic of Gilgamesh* from the monster's point of view.'

'We can't help it: we're modern,' Runner said. 'In the old days, nobody would have socked Gilgamesh in the jaw for slaying Humbaba.

'Don't make fun,' admonished Missy. 'He could really be hurt.'

'I'm not making fun, Missy. I'm only … '

Coby, emboldened by Romy's absolution, decided to take up her cause.

'Why are you talking about this like this?' he asked.

Runner turned to him with almost as much shut-up-warning in her voice as Missy might have.

'Talking about what like what?'

'This like this.'

'What like what?'

'I mean,' he ventured, 'that girl just left without — '

'Romy. Her name is Romy.'

'Sorry. Romy just left, without any ... without any of her hair. And Du's out cold on the ground. But ... here you are, and you're just — '

'We're having a discussion,' said Runner.

Instead of responding, Coby let out a loud sigh, as if to say, 'I was trying to appeal to reason.'

Emmy said, 'He's right, Runner. This might be a bad time.'

'But this is the Lacuna Cabal Montreal Young Woman's Book Club!' shouted Runner. 'We have discussions! We'd have discussions even if bombs were falling all around. I'll have discussions on my deathbed. Because our discussions can change the world! It doesn't mean we have no heart!'

'No, I never said anything about having no — ' (Coby, in over his head.)

'I'm simply attempting to divine for Emmy why we so immediately take the monster's point of view, even though they didn't in the old days! Is that so bad? Is that really so bad, mister? Is that so bad?'

'No!' said Coby. 'That's not — No.'

'For example, have you seen the Forest of Cedar lately? No? Exactly. That's because it's all gone. It's gone! Because you and your friend here killed its only guardian tens of centuries ago and chopped down all the trees.'

'Hey, that wasn't really me.'

'And now it's nothing but a windblown desert in the middle of Lebanon! We have discussions, mister, and our discussions are important! Our discussions turn the mistakes of the past into the achievements of the future! We need our gods back! Our exiled gods and our slaughtered monsters! Even if we have to make them ourselves. Even if we have to make a giant monster fitzbot and stand it in the middle of the last forest, with its head above the tops of the trees, stronger than you, stronger than him,' pointing to the supine Du, 'stronger than Romy's hair and stronger than the future! Something you can't kill because it isn't alive. If we can't bring our exiled gods back, then we have to become them and build them and make them up! Romy just walked out into the street of Montreal as a god.'

'Yeah, right,' said Coby.

'She did.'

'I think so too,' said Priya.

Runner said, 'We owe it to her to go on.'

There was going to be a little bit of a problem, though. A moment later, they didn't have a Gilgamesh.

Missy had been tending to him with water from her bottle, applied to his forehead with a T-shirt for a compress, cooling the embattled, overheated brow of Dumuzi, the king. When he opened his eyes, her face and hands were very close.

He yelped. (That was unfortunate.) And then he was on his feet.

'Hold still,' Missy had said. 'I'm trying to — '

'Forget it. Get out of my face. I've had enough of you people.'

And then he was gone too, like Romy. No, not like Romy, since it did not sound like he had wished them well.

There are those who say, when well into their cups with the subject of the last days of the Lacuna Cabal Montreal Young Women's Book Club, that the turning point in our story was a haircut. But they're just being clever. It is our considered opinion that the turning point was rather the departure of Dumuzi. Because with Dumuzi, we hate to say it, went all of Runner's hope and conviction and desire for life. It might have been embarrassing for Missy, sitting there on her knees, having put herself out, scuffed a nice skirt, tried a few tricks from Jane Austen. But for Runner it was catastrophic. When Dumuzi left, calling his blunt sayonara back to them like they were strangers, it hit home with forehead-slapping suddenness that there was not going to be any sex for Runner. No sex for Runner Coghill to drag her from the darkness into the light, from sickness into health, from death back into life, from skittish youth to full-

169

blooming maturity. It was unreasonable to have expected it, especially since (let's be honest) the boy had hardly ever even looked her in the eye. But still.

And his leaving meant there would be no Anna either, which was even more unbearable. So, no sex, and no Anna either. Du and Anna had represented life times two for her. New friends, unknown to her two weeks before. Hope for the future. Possibility. A reason to live. Scratch one, scratch two. Nothing left to do except skip all that was left of the fun and get straight to the serious shit.

After a moment of gathering, Missy spoke. 'Can we adjourn, please?'

'Missy,' said Priya, 'Runner wants us to go on.'

'Right. Sorry. Let's go on.'

Runner was staring off into space. Priya said, 'What happens next, Runner?'

After a second in which Priya thought she had not been heard, Runner said quietly, 'It's okay with everyone that we go on?'

'We'll vote on it.' (Priya.) 'All in favour of going on?'

Runner turned to look at the hands going up. She was pale. They were all up. Even Coby's.

There were more hands up than people present.

Ruby was there and her hand was up too.

Ruby's hand was up and indicating that they should go deeper into the dark part of the story. Ruby wasn't sitting quite with the rest of the group. She was more or less surrounded, in Runner's view, by a kind of cave. She was on the wall of the cave, in fact. Hanging from a nail.

Where they put forgotten people.

The nail did not allow her to raise her head easily. But she could raise her hand. Her hand was white against the darkness of the wall. And it was up.

Making it unanimous.

They would go on.

'Maybe we should wait,' said Runner, very quietly. She was looking at Ruby, who rolled her eyes up to look at her and smiled and had no teeth. Ruby, who wasn't supposed to be a nightmare. Ruby, who wasn't supposed to represent the fear of death.

'No, Runner, it's okay,' said Priya. 'We said we'd go on.'

Priya was sweet. Runner turned to her, weakly. 'I know,' she said, 'but it's the hard part now. We have to get through the hard part. Up till now, it's been an adventure, but then somebody dies and everything changes.'

'Who dies?' (Coby.)

'Enkidu. He dies.'

'Oh, great.'

'Enkidu dies. Punishment from above from the goddess Inanna, for the killing of Humbaba, protector of the forest.

'How does he die?' asked Coby.

'He gets some terrible disease and Gilgamesh watches him die and it's awful,' said Runner.

'Just because he killed the monster?'

'I'm afraid so,' said Runner.

'But everyone made him do that.'

'It doesn't matter.'

'That's not fair,' Coby protested. Beside him, Emmy could barely refrain from rolling her eyes.

'Don't take it personally!' yelled Runner. 'You don't understand! Enkidu is just a person and Gilgamesh is just a person and people die! People just up and die. That's the point. It's something they discovered a long time ago and we still haven't gotten over it. Enkidu dies, and then Gilgamesh mourns him and realizes that he himself is mortal. And so he goes on a long journey ... '

Now it was Neil's turn to be upset. He must have been upset, since he spoke out of turn.

'Wait a minute,' he said.

'What, Neil?' (Impatient Runner.)

'You're leaving so much out!'

'No I'm not,' said Runner, who was tired, tired. 'They're unnecessary details.'

'But you left out the Bull of Heaven!' protested Neil, as if the Bull of Heaven were his favourite part, though Runner knew it wasn't.

'Don't worry about it, Neil,' she said, closing her eyes like a ghost.

'But they fight the Bull of Heaven!'

'That's just another stupid adventure!'

'That's what's good about it! Why are you in such a hurry?'

'I'm not in a hurry.'

'You are!'

Runner was nearly falling over. But she had one more bit of fire in her, hating to lose an argument. 'You want to bet, Neil?' she asked. 'I'll prove it to you that I'm not in a hurry. I think maybe we should adjourn today and come back to it tomorrow when Romy's here and … and we have all the boys and … things aren't so … you know … '

She started to cry.

'Okay,' said Neil immediately.

The tears were real. Nobody was quite sure they had seen that before, not even during the previous September when the death of Ruby had turned the Cabal upside down.

'Can we meet tomorrow and go on?' asked Runner meekly.

'Okay,' said Neil, even though he didn't have any authority in the matter.

'I'm just a little tired.'

'Okay,' said Priya.

'Okay,' said Missy.

'Sure,' said Aline, still slumped on the floor.

'Okay, Runner,' said Emmy, who had not been looking at Coby for quite some time.

'Okay,' said Coby, so it would be understood that he bore no ill will. He just wanted to get the hell out of there, go sit in the near dark somewhere and take in the light show of Emmy's skin.

'Okay then,' said Runner.

Okay then.

'Okaykayay,' echoed Ruby, disapproving, disapproving, disapproving.

✝

Dumuzi chose to walk out through the fourth floor for much the same reason as Anna had chosen it: he wanted to evade any Cabal members who might follow him. He wasn't doing a great job at being surreptitious, though, since he was speaking out loud, full voice, as he went.

'Jesus fucking Christ, these crazy fucking girls, I swear to God. It's like getting caught up in a hurricane or a tornado or a — '

And then he saw Anna. And the john. They had seen him first and heard him before that, so by the time he saw them it was as if they were inside a single pair of pants trying to get out. Except that wasn't what they were doing. The john's pants were around his ankles and he was falling over and panicking, shouting accusations at Anna about how it was a trap.

Dumuzi, grasping the matter perfectly, stepped directly into the fray: 'Yeah, it's a fucking trap, it's a fucking set-up, you get the fuck out of here, you fucking — '

Anna was screaming, something about how Dumuzi should not be upset and leave him alone and why wasn't he upstairs.

'Because they're fucking freaky upstairs!'

Freaky. He had paused and was looking at Anna's body and thinking of Missy upstairs, up close with her eyes and her mouth, her chin and her breasts; he had felt her hands on hisface. It had been a long time since he had felt a girl's hands on his face. He was thinking of Romy and the sudden explosion of Aline. And now here was Anna, with her shoulders and her waist exposed, and more besides, and what little light there was casting a glow off her skin like layers of glaze on a Raphael painting.

The john scrabbled away, half-pulling up his pants and stumbling and falling down the stairs, cursing and weeping and plotting revenge. Dumuzi was already forgetting about what he'd just done, weakening in the face of pure, jealous love.

'Anna,' he said.

And then there was a crash behind them. Something had fallen between the fifth and the fourth floors, without any help from Du punching walls. They knew before they looked: Runner had fallen through the floor again, beckoned by the weak spots and the underworld.

Anna said, 'Now look what you've done,' to Du. Which was, as we all know, not fair. And then she ran to Runner, calling over her shoulder for Dumuzi to help. He remembered and discarded his old wish for cities to collapse around his anxiety. *You did not wish for this to happen.* And his mind was not blank either — an improvement from Chapter One.

Anna knelt down by Runner, who was crumpled, eyes closed, wrapped around a waterlogged cardboard box. Anna pulled the box away and knelt into the curl of her body.

'Runner? Kid? Runner? Are you okay?'

Runner's eyes stayed closed. She was, we think, afraid to open them as she contemplated the perfection of the moment. 'What are you doing here?' she asked, feebly, gratefully. Awed by this miracle from the upper world.

'I … ' said Anna, her honesty drawn out. 'I'm stupid. I had my first client.'

She evaded Du's eyes, which were evading hers. They both watched Runner's brow furrow slightly, confused, her eyes still closed.

'Your first client for what?'

And then she smiled. Grinned, really, a sizable one, as if she weren't in any pain at all. 'Oh … '

And then she even laughed a bit, managing high mocking dudgeon: 'Hoor.'

She laughed again. And then faded for a moment. Practically disappeared, in fact. Then her eyes opened, black pools, and looked straight up into Anna's. 'You're pretty. I wish I was like you.'

And then, 'I was like you.'

Anna saw this girl's eyes cast over her like she was the angel of her devotion. And she loved it. God, she loved it. If she could manage even a small portion of this potential that Runner's eyes formed in her, she would accomplish great things. All she had to do, really, was start hanging around her, and excellence would follow. It was inevitable. Runner was a sun around which to swing her own earthy self.

She said, 'We're going to get you to the hospital.'

'Wait for Neil,' Runner said, brow furrowing again, eyes closing. 'He'll be mad at me.'

Anna looked up at Dumuzi. He slid his hands beneath the tiny bones-broken body.

'I'm going to pick you up now,' he said. 'No jokes.'

Runner gave herself sensually over to his arms. 'I only flirt because I like you.'

'No shit,' said Dumuzi, working his hands further in. She winced. He felt a small jolt, but she made no sound of pain.

'I just want you to fuck me. Is that so bad?'

Du was surprised to feel a surge inside him, a shot right through him, incoming from Runner and out toward Anna. He was suffused with it but pretended it wasn't happening. Up she came, into his arms, without so much as a cry, like a small pillow full of bones.

'Does that make me a bad person? She's busy fucking other men, anyway.'

Du nearly dropped her, though he should not have been surprised by what came out of her mouth. He glanced up at Anna to check if she had clocked the remark, and caught a — could it be? — guilty sort of expression; he wasn't sure, since he'd never seen the like on her face before.

'Du,' she said.

'Can we talk about it later?' His voice was high and reedy and his knees felt weak. He had liked that tone, though, the one that had just come out of Anna. Loved it, really. But he didn't want to risk dropping the girl again, so ...

And then the others came.

Missy was the first to appear. 'Runner, what happened?'

For Runner it was the most natural thing in the world to be back in these arms, eyes closed. Dreamily dreamily. 'I was experimenting with the structural integrity of the building.'

The others were close behind. Dumuzi said, 'Can somebody help us out here? Get the door.'

Aline said, 'Yes,' and went to get the door. Then Neil arrived, finally, looking white as a ghost himself.

'Sorry, Neil,' said Runner.

'That's okay,' said Neil softly.

'Don't be mad.'

They heard the distant sound of thunder. Aline came back, feeling awkward in the presence of Du: blocky. Sorry. Failed female. Male.

'It's pouring out there,' she said. And they started to go. There had been a low thrum of distant rain for some time now, they all realized. The streets of Montreal being washed of winter soot.

'Don't be afraid, Neil,' Runner called over Dumuzi's shoulder, in a voice that made her sound like she wasn't hurt at all. Du glanced at him. His expression was inscrutable as they filed into the stairwell.

✝

Coby was waiting for Emmy, who hesitated, so he hesitated too. Then, after the rest of them had gone through the door, she started to go too. Coby was right behind her. She stopped and turned. She said, 'I don't want you to come.'

This was a bit of a shock.

'What?' said Coby, surfacing. Laughing, almost, at her presumption.

'This is serious business between me and my friend. I don't want you to — '

'B— I know her too.'

'Not really. And Romy … '

He started to protest the Romy angle, citing absolution, but she interrupted him.

'I have a lot to think about.'

'But,' said Coby, grasping, 'but I thought we were — '

'Well we're not, I'm just numb. Sorry.'

And then she was gone. Coby was alone on the fourth floor of some ratty, dangerous building, somewhere in the city, who knew where, wondering how much time had gone by and where it had gone and whether it could be recovered. He stood quite still.

'Oh god … ' he said, 'I just … I just wanted to live in my skin!'

Outside it was raining. A torrential rainstorm, through which the Lacuna Cabal was making its way, bearing the burden of a broken Runner, Emmy catching up, alone. Coby saw it all clearly in his mind's eye. Nobody asked, 'Where's Coby?' They were too busy.

✝

Though we wish to always be moving things forward in this narrative, it has become necessary to pause where Coby is concerned, and go back. We find we can't leave him standing there in the doorway. That would be uncivilized, and we're supposed to have been the civilizing force in his life.

Coby walked home, distracted, to the apartment he'd barely seen in his new life, sat down on the toilet and, still distracted, urinated on himself. All over his legs and his pants and the floor of the bathroom. And then he cleaned himself up, sat down at his desk with an exercise book, tried to summon his scientific mind back from banishment and made some notes:

He wrote: *bioluminescence* and *Common Wood Louse*. And then he wrote, *If you love nature, then you will come to love 'whatever is twisted and capricious in nature.' Mondrian, something like that.*

> *I have concluded that Emmy is a common wood louse, of the light-sensitive, bioluminescent sort, based on the following evidence:*
>
> *1. colour/texture sensitivity: to Emmy, a certain combination of colour, shade and texture has moral connotations. If a complexion is both dark and rough, then it has the chance of seeming cheerful and trustworthy, but the only chance anyone has of entering a long-term relationship with Emmy is an individual who is both pale and smooth. My skin is both pale and rough, what she calls 'hypocritical.' She can't help it. I don't see anything human in this, though it's true I don't have a lot of experience.*
>
> *2. physical structure: the third night we were together, I turned over and noticed that she was curled up in a ball beside me. A tight orb, a sphere. I could perceive her limbs enfolded within this enclosed part of herself. I hadn't noticed before that she had an outer shell, blackish mauve, tougher than a callus and covered with small pimples. It looked like I had a small round steel bomb in the bed beside me. Very strange.*
>
> *It was, as it turns out, a usually well-disguised exoskeleton, which fans out from her spine when she curls up into a sphere.*

This explains a lot.

Possible solutions to rejection by common wood louse:

I've read somewhere that when a male ungulate is kept alone in a pen, he will start to go mad, rub his neck raw against a post or nod his head back and forth into oblivion. The ungulate's keepers handle the situation by placing a chicken in the pen with the ungulate. Then, reportedly, the ungulate will feel like he is protecting the chicken and it will stop him from going around the bend. Technically I am not an ungulate, but I am alone. I'm going to be alone forever, and beauty has been banished from my life. Also love. Conclusion: I need something small and animate to look after. Something like a chicken.

QUESTION: *What AI life form most resembles a chicken?*
ANSWER: *Fitzbot.*

And so we bid adieu, for the moment, to Coby, wishing we could whisper in his ear that he will play a part again in this story, that his fitzbot — designed to head toward the shadows and find comfort there — will fulfill one of the most important tasks ever for a member of the Lacuna Cabal, whether that member be animal, vegetable, mineral, goddess, human or (in)animate object. Still, we will leave him to do his laundry and refamiliarize himself with his textbooks. And find his fitzbot, since he had misplaced it yet again.

Chapter Thirteen
Weather

Runner opened her eyes at one point and said to Anna, suddenly all seriousness, 'Hey! You came to a meeting!'

Anna said, 'Well, sort of.'

And Runner said, 'Don't be afraid, Neil.'

And Neil pretty much ignored her.

They were travelling through the city. South on Saint-Laurent in the freezing rain. Toward the Royal Vic. A bad idea to go on foot, but everyone was blindly following Dumuzi and Dumuzi was answering the call of panic by exerting himself.

As they approached the corner of Laurier, Aline said, 'We should stop at the bank machine and call an ambulance,' but they ignored her. Then, as they were crossing the street, Missy pulled out her cell phone and said, as if it were the first time, 'Let me call an ambulance, I'll pay for it.' Dumuzi was saying, 'No, it's not a problem, we can get her there.' But Missy had already trotted ahead and buzzed open the door to the bank. Du wasn't going to ignore that, not with Runner shocked and shivering in his arms. So he crossed the threshold of Missy's control and everyone filed in after, leaving Aline outside to roll a cigarette[29] in the rain. In her skirt. With her makeup running into the collar of her blouse.

We're not saying Aline was paranoid or had no right to get upset for being ignored. Aside from the fact that there was

---

29 Yes, Aline smoked. She rolled her own Drum Tobacco with Export papers. A filthy habit. She rolled to save up a bit of cash for her sexual reassignment surgery, which is, for all intents and purposes, not covered in Quebec.

understandable tension between her and Du, her constant state of depression made her invisible to her friends — yes, her friends — during a crisis. She often mumbled. That was the truth of it.

They were all inside the shelter of the bank machine, doting over Runner, waiting for the ambulance, while the mumbling Aline was outside, smoking in the freezing rain. She'd even wandered a little way down Laurier, away from the bank. Which is why nobody saw what happened next. There was a power line there, heading north and south along Clark. Aline bent over, cigarette stub gone out in her mouth, unlaced her prized Pro-Ked sneakers, slipped them off, picked them up, pulled the laces taut, knotted them together and, without giving it a second thought, threw the whole double-shoe contraption up into the air. One shoe caught the power line, wrapped itself around and flipped off just as the other shoe caught. Thereby setting Aline's only reliable icon of androgyny safely out of her reach. Aline stood in her sock feet and began to notice that the rain had turned to sleet, the temperature had dropped, and though the socks she wore were wool, they weren't going to help for long.

If this were the movie of our lives, the camera would fade here to black and we'd cut to inside the taxi, a view through the front windshield toward the ambulance in front, tail lights diffused by the wipers against thickening droplets of snow, as they follow the ambulance south on Saint-Urbain.

It was Priya and Anna and Aline in the cab. Anna and Priya were talking but Aline was in an accustomed silence. She had a good deal on her mind. As they drove past Rue Rachel, she said, 'I want to get out.'

Priya said, 'Aline, don't you want to see if — '

Aline interrupted her. 'She's going to be okay. I'll come visit in the morning. Stop the cab.'

As she slipped out into the night, Anna said, 'Is she not wearing shoes?'

And the cab drove on.

Then Aline was padding alone down a deserted Rachel toward Parc Lafontaine and her home, and the air had turned to puffy white. The snow on the ground was starting to stick to the slush below it and Aline tried not to think about her feet. There was a lot to think about that was not feet.

She was concerned about Runner, but they had never been that close. And Runner had recently been callous toward Aline, who struggled to ignore the subtle taunts regarding 'illusion' versus 'reality' by considering that Runner had taken them up only in the months after the death of her sister.

Aline forgave Runner her failings. Judge not, she thought, lest ye be judged. And although Runner was herself doing some pretty heavy-duty judging, she was also herself pretty judgeable, and Aline knew the two of them had more in common than not, and that whoever judged either of them stood against individuality, idiosyncrasy, the intrepid spirit and the impulse of life itself. Stood against the very muscle that pumped the blood through Runner's thinking brain, and Aline's too. She thought of that and it gave her peace, as she sloshed along.

But what about the boy? What about Dumuzi? That represented a failure on Aline's part. Physical confrontation represented the masculine in ascendancy: the yang sloshing across the divide to overwhelm the yin, like some terrible tsunami. If Aline could not control her violent impulses — even Aline — then what hope for men everywhere?

Such thoughts were not helping her ignore her feet. So what about Romy? Was she out wandering in this weather too?

✝

Romy had come out the front doors of the Lighter Building, slipped over to Saint-Dominique and headed south. She had crossed Saint-Laurent at Laurier and zigzagged her way along the foot of the mountain. Walking along Esplanade between

Marie-Anne and Rachel, soaked and freezing, she spotted a lamppost with poetry glued to it, accompanied by a photograph of a bleak urban landscape that drew her to it like a beacon, even though it was dark. The poem was about travelling west into Ontario on a bus home.

'Home was a cold word,' it said.

Romy thought, Has it come to this? Bingotown, beckoning from a lamppost?

And then she tore herself away and headed down into the Ghetto, took off her wet clothes and fell into bed.

✛

Aline thumped across Saint-Christophe, thinking through a proposition: if she was going to make a transition from the whole idea of transitioning, if she was going to wilfully fail the humiliating RLT (the Real-Life Test) before the SRS (the Sexual-Reassignment Surgery), then it was good and right that she had started with her shoes.

Aline lived in a small bowling alley of a flat on the second floor of a four-storey walk-up at the corner of de la Roche and Avenue Bureau. The entire apartment focused in on a large window at the far end, which opened into an alley. When Aline had decided, several months before, to throw away her man clothes, she'd simply packed them into cardboard boxes and dropped them out the open summer window. The boxes had floated down, slightly heavier than air, and landed on the ground by the wall, ready to be picked through by passersby.

Now she let herself in without switching on the light and hobbled painfully into her little half-kitchen. She pulled a pot from the stovetop and filled it with water, dragged it back across to the element and turned on the gas. The pilot light was out. Her feet were already starting to burn inside the slop of her socks and the floor was slick with water. She found some matches, bent over to light the pilot. Nearly set her hair on fire. Wouldn't that be funny, she thought: ice feet, fire face. What was in between? she wondered. Nothing, maybe.

She had long struggled to believe that the mind was all that mattered. The night room of the mind, with the moon shining in, illuminating underneath. The mind of Aline, and her body, transformed and transforming.

But a recently published book was conspiring against her.

She sat on the floor and rubbed her feet, peeled off her socks and threw them toward the hall. The water on the stove sat quietly. She recalled sitting in a coffee shop last summer. A man had walked by and complimented her red socks. They'd been Christmas stocking stuffers from days of yore that had lasted forever because they were wool and her feet were, how to say, delicate. Suddenly they were no longer Santa Clausers but rather a banner of deep-cover Pride. Not so inaccurate, except the idea of giving blowjobs to boys had always made her want to puke. A confusing fact at the best of times.

Everybody always wanted to talk about sex. Enough already. There were more things on heaven and earth. But she'd worried about it. And now she'd pushed herself to a crisis by getting rid of the sneakers. Her socks were pretty much gone too.

How far along was she? It had been the end of last July when she'd shoved the boxes out the window. Eight months. Four more to go before she completed the RLT. But the truth was, she had never wanted to do it. Sure, it would be great to be able to choose the surgery, but it was all so garish and she wanted to be subtle. The only thing that had allowed her to make such a serious go of it (eight months!) was Missy's brilliant idea that had placed her in the bubble of a book club. Missy pretended otherwise, but she was, Aline felt, a deeply compassionate person. A leader of men, as they say. Or of womyn.

And the Pro-Ked sneakers. She had always imagined that if he had been born a girl, which if nature had been fair was what

185

would have happened, then she would have grown into the sort of girl who'd wear sneakers, jeans and sweatshirts big enough to swim in. A tomboy girl.

But jeans and sweatshirts were off-limits in the RLT. So the Pro-Keds were Aline's only bid for sartorial normality. She found that she would gaze down upon them for long periods of self-identification.

So she had been getting through it, and would have continued to get through it, despite the addition of boys to the book club. Contrary to popular belief, it was not the boys who had thwarted her best-laid plans so much as that book. March 2003 was a time of war for the Middle East and the transgendered community both.

The book was called *The Man Who Would Be Queen*; it was available in its entirety for free online, and its argument was basically that if a man had spent his boyhood as a boy but now wanted to be a girl, then his current desire to cross over was tied to a perverse form of onanism: the desire to fuck himself as a woman. Autogynephilia. A Gender Mirror. Puke.

The water was beginning to steam. Aline pulled the pot off the stove and placed it on the floor. She slid down the fridge and lifted her feet into the water.

Why didn't these people leave her alone?

Dumuzi had merely given her anger a target.

The last straw had been the disappearance of Aline's beloved Baghdad Blogger, lost among these new-falling bombs of March. Aline knew she should be concerned more for a whole country full of people. But she wanted to hear from Salam Pax again. These days she would sit and stare for minutes at a time at her own blog, pov.blogspot.com, wanting to blurt out words of concern and love and loss; sometimes she even wrote them, but the only entry she'd saved had been one from weeks before, while Pax was still posting.

Her feet, sitting in the warm water, were beginning to return to life.

She'd e-mailed him many times, but that was different from the public declaration — the blog — and, anyway, the Baghdad Blogger had never written back. Aline loved this stranger mostly for the fact that the bear of Baghdad seemed to have a certain amount of affection for himself, despite his gayness and his fatness and his bearness and his geekiness. Maybe she'd give the Baghdad Blogger a blowjob. Maybe she would.

As Aline sat on the floor with her feet in the fast-cooling water, she decided that, beyond her cut losses, what she had to do was recall her old secret feelings of beautiful androgyny. The only way to do that was to let a few of her male attributes stand out again, at least for a little while. RLT be hanged.

But what were they, her male attributes? Mussable mop of hair? Birdbone cheeks and shoulders? Violence?

Perhaps if the masculine were to be exposed, then the feminine would stop being elusive, become touchable again. Aline would remove the skirt and go with black sweats for a while. The black sweats. Just for a while. At least until she could pick up a couple of pairs of jeans.

The clarity of this thought made him cry, sitting on the kitchen floor, makeup running, though most of the light foundation he wore had already been washed away by the rain.

Chapter Fourteen
Inanna's Descent

, Royal Victoria Hospital.
At his place by the door, Neil wrote in his book:

> *Hospital. Runner in bed. Neil at the door. He's writing in his book. Girls have all left except Anna and, because of Anna, Dumizu [sic], who seems to be hanging around waiting for Anna.*

We have no reason to doubt the veracity of Neil's account, laconic though it may be. 'Dumizu,' though: that's hilarious.

Runner's eyes were closed. Anna said to Dumuzi, 'Will you stay with her for a bit?'

Dumuzi, despite everything that had taken place, felt the old anxiety, the panic: 'Why, uh? What do you ... ? Where are you ... ?'

He was ashamed to be prying. But the desire won out as always.

'I have class,' said Anna.

'Really? But it's like six-thirty or something.'

'It's a night class, Du. I'm already late. I don't want her to be alone.'

'But, uh,' gesturing to Neil at the door, 'her brother's here. I'll walk you.'

They were right back into the old struggle. Anna said, 'Please, no, Dumuzi. I'll come back. I just ... ' She was trying to be nice, after everything he'd done. She wanted him to be good. She wanted to be good too, but he was prying, and between these two extremes she lost her cool. 'Just stay with her a bit!'

Dumuzi, failed again. 'Okay.'

And then Anna went. Dumuzi sat. Neil was still crouched by the door. Dumuzi was distracted and so Neil pretended to ignore him, looked down at the floor, too self-conscious to even write in his book. Dumuzi was staring at Runner but it was obvious he didn't see her. He was thinking of Anna. When Runner spoke, abruptly, it seemed to be right out of a dead sleep. She said, 'Anna.'

Her eyes were still closed. Dumuzi regained his equilibrium and said, 'Anna's gone.' It was as if she didn't hear him for a moment, but then she smiled with satisfaction.

'She finally came to a meeting.'

'Yeah,' said Du. 'Sort of.'

Du was staring down at his boots for lack of a better place. Then he looked up to see Runner's eyes open and on him, black and flinty with mischief.

Neil spoke up from the door. 'She's tough, eh?'

'Anna?' said Dumuzi. 'Yeah, she's tough.' Neil tried to hide his pleasure in being agreed with.

'I'm tough too,' said Runner weakly. And then, with obvious pride: 'If I live through this, I'll have a chthonian cicatrix.'

'Really,' said Dumuzi, with no idea, even as Neil rolled his eyes so high they almost got stuck in his forehead.

'Oh, dream on, Runner.'

Dumuzi tried to ask, 'What's a … kithinian … kol … '

'It's a scar,' she said smoothly, choosing to ignore Neil. 'A scar from the underworld.'

'Why the underworld?' asked Dumuzi.

'Because it's the underworld that keeps trying to pull me down,' said Runner.

And then, in response to Neil's expression of disgust and disbelief, 'Neil, don't be rude.' And then she smiled a terrible, lying scowl. 'I'm just kidding.'

Dumuzi looked over at Neil, whose eyes were on the floor, clearly upset. 'Hey,' he said, not knowing why, 'she's just kidding.'

'Yeah, sure she is,' said Neil. 'Yeah, sure she is.'

Dumuzi turned back to Runner, who wasn't paying attention to Neil at all. She was fixing Du with a conspiratorial look. 'Can I tell you a secret?' she asked. 'A secret story?'

'That depends,' said Du.

'On what?'

'On whether there's any sex talk in it.'

'I'll try to keep it to a minimum.'

'Okay.'

Her voice deepened a semi-tone or two. 'It's a story that Gilgamesh would have heard from the priest when he went to church on Sundays.'

Dumuzi, misunderstanding, started to explain how he was pretty sure he didn't want to be their Gilgamesh anymore, but Runner cut him off and explained that she was only trying to illustrate how it was an old story, older even than the ancient king himself.

'You're sure?' said Du. 'Because if I suddenly find myself sitting in some, you know, church pew tomorrow, I'll know that, uh, I'll know.'

'Don't worry.' She smiled.

'Okay,' he said. Her smile reassured him. 'So, it's an old story.'

'Very, very old,' she said. 'And sacred. It's the oldest and best story of twins, which is why we became so devoted to the whole Sumerian and Mesopotamian pantheon in the first place. Because we discovered they have the best and oldest story of twins.'

'Really?'

'Yes.'

'So what is it?'

'It's about Inanna, goddess of life, descending to the realm of her sister Erishkigal because it was the only place in the universe that she had never been, and she was curious. So she went. To get there, she had to pass through seven gates. As she went through each, the guards would make her remove a piece of her garment, until when she came before her sister Erishkigal, Queen of the Dead, she was naked. I'm sorry if that embarrasses you.'

'That's okay.'

'She even had to remove her "fuck me" breastplate.'

'I get the picture.'

'She was naked and ashamed, and then her sister struck her dead and hung her body on a nail. That's how they tell it: hung her body on a nail. Erishkigal was jealous of her sister's primacy in the upper world, and wanted her to stay down there. These two women, though. They were so close as to be almost the same person. When Inanna's servants came down to claim the body, they found Erishkigal moaning and doubled over, as if she herself were experiencing the physical pain of her sister's death. And she wouldn't let her go. It was like they had to be together, the two sisters, but also they couldn't be together, and the only way Inanna could be returned to her place in heaven was if someone she loved would come and take her place. It's a great mystery that we fail to understand even after all these centuries. What is this ritual that bound these two goddesses together, one above and the other below?'

There was a pause. Dumuzi looked over at Neil again. He was writing in his book, though Du thought he saw fear in the boy's face. 'So did they have a little brother?' he asked, and as Neil looked up he winked.

'Who?' asked Runner.

'Inanna and Erishkigal?'

Neil stopped writing. 'Yeah, did they have a little brother?' he asked.

Dumuzi said, 'You should think of him too, you know.'

'Yeah, you should think of him,' said Neil.

Runner rolled her buggy eyes so that they looked for a moment like they might pop out and bounce away.

'You think we didn't? Neil has lived his life in the world we made. He didn't even have to walk on his own until he was six or seven. We used to swing him between us, up in the sky. In kindergarten they thought he was the biggest freak. Isn't that right, Neil?'

Neil nodded, beaming now for being the centre of attention. Horror forgotten.

'He got jealous of our games, though. It's true, didn't you, Neil?'

He nodded again, more gravely. Bent over to write a note in his book. Runner went on.

'His place in them was never cut and dried. So we told him he could be Neil Coghill the Real McCoghill. One of a kind.'

'And was he happy with that?' Du asked.

'It was okay,' said Neil, still bent over his book, and then they all laughed. And the laughter came like lightning to startle them all.

Until it exhausted Runner. She lay back on the pillow and closed her eyes. Dumuzi thought for a moment that she was done for the evening. But then, unexpectedly as always, she started up again.

'Sometimes I try to do that,' she said, and opened her eyes.

'Do what?' asked Du.

'Sometimes I try to bring my sister back. But I'd have to defy science to do that.'

'How would you defy science?'

She smiled. 'You take a small nuclear reactor's worth of energy called the Lacuna Cabal Montreal Young Women's Book Club. You use them to build the whole Sumerian universe, above and below, pantheon and people, women and men ... '

She paused long enough that Du thought she was finished. Then went on.

'Once that's done, in theory, all you'd have to do is wrench open a sewer grate somewhere and just climb down.'

'Climb down where?'

'To the underworld, of course.'

'Sounds like a weird theory,' said Du.

'Yeah,' said Neil. 'Sounds like a weird theory.'

'I know,' said Runner. 'It probably doesn't work. That's why I have a fall-back position.'

'What's the fall-back position?'

'You try to do instead what Gilgamesh did when the one he loved died. It's more down-to-earth.'

'What did Gilgamesh do?'

'Mourned the death of his friend. Became afraid of death himself. Went on a very long journey. Spoke to a very wise man. Eventually put his fear and grief behind him. Returned to his life.'

'Sounds way better,' said Neil.

'Yeah, that sounds way better,' said Du.

'Way, way better,' said Neil.

'You know, Neil,' said Runner, 'you'll always be Gilgamesh to me. You know that, don't you?'

✛

Later, it was late. Du and Neil had remained in their respective places, though the two of them were sound asleep.

Now that we, the two of us, are experts on *The Epic of Gilgamesh* and related material, we can tell you there is a coda to the story of Inanna's Descent. There was a pair of flies in that story that helped the goddess out somehow. They got down into the underworld to scope out the place for her, two little black flies. As a reward, the goddess Inanna allowed flies to go everywhere: flies are permitted in the halls of kings and in the bars with the drunks and on the naked shoulders of lovers loving. No gate shall keep the little fly out, for she is wise.

With us it is the same. With this account, with this — if we may so deem it — book, we have been granted a similar clarity of sight: we see things that took place, and the reader should understand that they happened just as we say, because it is as if we were there. And it begins with what Runner saw before she died, when she was alone, while Neil and Dumuzi were both asleep. March 31st, at about one o'clock in the morning.

Ruby appeared far away and was travelling closer and closer, until it became apparent to Runner that she was carrying a book in her hands. And she responded to everything that Runner said, using the book: opening, closing, writing, offering. And what Runner said, as she travelled herself through the seven gates to meet her sister, was, 'Be nice.'

And then she said, 'I wanted to tell you. I read a book ... I read this book ... I'll bring it. If I can. It's about two women who loved each other, loved each other in November. And one of them died. I thought of you a lot. Wish you were here. Do you want to read it?'

And then they reached and they reached, and their hands found one another. They grasped and held. Runner hesitated, looked back at the brother that her dead sister did not see. And then the two of them departed from this world. Runner and Ruby Coghill, together again, like the Beatles, only better.

Neil woke up. It was the middle of the night. Dumuzi was still in his chair, his head on the bed. Neil could see in the light through the window that Dumuzi was sleeping and drooling. He thought perhaps Dumuzi might drool onto Runner's arm. He stood up, walked over and poked him. Dumuzi did not wake. Then he looked at Runner. Then he looked away, walked all the way around the bed so that he could be up by her head without Dumuzi being in the way. And he looked at her again. He put a hand on her shoulder. Shook her a bit. She was loose and did not wake up. He put his face up to her face. Right up to her face, to feel that she was not breathing. He stood up and his hand came up and went over his mouth for a minute. And then another minute. She was the healthy one. He stood and stood and did not cry. Then he reached down and picked up her hand. Carefully lifted out the cuneiform stone on which it was resting and tucked it under his arm. Then he took off his glasses and put them into her hand. They were just fake glasses. Then he walked around the bed and went to find his bag by the door, rummaged around inside it until he came up with a small pair of scissors. He took the scissors and cut off a lock of his hair. Just a small one. Then he walked back around the bed again, reached and touched her other hand and then picked it up. Enclosed the lock within her palm. And that was it. He was done. He slipped quietly out of the room and was gone. Nobody saw him. He did, after all, know that hospital like the back of his hand.

PART THREE

Chapter Fifteen
In the Skin of a Lion

Dumuzi was in the front of the hospital when Missy arrived; he was crouched down against a pillar, surrounded by smokers. The weather had cleared, though the snow had stayed. It was below zero and getting colder by the minute. Du stayed outside, though, hoping the cold would whisk away his tears and obscure the puffiness around his eyes. He didn't like it much inside, anyway.

Missy appeared a few minutes before nine, which was what he'd thought would happen, since she'd said she would be there at nine and, clearly a punctual person, would have needed the few extra minutes to travel up the elevator and make her way through the wards.

He had never told anyone that someone was dead before, and he soon realized that he would do certain things differently next time. Like not beginning ambiguously ('It's pretty serious'), thus avoiding the question 'Is she going to be okay?' The effect, ultimately, of his unschooled method was a dizzy spiral downward, with the listener (Missy, in this case) grasping at roots and vines all the way down the crevice wall.

After the first burst of tears, Dumuzi told her what the doctors had said: Runner had shattered some bones and there had been some internal bleeding but, worst of all, she hadn't been taking her medication, so her thyroid levels were catastrophically high when she arrived at the hospital. Missy wanted to know what Dumuzi meant by her thyroid levels and Du explained that apparently Runner had been suffering from Grave's Disease, a condition she had apparently managed to keep secret from everyone she knew, except, presumably, Neil, and which was the very condition that had killed her sister. It was a serious disease that caused the thyroid gland (regulator of energy levels in the body) to become overactive, inspiring eccentric behaviour and causing other serious conditions like osteoporosis, high anxiety, mood swings and a bugginess of the eyes. Runner had suffered from all these things, a fact that should have been obvious to anyone who knew her, even Dumuzi, who had known her for only two weeks. The disease had also weakened her heart muscle, which, in the end, had been the cause of death.

While very serious, Grave's Disease was also highly treatable, though the doctors had found Runner to be an extremely unreliable patient, who failed to look after herself at every turn. They were grief-stricken themselves, the doctors, as they had lost Runner's sister in a similar fashion six months earlier, when Runner had been nearly as healthy and robust as any twenty-three-year-old could ever wish to be. Her decline had been inexplicable to them.

They were intimately familiar with the sisters and also with Neil, who was now missing.

Dumuzi told Missy about Neil's glasses, which he produced, expressing some concern about how the kid was going to get by without them. Missy asked Du politely if he had noticed that there weren't any lenses in them. He hadn't and was so relieved to learn that Neil did not need them that he ignored Missy's subtle mirth, endearing himself to her in a way that erased his terrible slight of the day before (was it just the day before?). Here was an impulsive man, she thought, not much given to reflection, but always solving problems. That wasn't so bad. More importantly, he was a faithful man, a most faithful man; he had stayed all night by the bedside of Runner Coghill. It would be so noted in the Lacuna Cabal Book of Days: a semi-member had comported himself in a most distinguished manner.

The two of them stood and waited in the deepening cold until Priya came, and then they told her together. Priya had barely finished crying when Aline and Emmy arrived at about the same time, and so they all cried again for a while until someone noticed that Aline was wearing no makeup, had sprouted black sweatpants on her legs and was giving the impression, all in all, of a rather conventional-looking young man. What's more, his only effort to hide this fact was to keep the hood of his hoodie pulled up over his head.

This distracted the mourners for a couple of minutes as they tried to figure out what the hell was going on with her. Him. Him. Her. Him. They managed to learn that he would continue to answer to Aline, at least for the time being, and that generally what was going on with him was not as important as what was going on with them.

And then they recalled what was going on with them and the tears came again.

After that, they all waited a little while for Anna, feeling their tears dry up in the cold, their skin wrinkle and chap.

Anna didn't come. Aside from Du, there was no one who should have been disappointed by the fact that Anna didn't come. And yet they were all disappointed. Runner had loved Anna, it seemed so clear now, and Anna didn't come.

The next problem: what about Neil?

✚

Neil had gone home, let himself in, slept, got up (early), eaten some Ichiban, grabbed a piece of paper and wrote on it:

Dear Runner, I am too strong enough. You'll see.
  Love Always, Neil

Then he folded it up into an origami butterfly, a thing he had learned how to make in order to remind Runner of the little butterfly of a thyroid beneath her throat — its delicacy and her need to take care of it. He'd made hundreds of them in the previous six months. He'd made a few for Ruby too, though he'd known that Ruby had really been trying. The same could not be said about Runner, whose death wish had been clear to him the whole time.

This one would be his last. He went into Runner's room and placed it on her pillow. Saw that the bed beside Runner's was not made — she'd been sleeping in Ruby's again. He crawled up onto it. Felt for a moment like sinking down into it, but instead he lifted his knees one by one to pull up the messy blankets and made the bed as best as he could. Then he climbed down, left the room and closed the door.

In the front hall, he arranged all ten cuneiform stones neatly in his knapsack, which he called his carpetbag, packed around them with food and clothing, headed out to a bank machine, withdrew some money and walked back up into the city.

A long journey would require some girding. And he knew he'd have to lie low. No doubt there would be people out prowling for him very soon. He had time to kill, though, as he wanted to wait until nightfall, which would not come until twenty minutes after six.

So he went and sat in Wallenberg Square, behind the Christ Church Cathedral. He sat on a bench beneath four small gargoyles. His feet were tired already. The carpetbag was heavyish. He took it off and went over to the plaque to read about what Raoul Wallenberg had done. He read the quote from the Talmud that was carved there in stone: 'Whoever saves one life, it is as if they have saved the entire world.' He thought, I wish I could save somebody like that.

Then he went back and sat down on the bench to rest his feet. This is where he was when Dumuzi, Missy, Priya, Aline and Emmy were standing together in front of the Royal Vic.

Missy had managed to retrieve Runner's house key from her personal effects, and the five of them made the trip down to Champ-de-Mars Metro in Old Montreal and the fabulous third-floor apartment of Runner and Neil Coghill. It stood above the cobbled street of Rue Saint-Gabriel and featured exposed brick, hardwood floors and four oriel windows, two for each of the outside walls. Neil loved the oriels so much that Runner permitted him to set up an encampment around one of them as a sleeping area. Neil's belfry, Runner called it.

It was the kind of place normally owned by rich American tourists as a *pied-à-terre*. A place to hang your hat when you're visiting the city. 'How did they end up with a place like this?' asked Dumuzi, for whom it represented everything he'd ever dreamed of in a Montreal apartment.

'Insurance,' said Missy.

'Insurance for what?'

'Their whole family died.'

'Oh,' said Du, stopped short. 'When?'

'Does it matter?'

'Well, like, was it recently?'

'When they were sixteen. A building fell on them.'

'A building?'

'I don't want to get into it right now.'

'Okay. Sure. Okay. Fair enough. Wow. Shit. That kid. I should have kept an eye on him.'

'You didn't know.'

Missy had never been here, either, and she was amused to discover a window in the bathroom shower that went all the way down to the floor. It was all glass brick and therefore translucent, but she could still get a sense of the movement in the street below. How that must have thrilled Runner, right to the marrow of her brittle bones. She must have been an exhibitionist, Missy thought; she must have showered with the bathroom light on after sunset. No question about it. Grave's Disease may have induced low sex drive, but Runner would have induced the sex drive right back. No thyroid condition was going to prevent Runner from being as dirty as she wanted to be.

The shower stall would have embarrassed Neil, though, Missy imagined. Sure enough, the sink was coming away from the wall, as if someone had been doing an undue amount of bathing in it.

'What are you grinning about?' asked Priya as Missy came out of the bathroom.

'Nothing,' said Missy. 'Nothing.' Though if she had said something it might have surprised Priya into endearment.

In the vast and sunny apartment, the others were searching for some clue as to Neil's whereabouts. One of the spartan inner rooms contained a dresser with turned-out drawers, but things outside of Neil's small encampment seemed to have been left untouched. Priya opened the door to Runner's room and saw two made beds, then shut the door again. Everyone left the door closed after that.

Dumuzi had found an origami butterfly in the boot rack by the door. He was about to unfold it when Missy swooped down and whacked him in the forearm — a distinctly Coghillian gesture.

'Don't do that,' she said.

'Why not?' he asked.

'Don't do it unless you know exactly how to put it back together.'

'Well, I don't,' he said, 'but it looks like it was only recently made.'

'How can you tell?'

'I don't know. It just looks like it — it looks like the edges are new and ... I don't know. It's so white. Why do you care?'

'It's origami!' said Missy.

'So? It might be a clue.'

'Put it down.'

In a small, swift move, Dumuzi opened the sheet. There was nothing inside.

'Now look what you've done,' said Missy.

'It was all we had,' said Du, as he began to try to fold the sheet of paper back up again.

Missy turned to the others. 'I think we should head back to the Lighter Building to see if he's there.'

'You think he might be there?' asked Emmy.

'That's where he knows to find us,' declared Missy. 'He knows we're his friends.'

'Does he?' asked Du.

'Yes! He does! What's that supposed to mean?'

'I'm just asking.'

'Fine. Let's go.'

They went.

✝

But Neil wasn't at the Lighter Building. While the truncated remnant of the Lacuna Cabal was making its way up through the city, Neil was attending a service inside the cathedral, mostly for warmth. He didn't take this ancient religion any more seriously than the Sumerian one espoused by his sisters. But he knew prayer was becoming a popular form of communication these days, and he wondered whether we weren't all gearing up for a religious war fifty years down the road when we'll all have forgotten why we started praying again in the first place. That, Neil felt, was how it had always happened, and there was no reason to think it wasn't going to happen that way again.

That's what he was spending his time thinking during the noon service, and also, apparently, during the five-fifteen one. At least that's what he recently told us. He's a little older now, and we think the responsible authorial thing to do is to take such assertions with a grain of salt. He was, after all, ten years old. But then again, he was Neil Coghill the Real McCoghill. And brimming with gravitas.

Several hours later, Missy, Du, Emmy, Aline and Priya were still pacing around the fifth floor of the Lighter Building where Neil was not. Or, to put it officially: March 31st, 5:43 p.m. Pacing Session of the Lacuna Cabal. Dumuzi was berating himself.

'It's so bad,' he kept saying. 'It's so bad.' And, 'Shit, shit, I'm such a loser.' That word, 'loser,' connected him forever to the absent Anna, from whom he'd learned how to use it, about himself, with conviction and authority.

Priya said, 'Do you think he'd still be following the Gilgamesh story?'

'I don't fucking know,' said Dumuzi, who felt, quite reasonably, that they were all well past the Gilgamesh story, along with all other books. Yu Xuanji even, though he had an impulse to go home and tear out her pages and keep them folded up in his wallet. You never know where you're going to end up next.

'Who gives a fuck about the Gilgamesh story?' he said.

'Well, he does,' said Priya.

'Who?'

'Neil!'

Dumuzi turned to look at her in slow motion.

'I mean, wouldn't he?' asked Priya. 'If I were him, I would think it would be all I had.'

Du was nodding. 'Yeah. Oh yeah.' He was impressed, grateful, speechless. He'd always thought that Priya was a flake who spent half the time talking to herself, but this was clear evidence of ... what did they call that? Empathetic intelligence. Grace.

He was about to mumble words to that effect when Priya continued.

'Okay, so the Gilgamesh story ... '

Missy said, 'Enkidu dies and Gilgamesh is the surviving friend.'

Du said, 'Maybe he ... You don't think he's ... g ... Uh ... Oh god: Gilgamesh is the surviving friend. What happens next in the story? I feel like it's exam time and I slept through half the semester.'

Priya said, 'The king's friend Enkidu dies.'

Missy said, 'And the king becomes afraid, goes for a long journey — '

Du said, 'Oh god … '

Missy said, ' — across the ocean, in search of eternal life.'

Du shouted, 'He's gone down to the water!'

Priya asked, 'What water?'

'The water. The river.'

Emmy: 'The river!'

Aline: 'The river!'

Missy commanded, 'Let's get him!'

And as they went. Dumuzi mumbled, not quite under his breath: 'That kid's not going to make a Gilgameshaster out of me.'

✝

Heading down University, just as he got to René Lévesque, Neil saw Romy. She was standing across the street, beyond all the traffic, looking at the Farine Five Roses sign, steam coming off her in the cold.

Ever since he'd left the cathedral's five-fifteen service, Neil hadn't been able to shake the feeling of being followed. The follower, he felt, was something creepy, not quite human. He had wondered, with a small plummet into mute grief, whether this was how Runner felt to be followed by a ghost. If he was being tailed by his sisters, he thought, then he wanted them to pull him down and get it over with. His teeth started to chatter. He realized he was afraid. He wanted company. And that's when he saw Romy. Like, fifty feet away. But he thought if he moved toward her she would recede. This was already how his mind was starting to work. So he stood there for three minutes until she turned and saw him.

'Neil!' she called. It was very satisfying. 'Neil!'

'What were you looking at?' he called.

'Nothing in particular,' Romy called back, crossing. 'I was looking in the general direction of the port.'

'Why?' called Neil.

'I was down there earlier,' she called. 'I overheard two French dudes talking about tugging a boat to Owen Sound.'

'Oh yeah?' he called.

'I'm thinking of hitching a ride,' she said, arriving.

'You mean stowing away?' he said, as his heart skipped a beat, since he himself had formulated a plan to stow away on a boat.

The water. The river.

'Yeah,' she said. 'Owen Sound's a lot closer to Bingotown than we are here. And I saw the boat, Neil. It's a big boat. Way better than the bus. There won't be any sailors on that boat. They're all going to be over on the other boat — the tugboat. I'll have the run of the place. It's an old ferry, I think. Looked like shit on the outside but I bet it's got a stellar interior.'

'Then what are you doing up here?'

'Considering my options. Do I really want to give up and go home to the colourless cities of Ontario? Or would I rather stay here in the bleak, perpetual winter of colourful Montreal?'

Neil looked at Romy. She was still looking distractedly toward the port, chewing gum. Steam was coming off her head in the cold. She was different. Her hair was cut more smoothly against her scalp than it had been the last time he'd seen her. And she was wearing a multi-zippered leather jacket over an enormous wool sweater and brilliant black-and-white-striped jeans. She looked cool, he thought. She looked like a dyke.

'My sister died,' he said.

Now he was looking at her very carefully, though he pretended not to be. He saw her look at him like she didn't quite understand what he'd said. Then he saw her want to ask and then he saw her decide not to. Then he saw a plummeting emotion pass so fast over her face that he knew he wasn't alone because he'd seen it. But she hid it after that.

'Come with me.'

'Okay.'

Neil shivered suddenly and turned to look up the hill.

'What is it?' said Romy. 'What's there?'

'Something's following me,' said Neil.

'Really?'

Neil nodded gravely.

'Hold still.'

Romy glided up the block a bit, watching intently. She disappeared for a moment up onto a cement partition at the edge of the sidewalk. Suddenly she let out a yelp and scurried back, composing herself.

'It's the fitzbot thingy,' she said. 'The fitzbot followed you here.'

'Really?' said Neil.

'Weird,' said Romy, gripping his shoulder protectively. 'I don't see it now, but it's up there. I saw it.'

'That is weird,' said Neil.

'Weird, all right. Are you carrying some sort of chip or something?'

'No.'

'Well … as long as it doesn't come any closer,' she said.

She looked intently down at him.

'What did you do to your hair?' she asked.

'I cut it off. Just a bit off the front.'

'And your glasses — where are your glasses?'

'They weren't real,' said Neil, to let her know. 'They weren't even real at all.'

Romy went down on one knee and enclosed him in a furry, leathery, spiky, full-body embrace. This was one mouse that wasn't going back to the store.

✝

If the reader will permit us to go back a bit: 4:30 p.m., March 31st, we figure, is about when Anna arrived at the Royal Victoria Hospital to visit Runner. There was a single nurse at the nurse's station. Anna's arrival caught her by surprise.

'Hi,' said Anna. 'My name's Anna Lighter. I brought my friend Runner Coghill to the hospital last night, and I was wondering … '

'Are you a relative?' the nurse asked.

'No, but … '

The nurse was inscrutable. Like a stone sentinel guarding the gate of a palace, weighing Anna's importance on invisible scales. Anna was starting to get a bad feeling. The nurse made a decision.

'I'm very sorry to tell you that Runner Coghill passed away this morning. She was very, very sick. She had a very serious thyroid condition.'

Shocked now, Anna was barely listening. 'Thyroid … '

'I'm very, very sorry.'

Anna was chewing her lip. 'Right.'

Chewing her lip wasn't going to contain it. Funny, it had always worked before. A little bit of self-defacement to show she was being thoughtful. But now she found she didn't want to be thoughtful or show anything at all. So this was what feeling was. 'Ah, shit,' she said quietly. 'Ah, fuck … Ah, kid … I am such a loser.'

The nurse was starting to look uncomfortable. The phone on the desk was flashing. 'Is there anything else I can do for you?' she asked.

Anna wasn't listening. She was being overwhelmed by an unfamiliar feeling. It was causing her to shake and weep. Her display was so over-the-top that the nurse didn't seem to believe it.

'I really wish you wouldn't make a scene,' she said.

Anna, who had never yelled before: 'I'm not making a scene!' She didn't know what she was doing and felt the need to explain.

'She just wanted to be my friend, you know?' Sobbing now — Dumuzi would not have recognized her. 'But I live in a fog! I'm incapable of figuring out what I even want! Do you know what I mean? Do you know what I mean?' Now she was rummaging around in her bag. 'But I got a copy of the book.' She pulled out the slim paperback Penguin Classics prose synthesis of *The Epic of Gilgamesh* by N. K. Sandars. 'I have the book. I know it's the wrong version; it's like the loser version of *The Epic of Gilgamesh*; but I had to catch up somehow. Ah, shit. I am such … I am such a … '

The nurse apologized firmly and told her that she could refer her to the office of a grief counsellor connected to the hospital, that she couldn't help her in any other way, that she was very busy, that Anna was disturbing the other visitors on the floor, that her language was inappropriate and that it was best she went home.

✝

'Where is everybody?' said Neil.

The pier looked like it had been abandoned for decades.

'Near as I can figure, Neil, this isn't the real port. Just a storage place. This boat's been sitting here for a while, I guess.'

'Sure looks like it.'

'Doesn't it, though? Don't worry. They're going to tow it out of here tonight. I heard them.'

It was sitting at a dock behind a rickety gate with a No Trespassing sign on it. In fact, only the rear two thirds of the ship was behind the gate; the whole front part of the hull from the forecastle to the high windows of the pilothouse was right there in front of them, tied to a rope that sloped down to an iron post by their feet. Somewhere to the west, beyond the dark passenger quays, they could make out the beams of the Old Port.

Their boat was a big boat and it was white with blue stacks. Even in the semi-dark Neil could see that it was in dire need of a paint job. It was an expressive and spectacular ruin. Among the peeling paint on the port side he could see the remnants of slanting block letters: *Manx Lines*. That was all the detail he could make out, but Romy told him that on the other side even the name of the boat was obscured, though you could still see it: *Nindawayma*. Though it looked, she said, like it had possessed other names before that, roughly painted over in blue, with Owen Sound written underneath.

'Owen Sound. That's where we're going,' said Romy.

But the *Nindawayma* didn't look to Neil like it was going anywhere. It looked like it had grown roots in the river.

'I thought you said there was a tugboat,' he said.

'There is,' said Romy. 'Departure at midnight. Question is, are you ready to go?'

He nodded.

'Then we'd better get on board, try and find a place to hole up.'

'Okay,' said Neil. 'Do you think the fitzbot will … ?'

'No, Neil. That thing's not going anywhere. The lady promised.'

The gangplank was beyond the gate, lowered to the dock. The fence was hoppable, but Neil had a better idea: before Romy could stop him, he had climbed onto the big rope that was keeping the ship tied to the dock. He shimmied up it, not even budging the boat, and jumped onto the foredeck.

'What you do that for?' called Romy quietly.

'Didn't want to trespass,' called Neil as he ran up a brief set of stairs and disappeared through a door below the pilothouse.

'Fuck that,' said Romy, and jumped the fence. Her ears were burning. She pulled a toque out of her coat pocket and donned it, walked down the pier and up the gangplank, through an opening in the fencing and onto some kind of rear deck behind two enormous smokestacks.

The *Nindawayma* was large and impressive. Well over three-hundred feet long and fifty-six feet wide. It could carry up to four hundred passengers and 125 vehicles. Romy felt a bit of déjà vu when she stepped onto the deck: she'd been here before, though it would take her some time to figure that out. The déjà vu was spooking her and she was beginning to wonder how she would ever find a ten-year-old kid in the dark on this big boat.

'Neil!' she called, and climbed a ladder up to a higher deck. She stumbled through the dark, past the smokestacks and two lifeboats. 'Neil!' she called as she came to yet another ladder and climbed up to an upper deck that still wasn't the highest.

Neil swung through a door, out of breath. He said nothing, but his eyes were luminous. He had been perhaps as spooked as her, but it was mostly excitement about being on a big empty ship. He could climb ladders and go through off-limits doors. Now they were aboard, it didn't look quite so beat-up; it looked capable of heading off to any destination one might imagine. Romy wondered if anyone had ever squatted on an abandoned ship before.

'That's the pilothouse over there,' said Neil, pointing up and behind himself.

'Do you want to show me?' asked Romy.

Neil nodded.

In the pilothouse, with its captain's wheel and its windows all around and levers and panels in the half-light, they found a treasure to outdo all other treasures: a box full of mitt warmers. They stuffed their hats and coats and gloves and pants and socks with them — there seemed to be an endless supply. It was a great relief because the weather had stayed unseasonably cold and was getting colder. Romy decided they could be generous with the mitt warmers on the first night, but if it turned out to be a long stretch of cold they'd have to start rationing. This was all reminding her of a children's book she'd read a long time ago.

And then they were on top of the pilothouse, looking up at the stars. Except there were no stars — it was overcast. 'But they're still up there,' Neil observed. They were starting to feel the pleasantly burning effects of the mitt warmers.

Still, Romy said they couldn't stay.

'Why not?' Neil asked.

'Because, Neil, I figure that your pilothouse is the one place where any self-respecting tugboat captain's assistant is going to station himself to assist the manoeuvres of the tugboat. You can see the whole ship from here.'

'Do you think he'd stay here for the whole trip?'

'We'll see.'

They went down onto the next deck and then the next, slipped through one of the doors and found themselves in a large dark room full of swivel chairs fixed to the floor. Romy thought it might be safer to go even lower, but it was already dark where they were and she could imagine how dark the lower decks would be. The thought of the empty car-park decks made her shiver.

So they stayed there, in the swivel chairs of the snack bar, enjoying the effects of their pockets of heat and settling in to wait. Romy knew that nobody would come looking for them there: who would want to stow away out of Montreal, the most beautiful, colourful city in the world?

Romy would, that's who. And Neil too.

Just before midnight they heard the engine of the tug start up and someone calling from the deck, hard to tell what language, and then the sound of a winch. At this point they were strewn out on the floor among their bags and blankets and a few well-placed mitt warmers. They sat up to listen, ears cocked, ready to gather and run.

They felt the unhurried lurch of the ship as it was pushed into the dock by the rubber nose of the tug. Somebody was up on the foredeck. 'He's handling that hawser,' Neil whispered.

'What's a hawser?' Romy whispered back.

'That big rope I climbed up.'

There were times over the course of the next hour, as the ship lurched back and forth, when Romy wondered whether there weren't two tugboats manoeuvring around out there.

'Most likely,' whispered Neil.

'How come you know so much about it?' asked Romy.

'I grew up down here,' said Neil. 'By the docks.'

'Oh,' said Romy. And she wanted to ask: Are you all done with growing, then?

Eventually the lurching stopped and the human sounds fell silent. Romy could hear nothing but the easy sigh of the hull adrift and Neil asleep against her stomach, where he could hear the occasional burble that guarded against ghosts.

Chapter Sixteen
Shiduri

Our Cabal Remnant was less knowledgeable than Neil in the practice of waterfront wandering. So they split up the search. Three of them headed south to make their way along the waterfront to the silos and the port, while Priya and Missy worked their way through the populated part, scoping restaurants and such.

It was perhaps fortunate that Missy and Priya had so little to say to each other. They might have been chatting. As it was, the two of them had held an awkward silence for some time when, just above Rue de la Commune, they heard something above them, a very quiet triple click that made the hairs on the backs of their necks stand up.

Missy turned to Priya and said, 'Did you hear that?' And together they heard it again. Above them there was a balcony and a light shining through the windows. On the balcony there was an old shed, and that was where the sound was coming from. And there was a woman up there too, looking down at them. She stepped outside for a moment, and behind her the apartment cast a warm light. She saw them looking up at her and gestured with a delicate hand for them to come.

✛

By the time Emmy, Du and Aline arrived empty-handed at the silos, it was very late. They kept walking, along the tracks, past the Empire crane, past a fence with barbed wire and a bunch of mobile homes behind it. Beyond that, there was a gate that was chained shut. The chain was loose enough to accommodate a small person, though not loose enough to accommodate the young man who was at that very moment attempting to squeeze through to the other side. He had just gotten his left arm, head and chest through when the three Cabalists arrived.

'Oh my god,' said Du. 'It's Coby.'

'Oh shit.' (Emmy, quietly.)

Coby heard the voices and thought he'd been caught. He tried to wrench himself back though the opening, but he was really stuck.

'Oh,' he said, realizing who they were. 'Hey, Dumuzi. Hey,' (to Aline). 'Hey, Emmy.'

'Hey, Coby,' said Emmy.

Dumuzi was floored. It was occurring to him for the first time that Coby had disappeared, that he hadn't seen him since the incident on the rooftop with the hair. The night before. (Could it have been only the night before?) (No, it was the day before.)

'What's up, Coby?' he said, feigning casual.

'Oh. Yeah,' said Coby as he worked to extricate himself from the gate. 'A guy told me he saw my fitzbot down here.'

'Your fitzbot?' asked Du.

'That's what he told me.'

'What guy?'

'At school.'

'You were at school?'

'I went back.'

Coby was still stuck. They were all too stunned to give him a hand.

'You're kidding me,' said Du. 'What happened to you?'

'Well, like, I guess you didn't really notice, but, like, Emmy and I, like, broke up right in front of everyone.'

'Uh,' said Dumuzi, who hadn't. Emmy was looking back toward the mobile homes, as if to ascertain whether someone over there would take her in.

Du changed the subject.

'Have you seen Neil?'

'Who's Neil?'

'The kid.'

'The … You mean from the book group? No. No, I haven't. Hey, have you seen the fitzbot?'

'No, Coby.'

'I thought we'd left it in that warehouse, but it's gone. I've got to get it back.'

'Sorry, Coby.'

Somebody was coming. They could see shadows and hear feet running down the track, voices out of breath but talking. It was Missy and Priya. Running and laughing like they were best friends. Emmy and Aline exchanged a look. And then they heard what they were saying: someone had seen Neil.

'No, it's totally wild,' said Priya as she came abreast of them. She was carrying a cardboard box. Everyone looked to Missy, who was just behind. She looked a bit mussed, but also amused and content to let Priya do the talking. Weirder and weirder. Priya went on. 'It was this woman who lives right on Rue de la Commune. She saw him. She said he wasn't alone, that he had an older girl with him.'

'Anna?' said Du, hopeful.

'Romy, I think,' said Priya. 'Also a small mechanical thing, she said. She said they came up from the piers to talk to her.'

'A mechanical thing?' (Coby.)

'Yeah, the fitzbot.'

Coby renewed his efforts to get free of the fence.

'You mean that fucking kid took my — ?'

'Just shut up, okay?' said Emmy. 'His sister died.'

Coby stopped struggling. 'She died?'

'He didn't take it,' said Priya. 'They left it with her. They locked it in a shed.'

'Is it still there?' asked Coby.

'Just let her finish!' (Emmy again. Poor Coby.)

'Sorry, I … Sorry.'

'So this is totally wild,' said Priya, checking in with Missy, who was letting her carry the story. 'So, this woman we met, she said that the little boy looked so sad and pale and he had a jagged haircut and she asked him, you know, "Why are you so sad and pale and why do you have such a jagged haircut? You're just a kid." And the two of them told her that the boy had just lost his sister. And so she knelt down before him and she said – I mean, I've got to tell you before I say this that she looked like a total flake, but on the other hand … on the other hand … '

'What did she say?' asked Emmy, patiently.

'Well,' said Priya, checking with Missy again, who was nodding, 'do you remember when I said I wanted to be the minor goddess who has the bar by the waters of death because she was a rock star who didn't sell out? And we voted on it? Well, that vote's toast because the part is taken: Shiduri. Do you remember Shiduri? Who said to Gilgamesh: *Don't go drifting. Don't go wandering in search of the wind. When the gods made life, they withheld the secrets of death. We can't grasp them.*

'So Missy and I, we were sitting there with this woman, and she was telling us that she told Neil all this. And she was handing me these orange slices, and all of a sudden, right out of the blue, she said, "You know, Leonard Cohen wrote a song about me once."'

'Leonard Cohen?' asked Du. 'What does Leonard Cohen have to do with it?'

'That's what we wanted to know,' said Priya. 'What the heck does Leonard Cohen have to do with it? But then I remembered what she said her name was when she – '

'What did she say her name was?' asked Emmy.

'Suzanne.'

'Who?'

'Suzanne. Suzanne. Who has a place by the river and you can see the boats go by and spend the night beside her and you know that she's half-crazy but that's why you want to be there, because she lives up top of this incredible converted building, in a warm house that's high enough to overlook the whole port, and she's like a minor goddess who gives you a drink and advice before you head out over the waters of death. Suzanne. Shiduri. Shiduri. Suzanne. The honorary membership of the Lacuna Cabal is expanding in unpredictable ways.'

✝

Now, if you'll forgive us, we have to stop and go back. The following was learned only recently, from Missy. We didn't know about it before because it seems we omniscient narrators have been barred access to the den of a certain minor goddess. And Priya, sworn to secrecy from that day to this, would not speak of it even once Missy had released her. Still won't.

Priya had seen Missy cry, something witnessed by no other mortal. Akin to Perseus glimpsing the face of the gorgon in his shield.

The way it had happened was like this: while feeding them tea and oranges and telling the story of Neil and Romy's visit, Suzanne had somehow (we can only imagine by inadvertently characterizing Romy and Neil as a surrogate mother and son, or else merely by divining) drawn some information out of Missy that no one had ever suspected — first that Missy's age was older than we knew.[30] Then, more shockingly, that Missy was experiencing some kind of malady that was jeopardizing her lifelong wish to have a baby. This revelation was witnessed by Priya, who must have been beside herself with shock, Missy's demeanour generally being one of consummate perfection.

Suzanne had then discussed with Missy a scenario that placed Priya's jaw squarely on the floor — that of Missy meeting

30 Thirty-three. But Missy didn't look thirty-three. Or, another way of putting it is, she'd looked thirty-three since she was twenty-two.

drunken men in bars and letting them fuck her in back alleys. They spoke about it rationally, weighing pros and cons, as if it were something that was really happening.

At first, Missy had behaved like her usual self, mocking Suzanne for lecturing her, since, 'I don't see your children here, sitting here, sitting at your feet.'

To which Suzanne had responded that she was barren, or at least had been so far, citing the example of the Biblical Sarah, who was ninety years old.

Ultimately, Missy's defence of her alleged after-hours behaviour came down to the belief, she said, that 'beggars can't be choosers.'

Leading directly to the exchange that changed Priya's vision of Missy forever:

'Even beggars know what they're bartering.' (Suzanne.)

'I know what I'm bartering.'

'Raise your price. You're a beautiful lady.'

'No. I'm not.'

And then, like a dam that hadn't shown a crack suddenly breaking, the tears came. Like you would not believe. Everyone got in on the act.

Missy went on to explain, through tears, that she would never change her behaviour, that since the most important thing in her life was to have a baby before her ovaries went the way of the dodo, then she was going to go about it by being reckless and/or deceitful and/or any way that would get her to her goal, because her goal was the ultimate good. And what she did in her leisure time while devoting most of her life to this goal was her business as well. Men mostly sucked. A women's club was a breath of fresh air. An extracurricular (read: daytime) activity.

Missy revealed all this to us recently. We're still in shock.

Later, as they were walking away from Suzanne's, Missy said to Priya, 'Don't tell anyone.'

And Priya said, 'I swear.'

And then, to level the playing field, Priya told Missy about her audience delusions.

Missy, who always felt like all eyes were on her, was pleasantly unsurprised. And sympathetic. She even compounded her vulnerability by suggesting that, if Priya really was in a movie, then, by extension, so was the whole Lacuna Cabal, and so perhaps their adventures were currently being shown at an outdoor screening on the top of the mountain. Further, if they were up on a screen on top of the mountain, that meant their faces and eyes, poking up above the trees, could look out over the audience and down past the university and the Royal Vic — like real goddesses, not just movie ones — and seek out a lost little boy on the waterfront. If they were goddesses, Missy said, then they could do that. And then they would find Neil. Wouldn't that be great, Priya said. That sure would be great, Missy agreed.

And then they walked a little further in silence, both feeling mildly but not unpleasantly embarrassed about their disclosures.

Then Priya asked, 'Do you really hawk?'

'My dad got me to learn. He said it was something we would do together.'

'And did you?'

'No.'

A bit further and then Missy said, 'Don't you live with a single mother?'

'I do. She lives right at the top of the house. There's another baby too, on the second floor, but that's with a couple.'

And Missy said, 'Still, that must be nice.'

Priya said, 'Yes, it is.'

And then they walked still a little bit further. And Missy said, 'I'd like to meet them sometime.'

✝

So then it all happened like we said before, with Coby getting stuck in the fence and being discovered by the others, and then the two pairs of feet that came sounding down the railroad tracks, which turned out to belong to Priya and Missy. And Missy knew that for Priya the next best thing to playing Shiduri was telling the story of Shiduri. Missy felt that this is what friends should do for friends. Priya was her friend now, whether she liked it or not.

Coby had finally succeeded in extricating himself from the gate: Priya put down the box she'd been carrying. Coby, as casually as possible, sauntered over and had a look inside.

'Oh my God,' he said. 'There it is.'

Priya said, 'Neil said it was following him.'

'My fitzbot?'

'That's what Suzanne said he said.'

And Missy spoke up at last — the superheroine who had endured a dark night of the soul and regained her powers, stronger than ever. 'And that means it can follow him again.'

Coby looked up from the box into Missy's determined eyes and realized what she had in mind.

'Oh no,' he said. 'No, I'm sorry, I've got to get that thing back to school in time to … It was due more than a … '

'I don't give a shit,' said Missy. 'It followed him before, it's going to follow him again.'

'No way, man,' said Coby, confused again already. 'I … '

Missy said, 'Don't call me "man."'

Emmy cut in. 'Don't say you need it for school.'

'I do need it for school. I'm sorry. I'm not a cowboy in the city anymore. I made this thing. This is a thing that I made. I'm a bright guy,' he went on. 'I mean, in my own way. I just have to face the fact and not get all broken up about it. I made this thing.'[31]

---

31 In truth, his heart was bursting in the presence of the bioluminescent Emmy. But that is cruelly irrelevant to our story.

Aline's turn now. Coby, with his notorious lack of attention to human detail, hadn't noticed anything different about Aline. Aline liked him for it. Now he tried to reason with him.

'Don't you want to test it in the field?' he asked.

'I have tested it,' said Coby. 'I tested it already.'

'Obviously it's evolved beyond its original parameters.'

'It can't evolve — it isn't alive,' Coby countered, dully.

'Then why is it tracking Neil?' Aline was starting to change his impression of Coby, who was refusing to look at him.

'It's not,' said Coby.

'I think it is,' said Aline.

'Why would it do something like that?'

'I don't know. Maybe he casts a really epic shadow.'

'That's got nothing to do with anything,' said Coby, in a tone that was the last straw. Aline rushed in, collaring Coby. It took everyone else to pull him off.

'The thing is following the kid! It's just a fact!' Aline was shouting from among the arms, still hanging on to Coby's collar.

'I don't believe it,' said Coby.

'Just try it! Just try it!' They managed to pull him off. 'Just forget I was wearing a dress, for fuck's sake!'

Everyone froze. Aline went on. 'I see reality! I am capable of rising above the limitations of my body and my surroundings, through the strength of my will and my desire! But I also have eyes, ears and a brain! I can look at the world and see it as it is!'

All of which was too much for the collared Coby to absorb. 'Whoa! Okay! Jesus!' It was the perfect argument, perhaps. Abstract thinking was his domain too, even if he didn't use it as an excuse to wear a dress.

'Give it a chance,' pleaded Aline.

'You think it will follow him,' said Coby, wavering.

'I'd stake my life on it.'

'Okay,' said Coby. 'Okay.'

There was a pause as everyone withdrew from the scrum around Coby's collar, which had remained miraculously intact. Coby crouched down and turned over the box. There was no movement for a moment. And then his little chicken scuttled out. It paused for another moment. And then scuttled off.

They all watched. Coby said, 'It's not going for the shadows, is it?'

Aline said, 'No, it's not.'

It was after midnight. Unbeknownst to them, the *Ninda-wayma* had embarked. So the fitzbot was going for the water.

✝

And that's when Missy revealed the most useful of all the skills she had acquired to win a spot in her father's daytimer: a yacht licence. For a while it had seemed the most promising, since he really did love the water, but he was a very busy man, her father, and the yacht was shaping up to be something he'd pay more attention to in his retirement, along with the gardening, the flying, the skiing, the camping, the hunting, the hawking, ball-room dancing, birdwatching, spelunking, shooting documentaries, going to the symphony and taking a trip to Patagonia.

Missy's father may have been absent, but the yacht was not. It was docked in the marina of the Old Port. Port d'Escale. A stone's throw away.

And so, Missy decided, with the fierce improvisational swiftness of a great leader, that she would take this yacht of her father's and steer a course to follow that fitzbot, wherever it would lead her, the destination being Neil Coghill the Real McCoghill. And if she never returned with the yacht, then her father was going to have to find something else to do with his retirement. And anyone who wanted to come, she said, was welcome.

Chapter Seventeen
Nindawayma

Neil and Romy awoke on a purple floor. Nearby were the swivel chairs, which were green, and tables the colour of fake wood. Also a blue-panelled information kiosk with two empty soda dispensers and a map of Georgian Bay. It was all surprisingly colourful, considering the state of the outer hull.

They were stiff and cold, but their mitt warmers were still functioning a little bit. Happy April Fool's Day. It was still very cold.

Romy could feel the ship moving, which seemed like a reasonably good sign. They weren't about to be confronted with any shipboard workers. There was perhaps some time to explore.

They replaced their fading mitt warmers, pulled a couple of power bars out of Romy's pack and went off in search of supplies. Neil insisted on carrying his carpetbag with him. He didn't want to be separated from it in case they were caught.

'Suit yourself,' said Romy. She was fuller and bigger in her skin.

They walked through sitting rooms and up and down stairs and passed some windows that displayed the far bank of the Saint Lawrence River fairly rushing by. They did not yet notice that it was going in the wrong direction. They avoided all doors that led directly outside and soon found the dining area, stately in its emptiness but lacking in basic amenities.

There were no windows in the kitchen, but in the spill from the restaurant they found, under the counters, several large buckets. Neil produced a headlamp and they pulled up the lids, revealing a tub of white rice that still looked good and a bucket of rot that had once been brown rice; lima beans and powdered milk and macaroni, all good; and a rotting tub of rolled oats. Very little that did not require boiling water, Romy figured, although if they got desperate and bored, they could spend their days trying to chew through all that fibre.

'Can you eat rice raw?' Neil asked.

'Yeah, but not much. It cooks in your stomach and then bad things happen.'

'What bad things?'

'You swell up like my mother.'

'Isn't that a good thing?'

'Not unless you want to pretend you're the first pregnant ten-year-old boy.'

There were also a number of cooking pots, which they surreptitiously assembled on the upper deck to catch rainwater. Then they went back inside, walked around and up and down, until they found the crew area. This featured linen closets and beds and a feeling of comfort in the half-light. Inside the cupboards of the crew's mess they found cans of chicken and tomato soup, which were very exciting at first blush, until Romy realized that they must have been more than a decade old.

'It's too bad, though,' said Romy. 'Wouldn't have been as crunchy as that pasta.'

'You could soak the pasta,' said Neil.

'Sure. Soaked dry pasta. Sure. Very tasty.'

And there were three more boxes of mitt warmers.

It was enough exploration for one day. They weren't going to go down into the darkness of the car decks and the engine room. Neil wanted to head back up to the pilothouse and Romy said no. They decided, however, to move their campsite to the crew area, which was more comfortable and had a more muted colour scheme. They grabbed all the blankets and pillows they could find in the linen closets and laid them out on the floor close to some windows. Neil sat down to read while Romy attempted to recall from memory the entire plot line of *From the Mixed-up Files of Mrs. Basil E. Frankweiler*, by E. L. Konigsburg, which, she realized, was the book this experience most reminded her of.

She contemplated how *The Mixed-up Files* wasn't really a kids' book at all. Wasn't Mrs. Frankweiler an accountant or something? No, she was an heiress, in correspondence with her accountant, or was it her lawyer? Whoever he was, she treated him with unveiled contempt. Did that make it a children's book? What was so childish about that? It was more of a survival handbook really, whose main characters happened to be children. Romy wondered why there always had to be this invisible line that prevented a book from being taken seriously as an adult book by a vast and small-minded segment of the population, which happened to include everyone she knew, including and especially Missy.

Neil was reading the tenth stone of the Gilgamesh epic. Romy asked him whether he could really understand the cuneiform. Without lifting his eyes from the stone, he assured her that he could. Boasted about it, in fact.

That's also when he told her there was a stone missing. An eleventh stone. In the tenth, Gilgamesh goes on a long journey over the waters of death and finds the oldest man in the world — Uta-napishti — so he can sit down with him and ask him why people have to die and how he can avoid it. But Neil had never read the eleventh stone, which covers the conversation between Gilgamesh and Uta-napishti.

'Ah,' said Romy, and wondered how they were going to find the oldest man in the world in Owen Sound, or Bingotown for that matter. She felt a spasm of guilt for not being more adventurous in her choice of destination.

But Romy was wrong about the destination of the *Nindawayma*. The sailors she'd overheard had been speaking French, and Romy had a tendency to get her *to*'s and *from*'s mixed up, or rather her *à*'s and *de*'s. Not *à Owen Sound* but *de Owen Sound*.

So, when on the third day she looked out the port side, saw the whole ocean and felt the warmth of the sun on her face, she didn't think, Where the fuck are we going? She thought, immediately, This is going to be way better than Owen Sound, and went back down to tell Neil, who agreed.

On the seventh day, they pulled into a port where they stayed overnight. They had no idea if this was their final destination, but Romy decided that if the ship did not budge again for a day and a half, then they would emerge. The layover was less than twelve hours, and then they were off again. It turned out to be Bermuda, but they didn't know that. All they knew was that winter was over and it was warm.

✛

They got a little bolder after that. They came up at night to lie on the deck hidden behind the higher decks and look up at the stars. One night they stayed up later than usual. Neil pointed up.

'See that up there?' he said.

'Yes,' said Romy, though she wasn't sure.

'That's the constellation Taurus,' he said. 'That's the real Bull of Heaven.'

'Oh yeah?' said Romy, wondering where in the world Neil was hiding his grief.

'It's in the book too,' said Neil, 'even though we skipped that part. Some of the book is because of real things like that.'

'Oh yeah,' said Romy. She turned and looked at Neil. 'Hey, Neil, it must be ... '

He didn't move. She shifted and touched his shoulder, but he continued to look up at the sky.

'Um,' she said. 'Maybe we should go down and get some sleep.'

'I'd rather stay awake,' said Neil.

'Okay,' said Romy, turning to look back up at the sky.

And then Neil fell asleep, right there on the deck, and he saw his sister Runner out on the water, holding a book and beckoning to him: opening, closing, writing, offering. For Neil, the trajectory of forever ended right there, in the pages of the book in her hands, close to her breast and her breathing, where he knew he belonged.

✝

The days that start from the night of March 31st and over the course of the month that followed are known in the annals of the Lacuna Cabal as The Time We Followed the Fitzbot. Wherein members of the Lacuna Cabal attempted to interpret the directional gestures of the fitzbot, perched on the forecastle of Missy's father's yacht, tied to a fishing line operated by Coby as insurance against its plunging into the depths. Coby wasn't really worried. Because of Du's habit of leaving the toilet seat up in their apartment, he'd programmed a subroutine to prevent the bot from entering water or stepping into the void. The Atlantic Ocean was both at once.

So the boat stayed with the fitzbot and the fitzbot stayed with the boat, tethered to its mooring, trying always to scuttle ahead, continuously checking to feel if the air ahead still carried the taint of sea spray and hadn't become land, unflagging in its pursuit of Neil Coghill's black and comforting shadow. And Missy was a good skipper — she'd sent them all home before setting out, to pick up passports and food — though the money she was spending on fuel was beyond belief. Not exactly with her father's permission, either. It took some nerve.

Behold the cosmology of the world: from the greatest of godly girls to the lowliest of fitzbot beasts. And the latter leads the former, further and further away from the narrators of this account, into the wandering part of the narrative.

Chapter Eighteen
To the Underworld

Romy and Neil had a bit of advance warning when the *Nindawayma* came to a complete stop, presumably right in the middle of the ocean.

'Hey,' she said.

'What?' said Neil.

'We stopped moving,' said Romy.

'I gathered that,' said Neil, poring over his stone.

'What kind of a thing is that for a kid to say? "I gathered that."'

'I did gather that.'

And then they heard the voices of the men who had come on board, presumably with no intent other than to find them. So they did their best, with limited destinations, to flee. Romy said they were going to have to face the lower decks. The car decks. Neil hesitated, citing a fear of the dark. But Romy told him that she was afraid of the dark too, and that, when it came right down to it, everything was going to be all right.

They felt their way down the stairs into the darkness and found themselves in the middle of an entombed highway with a yellow line painted down the middle. They felt their way to the far side of the deck. There were a thousand places to hide down here, Romy thought, and a thousand ways to get hurt. Before they settled, she stumbled across a small fire extinguisher and briefly considered wielding it as a weapon. Perhaps, she thought, against swift tears, that her experience on the roof of the Jacob Lighter Building would come in handy after all.

They were going to make it.

But she started to change her mind as they crouched in the dark, side by side against a wall, and Neil began to mumble quietly.

'How will we … ?' he said.

'How will we what?' asked Romy.

'Will we … ?' said Neil.

'I don't know what you're asking, Neil.'

Neil lowered his voice and continued to whisper. She looked at the side of his face, tried to make out his expression in the dark. But he would not turn to look at her. He seemed, rather, to be peering across the void of the deck. Romy remembered that there were gaps in the story of the stone, where the surface had crumbled away. 'A parchment partly eaten by rats,' Runner had called it. But that didn't provide an explanation for Neil's behaviour.

He spoke in low tones, sometimes whispering, sometimes urgent, sometimes plaintive, sometimes stoic, toneless, fateful.

Through sorrow ………… and scorpions ……… by sun and by cold …… Gilgamesh …… he followed his sister …… his sisters …… he followed his sisters ………… piled high …… he gave to his sisters ……… piled high ……… he gave to his sisters ……… piled them high for his sisters ………

Over and over in endless variations, until Romy was weeping silently beside him in the dark, worrying for his sanity and wondering whether she would have to carry him back up into the light after all.

We all know that what Neil saw there, in the belly of the *Nindawayma*, was not really Runner, who loved her brother, but rather a projection of his own desires and fears.

'Runner?' said Neil.

Neil, said Runner. She was gentle.

'It's Runner?' said Neil.

You found me, Neil, said Runner.

'I found you.'

Then he lost Runner for a moment, but then she was there again, flickering in the dim, barely. Barely there. The white glow of a leg cast. He focused on that.

Neil, she said.

'It's me,' he said.

I'm so happy to see you, she said.

'I'm happy to see you too,' he said as she faded again into the gloom.

I'm stuck here, said Runner.

'You are?' And indeed he saw her again, almost below the lowest horizon of his sight, flattened there, bound by darkness.

I have to escape, she said.

'You do?'

But someone has to take my place.

'Where?'

Here, said Runner. *In the underworld. And then I can escape to the Realm of the Gods.*

Her voice was so strange. But if this was a nightmare, why was he so happy?

'I'll take your place,' he said.

There was a pause. He started to think she was gone. But then her eyes moved, like a beetle on a glass, and he saw the gleam. These are images of horror, we know, but Neil's heart was all love.

Are you sure? said Runner. *You'll take my place?*

'Yes,' said Neil.

You'll have to sit down here in all this dark, said Runner. *All this dark forever.*

'I don't care,' said Neil. 'I'll take your place.'

A moment passed during which he worried that she had not heard him. But then she spoke again.

And I shall escape, she said.

'And where will you go?' asked Neil, hoping to hear it again.

I will go be a real goddess in the sky.
'You will?' asked Neil.

I'll have a crown,
(she said)
a throne,
the truth,
the loosening and binding of the hair,
the quiver, the art of the hero,
the art of power, the art of war.
Lots of other things too.

'All that?' asked Neil.
Yes, said Runner.
'Then I'll take your place for sure!'
Thank you, Neil, she said from the far wall. In truth, he could barely see her. But he knew she was there.
'You're welcome,' he said.
Now I must go, she said.
'Bye, Runner,' said Neil.
Bye, Neil, she said.
'Bye, Runner.'
Bye, Neil, she said, sounding further away.
'Bye, Runner,' he said, a little louder.
Bye, Neil, she said, still further away.
'Bye, Runner,' he said, through tears.
Bye, Neil.
'Bye, Runner.'

✝

And then they were found.

Yes, as it turns out, the *Nindawayma* had come from Owen Sound three years before. She had served as a car ferry between Tobermory and Manitoulin Island well before that, occasionally transporting the small Bingo-bound Romy, until the boat was retired and then sat in the Owen Sound harbour for almost a decade. Then she was towed up to Les Mechins and back down to Montreal, where she'd been sitting ever since, at least until the night she was boarded by Romy and Neil.

But if she wasn't heading for Owen Sound, where was she heading?

The night the *Nindawayma* began her midnight run from Montreal, she was christened with a new name, MS *Dilmun*, and registered under a new flag. The itinerary was as follows: she was to be towed down the Saint Lawrence to Newfoundland (one and a half days), where she would take a hard right and head down the coast to Bermuda (five days), thus avoiding the ninety-foot waves of the northern North Atlantic. Then across to the Azores (during which crossing Neil and Romy would be found), from there to the Mediterranean, down the Suez Canal and the Red Sea, around into the Arabian Sea and back up into the Persian Gulf.

The Persian Gulf? Wasn't there a war going on in the Persian Gulf? Surely they weren't allowing any ships in there?

Well, it's true the war was bad for business in the Persian Gulf (with one or two exceptions), but the business community of the Persian Gulf was no less tough-minded than certain members of the Lacuna Cabal Montreal Young Women's Book Club, and nearly all ports in the gulf were open for business. The managers of Mannanan of Manama, Bahrain's Second Best Shipyard, had offered the lowest bid for the Nindawayma Project, along with underwriting war-risk premiums and offering a flag of convenience. And the ferry's new owners were elderly, dispassionate Danes who had seen wars come and go. As for the tugboat crews, the Danes paid well.

So the car ferry *Nindawayma* was to be reformed, by the bored and underworked Bahraini (and Indian and African and Filipino) shipyarders, into a cable ship. It would have a Ferris wheel hanging off the stern to spool cable down along the ocean floor, mile after mile. In these days of fibre optics, somebody had decided that was the smart way to go. Somebody, most likely an elderly and dispassionate Dane, felt it was prudent to look to the future of the region, even as one of the region's countries was being stoned back to the Cuneiform Era by the hurling hands of a regressive and blinkered world power.

✝

The one who found them, down on the car deck, was a tall young Danish man. Turns out there'd been a second tugboat following the ship, whose captain had followed our two heroes in their efforts to hide behind the superstructure of the *Nindawayma*, collecting water, suntanning, et cetera. The supreme annoyance of the seafarer: stowaways.

'I have to stay here,' Neil blankly told the tall Danish sailor.

Whereupon the sailor picked him up and carried him, kicking and screaming and wailing, into the light. Romy followed along, feeling guilty relief.

They were marched up through the decks of the ship to the ladder on the starboard side that took them down to the second tugboat. When questioned, Neil said nothing and Romy explained that they had thought they were going to Owen Sound.

There was a conference between the captains of the two tugs. International rules for dealing with stowaways were so painfully convoluted that sailors sought to avoid them whenever they could. Their problem was further complicated by the fact that Neil and Romy were not carrying passports.

'It is often better,' said the more philosophical of the two captains to Romy, 'to simply dump you into the sea.'

Neil didn't care one way or the other. He was pale and silent and looked more bereft than ever. Poor Romy was not equipped to understand how he had, in a single hour of darkness, replaced the template of *The Epic of Gilgamesh* in his mind with that of the Inanna's Descent, the old mystery that Gilgamesh himself would have heard when he went to church on Sundays. Romy didn't know any of that and so she could not understand why Neil seemed to have abandoned his search for an old wise man. He should have been mocking the Danes for not being wise, or even so old for that matter. That's what he would have done, she thought, if they had stayed put at the campsite, glancing up from their reading as the sailors walked in. They should have stayed there. Instead they had descended into the darkness where Neil had lost hope. Romy had made a bad decision.

She wondered whether Runner had planned things this way: to leave her brother in the bosom of the Lacuna Cabal Montreal Young Women's Book Club. If that was true, then her duty now was as proxy for the whole group. If that was true, then perhaps she was unequal to the task. Perhaps she would fail.

But she had also learned, quite recently, that nobody really knows what's going to happen in a life. Not even the visionary Runner Coghill. But Romy knew one thing for absolute sure: she would stick with the kid. She would allow him to rave and fall down and foam at the mouth. She would let him grow long hair and wear lion skins and feel bitter winds blowing. If there was snow, she would piss their way through it; if there were hard men, she would fuck their way past them; if there were crowds, she would exhibit herself as a monster and let Neil slip through and she'd catch up with him later. And she would find him an old wise man, the real thing, one who had survived a deluge and could speak of it like in the eleventh tablet of *The Epic of Gilgamesh*; she would find this man and then she would kick Neil in the ass and force him to listen. She would stick with the kid and see him through to the other side of this fucking-piece-of-shit grave mess.

✢

The food was better at least, even if they had to work for it. Neil still didn't care. Some days they were obliged to return to the *Nindawayma* with ropes and buckets and mops to clean up the messes they'd made there.

The flotilla made one last port of call before making the final leg of the journey. The Azores. Both Romy and Neil stayed below in their quarters during the stopover, tucked well away. They didn't have to do any dishes that day. Nobody saw them.

After ten hours of refuelling, they embarked again. Several days through the Strait of Gibraltar and into the Mediterranean Sea, down the Suez Canal and the Red Sea, up past Yemen and Oman and into the Persian Gulf.

✝

And so Romy and Neil steamed around the northern coast of Qatar to alight at their destination: the northwestern tip of the small island hidden beside it; an island with no oil left except for what was lapping on her shores, and no underground water left, except for what they could convert from the sea; where farmland had begun to turn into desert; where people used to dive by the thousands for pearls; where, in a grave and mysterious coinci- dence, Uta-napishti the Faraway, known to people of the Ancient World as an old wise man, once looked out over the waters to see Gilgamesh coming on a raft and said to himself, 'That's not one of my men'; where the underworked shipyard had begun to take on jobs no one else wanted, such as pulling apart a fleet of contaminated and rusting American hulks; where the relatively harmless transformation of the *Nindawayma* from ferry boat to cable ship was soon to take place; and where Neil and Romy would be, much to everyone's surprise, arrested.

Chapter Nineteen
Bodies Changed

As we're about to enter the port of Bahrain's Second Best Ship-yard, open for business even though business is very bad, where we will see old ships in various states of dissolution, along with an American aircraft carrier that appears to be standing in three feet of water, and a speedboat closing in, carrying a man with a megaphone, first we judge it necessary to get caught up with a few individuals — mostly the six who are squeezed into the small pilothouse of Missy's father's yacht, looking ahead to see what is to come. From here on in, we won't have much time to spare for them.

Dumuzi,

for instance, who'd been reading and rereading the poems in his collection of torn pages retrieved from home with his passport.[32] He'd occupied himself lately by trying to conceal his reading from Missy. She'd noticed but pretended not to — a serious para-dox: it spoke in his favour that he read poetry, but that was no way to treat a book.

Du had never been so far away from Anna before, nor from the dizziness that rolled along behind her like an ice-cream

---

32 The poem Dumuzi read that morning was about a river and a pleasure boat, where Yu Xuanji works, drifting down the Great River, the Yangtze, passing an island of ten thousand homes in the early morning. She has finished her work for the night and all the customers are asleep. As she looks over the houses of the island, she imagines she's a butterfly fluttering through all their gardens. Du wondered whether Yu Xuanji's pleasure boat ever followed the river all the way to the ocean.

truck. It made him a little nervous, since he was never sure what she might be getting up to back in Montreal. But mostly he was feeling better.

Except occasionally he dreamt that she was up on the deck at night, under the stars, sitting on a horse. He didn't even know if she could ride a horse, but he knew she was up there, her horse quiet on the unsteady deck, bending his head to nose for grain, sleek with sweat from the trip, Anna asleep against his back, hat brim obscuring her face.

He told Coby about it and Coby's jaw dropped open. 'She's on the boat with a horse?' he asked. And Du said, 'Yeah.'

'Oh yeah,' said Coby, 'you're over it. Oh yeah, sure, you're over it,' and laughed a rare laugh.

Out on the ocean, Du felt calm for the first time since this whole Anna thing started. In the city, under the yoke of Anna, nothing he grasped ever had any lasting shape. But here he was on a boat with only five other people, a few torn pages of Chinese poetry and no yoke. No spike. It was different. In the city he'd become ragged, and the city itself was ragged and ever tumbling through chaos and more chaos. He felt now that maybe he'd finally gotten beyond that particular epoch. And he felt fine about it. He just wished he could refold that fucking origami butterfly.

Beside Dumuzi stood

Priya Underhay,

who'd been watching over Missy and had noted some softness come into her face even as it was bitten by the breeze; also the subtle pleasure residing in Coby's face; and the new mysteries of Aline, who didn't look quite as miserable as he had last year in that breakfast place, though he did look nervous and sad. She also recalled the glow of Romy leaving the Lighter Building as a god, also Runner's face, also Neil's fake glasses, and the glum looks of the whole Cabal on the day she first joined, last fall, wearing a lime-green kerchief on her head.

She recalled the book *Fall on Your Knees*, between the first twin death and the second. And the unease that was unfolding in the world at the periphery of her vision. She thought of her audience too. Not the one that included Freya, Geryon and the bear, or the one described by Missy, watching the adventures of the Lacuna Cabal in a mountaintop screening, but the real one, the one in the future. She wrote a song for them called 'We're in the Movies.'

At the end of the film, there's much to discuss
As we try to figure out what happened to us:
Did we win? Stay together? Did we cry? Did we pray?
Did we find we worked hard by the end of the day?
Were we good? Were we ill? In the movie, did we kill?
A conviction, an appeal? Was it fake, was it real?
Or maybe we just got one heck of a deal, and if you want
    more then there's always tomorrow and tomorrow.
If tomorrow comes tomorrow, then tomorrow can be
    borrowed for today, that's our way.

'Cause no matter what we do, we will always be young,
Like a book where you're always going back to page one.
'Cause a man came along from …
Built a marquee up above (um),
Set up a booth, sold tickets to our youth
'Cause we're young and we're young and we're young.

She played it many times on the trip. But quietly, quietly. Beside her stood

Missy Bean,

at the wheel, under Priya's discreet but watchful eye, haggard at the end of a long journey during which the lives of the others often lay in her hands — a fact she never stopped contemplating, especially since it had never happened before and she fucking

243

loved it, excuse the language. She figured it was high time. For example, Priya and Du both ran out of money two weeks into the trip, and they both approached privately to tell her as much. Since she didn't want their financial difficulties discussed by the whole group, and since the yacht was equipped with all the amenities to sit out the onset of, for example, a North American dictatorship, she opted to propose, for the sake of efficiency, that everyone stay on board for the duration of the trip. And they all gave their assent! Just like that! Without demanding any further explanation!

Now she was seriously considering a career in politics. How thrilling to hold the fragile lives of grown men and women in the palm of your hand! And to pull it off! Carry them through safely on the ship of state!

Still, it was no cakewalk. Missy's patience had been much tried during this trip. She was barely able to believe how swiftly they'd clipped across the Mediterranean, despite two fuel stops, even though she herself was setting the pace. The Mediterranean! Cradle of Civilization! Where Odysseus had been buffeted from port to port for seven years! And then she was annoyed that they'd had to take on a pilot down through the Suez Canal when she felt they didn't need any help. It was only at the other end, through the Gulf of Suez, that Missy wished she had him back. Navigating tankers and abandoned oil platforms on rickety legs, she often wondered privately whether they would make it at all.

The Red Sea figured to make up for all that, though, by presenting itself as stunningly beautiful. The breeze changing with the sun, east in the morning and west at night. But then the fitzbot ruined her fun by asserting a contrary agenda. It spent the entire southern passage straining its tether toward the port side, indicating that perhaps they were going to have to dock the boat at Jiddah and walk into the unknown deserts of Saudi Arabia. It occurred to Missy that perhaps Neil was making a pilgrimage to Mecca. She figured if he was anything like his sisters then that would be just like him. Someone dies and you up and do the Hajj.

This time she knew better than to express such sentiments out loud.

The plan she developed, perusing her father's charts, was this: Saudi Arabia would be the destination of last resort. As things stood, it was clear that Neil was on a boat, so if she held her course south and swung around Yemen, she'd come eventually into the Arabian Sea, where the fitzbot might ultimately be pointing. Or further north still, past Oman and into the Persian Gulf. If she found, once they got into the Arabian Sea, that the fitzbot was still straining toward Mecca, then fine, they'd go in, follow Neil all the way to the Kaaba. It was a good plan, and just like a Coghill to drag the Lacuna Cabal halfway across the world to within a stone's throw of a very serious war.

Then, after coming through the Mandab Strait, Missy was certain they were being tailed by pirates all the way along the southern coast. It was a long wooden boat that looked like it had been tied together with orange plastic. And it moved at a fair clip. But Missy's father's yacht had a lot of power. She managed to keep well ahead until Johnny Depp gave up, though it left the fuel gauge lower than she would have liked for entry into the Persian Gulf.

Beside Missy stood

Emmy Jones,

who had been sticking mostly to a deck chair through this journey, writing. Like Alice Munro on her couch, except this was Emmy in a deck chair on water in the middle of nowhere. She had been sketching the first scene of a play, maybe a play about gender issues, she didn't know. She'd also written a scene of Runner Coghill falling through a floor, though she had no idea what this could possibly mean. The underworld perhaps?

Always trying to pull her down? She liked this scene, though it was true it had nothing to do with gender issues.

Her skin was mostly fluctuating between ochre and green, brilliantly at times, though nobody thought anything of it. They all just felt bad for her seasickness. If you looked closely, you'd be able to see that she was beginning to develop scales. Ready to dive into the ocean at a moment's notice if things got too close.

Beside Emmy, helping to shield her from Coby, even though Coby was behind a pane of glass, stood

Aline Irwin,

who otherwise did not know what he was doing here. A perfect example of his luck, he figured, to be coming into the most male-identified part of the world. Several days ago, he stepped into the pilothouse, shocked, and said, 'You have Internet on this boat.'

'Sometimes,' said Missy. 'And wi-fi. Depending on how close we get to a resort. Grab the laptop, sit where you like.'

So he had sat, mostly below, protecting the laptop from the elements and searching the Internet when he could for some sign of Salam Pax's safe return to his Baghdad Blog. All for naught. The man is dead, he thought. The man is dead.

Beside Aline, sort of, in front of him really, in front of everyone, tethered to the end of a length of twine, tracing the vector of their motion ever forward, tugged the

fitzbot,

over which we pause to intone a blessing:

> *Fitzbot, we allow you to go everywhere. You will walk freely upon the earth and sail upon the waters. You will scuttle through our houses, fly through our skies, touch the moon, dive into our blood, pour through the sun, live on the earth as the lowest of creatures, but a creature nonetheless.*

And then, holding the other end of the length of twine in his right hand, perched on the forecastle in front of the pilothouse windshield,

Coby,

who believed none of this and all of it at the same time. He sat and held his piece of twine. Like the old man and the sea.

He was so excited by the prospect of where this marlin might take him, and had been for so long, in a steadily rising appreciation for the fitzbot's boundless capacity (over how many thousands of miles?), that he'd all but forgotten about his treatment at the hands of Emmy, nearly forgotten his cowboy-in-the-city phase. Coby's mind was more like Escher's than John Wayne's — how could anyone ever have missed that? Perhaps no one ever really did, except for him. So how did he ever miss that? He'd gone through a physical transformation of sorts, but found his way back in the swifter realms of his cerebrum.

The truth is, Coby too had a favourite book — a desert-island kind of book. He'd had it for years. Dumuzi had never seen it because Coby kept it wedged beneath the upper right corner of his futon.

When, in *Metamorphoses*, Ovid summarized and encapsulated two thousand years of Greek and Roman culture, he capped his orgy of physical and sexual transfiguration with a tribute to the imagination of a mathematician. Pythagoras: Coby loved that. He would have loved the book for that alone. We (that is, the two of us) don't know much about Pythagoras except that he said that the square of the hypotenuse of a right-angled triangle is, um, equal to the sum of the squares of the other two sides. But Coby tells us that the Pythagoreans divided the universe into two sides:

1. *square, masculine, limited, straight, resting, light, good, right, odd numbers;*

2. *spherical, infinite, unlimited, moving, crooked, dark, left,*
   evil, feminine, even numbers.

Feminine numbers have the 'stigma' of the infinite attached to them, apparently. Coby says this was his problem when trying to get over Emmy, who haunted his dreams for days in the form of the number two.

Ovid said that Pythagoras could see the stars using only his mind. Whereas Ovid used words to change boys into flowers and girls into trees and deer, Pythagoras imagined things that seemed not to exist but really did. According to Ovid himself, that was the difference between them, and that was what Coby took from the book when he'd been force-fed it in his high school Latin class. Through Ovid's Pythagoras, Coby saw the difference between the life of the body and the life of the mind, and he lashed his heart to the latter, just as he lashed himself now to the bot of the boat.

> *There is no greater wonder than to range*
> *The starry heights, to leave the earth's dull regions,*
> *To ride the clouds, to stand on Atlas' shoulders,*
> *And see, far off, far down, the little figures*
> *Wandering here and there, devoid of reason,*
> *Anxious, in fear of death, and so advise them,*
> *And so make fate an open book.*[33]

Coby wanted to make his fate an open book. What he could control he would, and what could only be left to chance and nature, like the fitzbot, he would see where it led him. When they made landfall, even as the immigration officers were moving in, Coby cut the tether to see if the fitzbot would really scuttle up into the yard. It did. He couldn't believe his eyes. It went like gangbusters through the open legs of several American Navy officers without them even noticing it. Coby realized that despite

---

33 Trans. by Rolfe Humphries.

the fact that he was about to get into a lot of trouble, it was all going to be worth it. All he had to do now — once they'd explained themselves, found the kid and got the hell out of there — was take his precious creation apart and find out what the bleep was going on in there.

Meanwhile,

Anna Lighter,

who had been ruminating for weeks, days flush with impatience and nights pale with grief, sat in a café, flipping through the pages of the slim N. K. Sandars prose synthesis of *The Epic of Gilgamesh*. Trying to work it out. She was past halfway in her fifteenth go-round of the book, muttering to herself, trying to figure out what she was missing.

'Enkidu ... dies ... Gilgamesh goes kinda crazy ... grows hair long, wears skin of a lion ... wanders wilderness ... People saying to him, You're a king, this isn't what you should be doing ... Goes across waters of death ... Meets old wise man ... '

She flipped back a few pages. 'The waters of death,' she said. 'I wonder if anyone ever called the Saint Lawrence River the waters of death.'

When Anna realized she'd missed the boat, she went for the next best thing: the library. She sat in the library, flipping through books on Sumer, Akkad and Babylonia, and mumbled to herself, provoking other patrons to occasionally shush her. Something along the lines of, 'We're in the wandering part of the narrative, where the king is looking for the oldest man in the world, who'll tell him how he survived a flood that wiped out the whole rest of humankind. And he'll tell him, too, that he won't live forever and he should stop worrying about it. So I haven't done that yet, so I'm going to keep looking. I mean, who wouldn't want to find the oldest guy in the world? Who wouldn't want to talk to that guy? One day, I'm going to find that guy and I'm going to talk to that guy. It's a fairly decent ambition, wouldn't you say?'

Beside Anna in the aggregation of missing members, there were

Jennifer and Danielle,

i.e., the two of us. Our brief return to the story. It was a full three days before we realized that anything was up. We'd been only a week away. And then it was a few more days before we decided to take over the day-to-day business of the Cabal, strictly as a temporary measure, until the others returned and could (ahem) vote us back in (ahem).

April 9th, 2003

Dear [André Alexis, Dennis Bock, Michael Crummey, Camilla Gibb, Sheila Heti, Michael Redhill, Russell Smith, R. M. Vaughan, Michael Winter],

On behalf of the Lacuna Cabal Montreal Young Woman's Book Club, we would like to thank you for your gift of eight copies of your book, _____ , for our reading pleasure. However, we regret to inform you that we will not be able to read, much less discuss, your book at the present time, and have therefore embarked on the prudent (fiscally for both us and you) task of returning the package, unopened, to sender.

If you might allow us a few words of explanation: we've had a few upheavals here at the Lacuna Cabal Montreal Young Woman's Book Club. There have been some deaths and some principled resignations, and, for the time being, the entire current membership has gone missing from the city of Montreal.

We respectfully request, therefore, that you neither malign us nor spread rumours of our demise. We still hold high hopes that everyone will be found and meetings will resume.

Also, we'd appreciate if you could let us know if you happen to learn the whereabouts of the list of people attached. Because of their general love of literature, we feel it is not completely out of the question to consider that your esteemed path might cross with one or more of them.

We do fear the worst, however, and ask, if you're given to such histrionics, that you please murmur a prayer for us. In truth, we fear the white-slave trade, though we know that is not likely or even really possible. Well, it is possible, but not likely.

Yours in Literature,

_____   _____

Jennifer H.   Danielle D.
Former Members
Lacuna Cabal Montreal Young Women's Book Club

p.s. Further to Russell Smith: we urge you to withdraw your comments on The Epic of Gilgamesh, printed in the Globe & Mail on May 25th, 2002.

Chapter Twenty
Theft

Somewhere around April 12th, while Neil, Romy, Missy, Dumuzi, Emmy, Coby and Priya were bobbing on the ocean, the director of the Baghdad Museum called a press conference in which he declared to the world that 170,000 artifacts had been looted from his museum during the American siege of the city. It was reported to be a cultural disaster on a millennial scale, comparable to the sack of Constantinople and the burning of the Alexandria library.

Then, a little later, it was speculated that the looting of the museum might have been an inside job. Doors had been unlocked with keys. Fakes had been passed over in favour of priceless artifacts.

Then it was reported that some of the missing artifacts were rumoured to have been removed by employees of the museum and hidden in a secret location.

When asked about the secret location, the museum's curator claimed it did not exist. A reporter asked about vaults. 'Who says there are vaults?' she replied.

An American colonel, sympathetic to the cause of restoring lost artifacts, managed to ascertain the existence of the secret location by having the museum's curator followed.

It was then reported that the museum staff had lied about the scale of the loss, that they were hiding artifacts, that they were perhaps acting in cahoots with a toppled despot, that their ultimate intention was to make American occupation forces look bad and enrich themselves in the process.

The reported figure of lost artifacts shrank from 170,000 to sixteen or seventeen. Not sixteen or seventeen thousand. Sixteen or seventeen, period.

The museum's director, source of the original press release, responded that although the initial figure had proven to be incorrect, there was still a serious crisis. He laid all responsibility for exaggeration squarely at the feet of the media.

That's when the shit really hit the fan, because then the press got really mad. Pundits called the museum employees thieves, liars and 'Ba'ath's apparatchiks,' suggesting darkly that 'the interrogation lights should be turned on all of them.'[34]

They all went home, sulked over glasses of milk and dropped the story.

Left alone, the museum staff eventually began to trust the American colonel assigned to the recovery of the missing artifacts (the actual number being 14,000), despite the fact that he'd had them all tailed like thugs in a Maigret novel.

They revealed to him, finally, after many months, that five senior employees of the museum had sworn on the Quran not to reveal the existence of the secret location of hidden artifacts.

The museum's director had not been included in the pact because he was a Christian, and it was felt by the others that swearing on the Quran would hold no meaning for him.

This, it turns out, was the reason the museum's director had given an inflated estimate of the missing artifacts. He had been kept in the dark. It was also the reason the museum's curator had answered the question about a secret vault by asking, 'Who says there's a vault?' She was being loyal to her oath.

The entire media-relations debacle had happened because of a secret pact among a cabal of five people, similar in standing and integrity to the Lacuna Cabal Montreal Young Women's Book Club. If members of the Lacuna Cabal Montreal Young Women's Book Club were to have been asked (by the media, for

---

34 martinkramer.org, May 1st, 2003.

example, or an occupying army), 'Where do sitting sessions of the Lacuna Cabal take place?' we would likely have responded, 'Who says there's a Lacuna Cabal?'

We might have sworn on the Lacuna Cabal Book of Days rather than the Quran, but otherwise the behaviour of the five senior staff was precisely akin to our own.

In our opinion – that is to say, the opinion of the two authors of this account, along with all former members of the Lacuna Cabal – the senior staff members of the Baghdad Museum behaved wisely, judiciously and with a grave sense of responsibility in a world turned upside down where they might have lost everything. As it turns out, they lost only the respect and attention of the Western media.

And so, after that, it was barely reported that countries all over the region – including Jordan, Syria, Kuwait, Saudi Arabia and Bahrain – mobilized immediately, before the end of April, in support of the effort to restore Iraq's cultural heritage. In co-operation with Interpol and the U.S. Task Force, they were able to seize more than a thousand stolen artifacts that were being smuggled over their borders.

Other operations were conducted with greater subtlety – authorities seizing shipments and then lying in wait for the buyers – thus expanding the dragnet. In this way, they made some surprising discoveries about the kind of people they were up against.

✛

The new task that had been thrust upon the Bahrainian Immigration Authority had yielded a lot of excitement, as well as a growing backlog of paperwork. One would, for example, lately expect to see Officer Seyed Samir curled over one of his written reports like an oyster fretting over a pearl. At the moment, however, he was being distracted by a pair of flies that were buzzing around his desk. He thought, If I cannot discover how these things manage to get into my office, how will I ever hope to catch a smuggler?

The two flies (let's call them Jennifer and Danielle) buzzed around the papers on his desk and landed again on the report he'd been drafting for the Immigration Authority. His every effort to shoo them away produced a double kamikaze frenzy around the office, at the end of which they'd alight back in the same spot. If he didn't know any better, he'd say they were trying to read it over.

One couldn't blame them for being curious. It was a curious report, of a curious situation.

Like many immigration officers in the Gulf countries, Seyed Samir had recently been trained in the practice of recovering stolen artifacts. The truth is, he was taking to it like a fish to water. To Seyed, this was the first really gratifying work he had ever done. Being an islander, he didn't generally run into a lot of trouble in his work. The most exciting thing that ever had happened at Bahrain's borders was when he and a couple of his compeers were asked to politely detain a diplomat and get him to pay his outstanding parking tickets.

It was also gratifying to Seyed that he should become a detective of sorts, because he had always understood that, to be a devout man, one must be prepared to see beyond the five senses of the body. What better profession, Seyed reasoned, than to become a sleuth, a seeker of the truth?

Seyed's Indiana Jones training, still so fresh in his mind, had painted a picture of desperate and hard runners working for shrewd criminal outfits with wealthy clients hidden away in Western countries. He imagined he would find himself in a tight spot from time to time, forced to phone his wife, Fatima, on a cell (he didn't even have a cell!) and tell her he loved her and their two children, Aisha and Abdel, and that if he ever made it out of this dastardly situation alive he would come home and immediately commence negotiations for a third.

It came as a surprise, then, when the first case he ran up against, just a couple of days earlier, was somewhat different from the template he had provided himself. He was handed the dossier for two young, English-speaking stowaways — one no more than a child — on a white paint-peeling ferry being pulled into the Mannanan shipyard by two tugboats manned by a Danish crew. They all claimed to have come from Canada.

Which itself was not implausible, except that the stowaways had in their possession ten priceless artifacts, certainly from Iraq and probably from the Baghdad Museum.

Iraq. Uruk. Uruk. Iraq.

All claims were therefore called into question: whether the stowaways were really stowaways, their true points of origin and disembarkation, even whether the Danes were really Danes, the Canadians really Canadians (though, admittedly, the Danes looked to Seyed like his impression of Danes, the Canadians like his impression of Canadians).

In fact, the managers of the shipyard confirmed almost immediately that the Danes were indeed Danes and that their point of origin was Canada.

Still, this didn't quite let the Danes off the hook, since it did nothing to explain their possession of Iraqi artifacts. The Danes claimed to have had no knowledge of the stowaways' possessions, despite the fact that the two youngsters had allegedly been caught and put to work. The Danes claimed to respect the possessions and personal space of all passengers and crew, including criminals, children and, apparently, galley slaves.

Seyed did not believe them. It seemed unlikely that the tugboat crew was unaware of the priceless treasure in their midst, and the fact that they were lying about it raised the spectre of a negotiated share.

This did not necessarily mean they were lying about the stowaways being stowaways. Seyed's theory, developed after much rumination, was that the tugs had picked them up during their scheduled stop at Port Said, while they were taking on Suez pilots to guide them down the canal. Such things happened from time to time. Perhaps the stowaways imagined the tugs were headed in the opposite direction, through the Mediterranean toward the west rather than back in the direction from which their booty had been looted. Perhaps they had made an error and were discovered by the Danes before they could correct it.

Still, the two stowaways didn't fit any kind of template at all. The child only ever made a single statement: 'You can't have them, they're mine!' He'd yelled that to Seyed as he was being taken into custody, and he had since refused to utter a thing. It wasn't because he was scared, either, Seyed thought. The boy spent most of his time on his bunk with eyes closed and hands crossed over his chest. Seyed would try to talk to him, ask him how he'd managed to gain possession of what appeared to be a single work, covering two sides of ten stones, in far better condition than any example Seyed had ever seen. The boy lay there and refused to respond. Looking from the stones to the boy on the bunk and back again, Seyed felt there was something taking place here that had not been covered in his training.

Then there was the young spiky-haired woman, who also asserted, with an unmistakable tone of moral authority, that the stones belonged to the boy, claiming no further knowledge of their origin.

'But, young lady, if you do not know where they came from, how do you know they're his?'

'He got them from his sisters.'

'Where are his sisters now?'

'His sisters are dead.'

'How did they die?'

'By being way too perfect for the world!'

And so on.

It was a conundrum. A cuneiform conundrum.

And then the yacht arrived, and Seyed should have been happy. After all, here was the rendezvous vessel. Here was a spectacular yacht, evidence of major financial backing and a well-organized smuggling operation. But the passengers on the yacht fit the template less than ever. They appeared, without exception, to be fresh-faced youths, though none were, on closer inspection, any younger than Seyed himself.

Perhaps, he speculated, this is how Canadians generally looked, the better to conceal their guile.

Whatever their innocence or guilt, there was something here to get to the bottom of. These cuneiform stones, somewhere between two and four thousand years old, were no mere holiday trinkets. All the Canadians were therefore detained separately for questioning, their yacht boarded and searched.

Seyed was a polite, patient man who enjoyed a good conversation.

One by one, from the first five passengers, the stories were virtually the same. All claimed the boy as the true owner of the stones. Their stories were highly detailed and plausible in every way except for how they'd managed to track their friends halfway across the globe to this port. All made reference to a small robot uniquely designed to track the child, 'because he casts a long shadow.' Two of his interviewees used this exact phrase.

'Who casts a long shadow? This robot?'

'No. Neil.'

'And why do you say Neil casts a long shadow?'

'Because his sister died.'

And so on. Seyed noted the discrepancy between 'sister' and 'sisters,' but alas, he did not know what to make of it or how to make use of it.

This story of the robot, on the other hand, struck Seyed as being of particularly dubious merit, especially since nobody could produce it for examination. Without it, or evidence of its remarkable tracking powers, the story lacked coherence and plausibility. Though he wondered why a group of professional thieves would commit to such an implausible cover story. He found himself hoping, irrationally, whenever he was approached by one of his compeers, that evidence of the little robot had been found.

The last passenger to be interviewed was the young man with the surname 'Aline', first name 'Joyce', middle initial 'I.' This one had a story that was different from the others.

✛

'You have the same name,' said Seyed Samir, 'as one of my favourite American poets.'

'Oh really?' said Aline.

'Mind you, he might not be my favourite if I were blessed with greater knowledge. As it is, my understanding is limited to the whim of my English instructor. However, you will want to know the name: Joyce Kilmer. Have you heard of him?'

Aline admitted that he had not.

'His poem goes like this: *I think that I shall never see / a poem as lovely as a tree.*'

'I had no idea that poem was written by anybody,' said Aline.

'Ah, then you have heard of it.'

'I do confess it,' said Aline, with no trace of irony.

'And you believed it was of anonymous authorship,' Seyed continued. 'No. He wrote the work in 1913 before continuing to die in World War One.'

'Continuing to die?' asked Aline.

'You are making fun of my English.'

'I am,' said Aline, startled and chastened. 'I'm sorry.'

'That's all right. Perhaps it is not such a beautiful poem as it seems to me. But, you see, his wife's name was Aline. So, my belief is the following: although you do not yourself know this thing, I have little doubt that your parents do.'

'Yeah, maybe,' Aline said, trying not to think of his mother. Perhaps this was a tactic of the wily interrogator. Make your subject sit and think about his mother, especially if she's a cow. So he decided to try to take control of the interview.

'Where are Romy and Neil?' he asked.

'You will see your friends very soon. You must understand: it is necessary to keep everyone separate until we have determined whether a crime has taken place.'

'No crime has taken place,' said Aline.

'Then you have nothing to worry about. Your friend Romy was worried as well: she demanded to know whether we were going to force her to wear a burqa.'

'Did you?'

'Ah. You have a similar tone of moral superiority. It is unmistakable. I myself do not believe in the burqa. I told her that the Quran advises women to cover up their jewels. I interpret that as the sexual parts, just as I seek to cover my jewels as well. It is reasonable. Do you not seek to cover up your jewels?'

Aline conceded that he did, laughed and then apologized for laughing.

'No need to apologize,' said Seyed Samir. 'I find it funny too. And so we have become acquainted, you and I. There are men who believe that everything about a woman is a jewel. In my opinion, such people suffer from overstimulation. But we have let ourselves get away from the subject at hand.'

Aline's story was like all the rest, right down to the strange detail of the robot. But he had something new to add. He told Seyed Samir that he believed there was an Iraqi citizen of Baghdad who possessed knowledge relevant to this case.

'Really?' said Seyed, who occasionally wished he smoked a pipe so that he could have something to do with his hands. This was one of those occasions. Things had suddenly gotten very exciting and he was afraid he was going to start fluttering in a way that Fatima occasionally mocked him for.

'Hey, Mister Butterfly, come here,' she would say. 'I'll give you something to do with your hands.'

In fact, Aline continued, this citizen of Baghdad, if found, could verify the truth of Neil's pre-war possession of the cuneiform stones on Canadian turf.

'If you can prove that,' said Seyed, 'then I will not have a case against you. But how do I know that your Iraqi witness is not simply a collaborator? Why, the very fact that you have an Iraqi witness suggests that you have been somewhere you should not.'

Aline's story went something like this:

Several weeks before, on the evening of March 18th, Aline had sent an e-mail to a resident of Baghdad who called himself Salam Pax. Salam Pax had not responded to Aline, but Aline continued to write him anyway, e-mail after e-mail, telling him all about the adventures of a certain group of Montreal residents who called themselves the Lacuna Cabal. Specifically, he wrote about their various readings and responses to an ancient Mesopotamian epic known to him at the time as *He Who Saw Everything*, though it had since been revealed as *The Epic of Gilgamesh*, written on ten cuneiform stones.

'Are you able to read these cuneiform stones?' asked Seyed Samir.

'No. I can't. Neil can, though, I think. And his sister, Runner Coghill. She was the one who brought them in. She was the one who interpreted them for us.'

Seyed paused to make a note. 'Salam Pax,' he said, 'sounds like a made-up name.'

'Why do you say that?'

'Because it means "Peace Peace." Surname in Latin, given name in Arabic.'

'I think it's a pseudonym,' said Aline. 'He wrote something about that.'

'And how had you become acquainted with this ... Salam Pax?'

'What do you mean, how did I become acquainted ... ?'

'Are you friends with him?'

'I don't know him at all,' said Aline. 'Not really.'

'But you wrote to him. Your entire defence is predicated on a body of evidence which you claim is in his possession.'

'It's a long shot, I know.'

'Your story lacks credibility,' said Seyed Samir. 'Why would you write such a letter to a person you do not know?'

And then Aline had to explain to Seyed what a blogger was, which was not such a simple matter. He explained that a blogger was the creator of a blog, short for weblog, and how a blog was a way in which you could write on the Internet, on a page that anyone could see, and all for free.

He explained that some people considered blogs the worst thing that had ever happened to literature and letters, while others had said it was the best, and in any case it didn't matter because blogs were here to stay.

'And what is your opinion of these so-called blogs?' asked Seyed.

'Oh, I love them.'

'No doubt.'

'I could show you mine,' said Aline, 'but I screwed up the layout, so it doesn't look good, and, anyway, it has almost nothing on it. Every time I try to post, I get self-conscious.'

'I see,' said Seyed, who could at least identify with the notion of writer's block, since he experienced it every time he wrote a report. He'd once tried to write a murder mystery. He'd formulated the idea, the plot, even detailed character descriptions, but when it came to writing it down, he found he could not do it. The story was about the murder of a ninth-century (or sixteenth, in the Christian calendar) painter who had skirted the rules regarding the depiction of Muhammad by painting him without a face, or rather with a veil over his face, riding through the night sky astride a horse with a human face. There was to have been a motif throughout the book of faces and loss of face and the faceless masses. But nothing came of it. He had been too afraid to lift the pen.

'Hello?' said Aline.

Seyed started, having fallen into a reverie. He cleared his throat and consulted his notes.

'And this Mister Pax,' he continued, 'was a blogger who lived in Baghdad.'

'Yes,' said Aline. 'They call him the Baghdad Blogger.'

'Ah. Did he write about the approaching war?'

'He did.'

'Was he for or against?'

'Readers who were against thought he was for. Readers who were for thought he was against.'

'And what did Saddam Hussein believe?'

'Saddam Hussein didn't seem to notice it. He wouldn't have known what a blog was, any more than you do.'[35]

Seyed confessed that it was no clearer to him why Aline would engage in a one-sided correspondence with a 'Baghdad Blogger' named 'Salam Pax.'

'I don't know for sure,' said Aline. 'It was an impulse.'

And he wanted to say, *I had a thing for him.* He wanted to say, *I knew he wasn't in my league since he wanted to get a bear paw tattooed on his neck, and I'm not the type to … I'm somewhat more … * He wanted to say, *I'm a bit of a femme, really, to tell you the truth.* He wanted to tell the truth, but he didn't, although he had a suspicion that this particular immigration official would not bat an eye to receive such information. He seemed far too cool for that. But there were bigger things at stake here than for Aline to test his

35 This turns out not to have been true. The Baghdad Blogger was monitored by the Mukhabarat which, for reasons that will never be known, did not expose him or his family

boundaries. So he skipped it, and instead he said, 'I thought he might be interested. He's from where these stones are from.'

'Do you think your Salam Pax is still alive, after six weeks of bombardment in that city?'

'I don't know,' said Aline. 'I don't know.'

'Your story, even if it is true, still does not explain why has this boy ended up here.'

'Sir, do you know the story of *The Epic of Gilgamesh*?'

Seyed found himself wishing he smoked a pipe again. Did he know the story of *The Epic of Gilgamesh*? Vaguely. There were one or two passages in the Quran that apparently alluded to it. A man makes a friend, the friend dies, the man goes on a long journey in search of eternal life and meets an old wise man.

'I know this story somewhat,' he said. 'Why?'

So Aline explained as best he could, with his limited knowledge of the epic, how the Lacuna Cabal had been acting out the story of *The Epic of Gilgamesh*, but then how someone had died and everything had changed; how the story had been abandoned by everyone except the young boy in question, Neil Coghill; how he was, after all, just a boy, so such an event would inspire in him such a peregrination; also how he had taken the story rather more seriously than anyone would have wished.

'If Neil were an adult,' Aline explained, 'you might be more inclined to believe me, since you'd be able to see for yourself how his cheeks were drawn; he'd have a heavy beard; his eyes would have a faraway expression, like anybody who had spent all this time wandering through the wilderness in search of the wind. But since he's only a kid ... Then again, maybe he does look like that now. I haven't seen him lately.'

'He still resembles the boy he is, I assure you,' said Seyed Samir, who was impressed by this new revelation. *The Epic of Gilgamesh*. 'Who died?' he asked, and then immediately answered his own question. 'His sister.'

'Yes,' said Aline.

'The reader of the stones,' confirmed Seyed, checking his notes.

'Yes.'

'And a second sister?'

'She died too, earlier.'

'Ah.'

Aline opted not to tell Seyed about the rest of the family, in case he was not believed.

'Now, doubtless,' said Seyed Samir, 'he is expecting to encounter an old wise man.'

'Yes,' said Aline. 'I think so.'

Whereupon Seyed looked up and realized the gig was up. The look on Aline's face informed Seyed that his story was to be believed, no matter how implausible. It was true.

Aline's face, you see, had acquired an unmistakably hopeful expression of the type that could not be faked. It reminded Seyed of the expression on Fatima's face when he had commenced negotiations for their second child, Abdel. He found it surprisingly, touchingly feminine.

'You don't expect me to ... ?'

'Could you?' asked Aline.

'Oh no,' said Seyed, blushing now at Aline's expression, 'such a task is not for me.' He was surprised at how swiftly this interrogation had gone off the rails.

Still, it was an important matter. The ancient epic of the region. A young boy's rite of passage. He was no longer in search of the origin of an artifact carved in stone, but rather a living, breathing story.

He took a deep breath. 'I must consider the possibility,' he said, 'that you are trying to distract me with this impressive tale so that my eyes may become dazzled and I might permit you to depart with stolen booty.'

Aline nodded, chastened. The trick of the interrogator, he thought. The good cop and the bad cop in one cop.

'And what about the rest of you?' Seyed Samir asked.

'We followed him here.'

'With the help of a robot.'

Aline caught the renewed tone of skepticism. 'You haven't found it?'

Seyed shook his head slowly.

'Have you looked in on Neil lately?'

The officer's eyebrows went up. Aline continued. 'Because I'm quite sure the next time you do, depending on where you're keeping him, you'll find it right there with him.'

Such conviction. It impressed Seyed again with the thought that this series of improbable claims was nothing less than the truth. Only one thing continued to nag at him.

'I want to sympathize with you people,' he said. 'But your story does not explain the improbable coincidence of a boy having in his possession priceless Iraqi artifacts, at a time when so many are going missing from that torn country.'

'Then I suppose you'll have to ask Salam Pax,' said Aline.

'I suppose I will,' said Seyed Samir. And got up and walked out.

Wow, thought Aline. After that, how tough could it be to be grilled by the doorkeepers of Sexual-Reassignment Surgery?

✝

The representatives of Interpol and the Bahraini government — at least the ones Seyed Samir spoke to — did not know who Salam Pax was and they didn't know what a blog was, either. Normally it would have taken a great deal of time, but Seyed Samir was intrigued by the notion of a sole uncensored scribe writing from Baghdad, in defiance of a dictatorship, during the lead-up to the war. He wondered whether it could be true: whether Saddam Hussein could have let such a thing slip through his fingers. He wondered if the man could still be alive.

If he wasn't, then Seyed felt sorry for young J. I. Aline and his band of quixotic claimants. They were all going to be charged with conspiracy and theft. The child at the centre of it might be let off, but as for the rest of them …

There was only one thing to do. There was a dial-up Internet connection in the on-site business manager's office. Seyed managed to secure the line for several hours.

And so Seyed Samir looked up the Pax blog. He read it, was annoyed, intrigued, scandalized, began to care and then realized that Salam Pax had not posted since the third week of March. It was now the 7th of May. So, whether or not these e-mails of Mister Aline were recorded on Salam Pax's server was something that would not be so easy to determine.

Of course, Aline could have told him that.

And, of course, Salam Pax was alive.

Uta-napishti.

Seyed finally had the bright idea of calling the British news agency in London for contacts in the Baghdad bureau who might be able to lead him to fluent English-speaking Iraqis. He made the call just as the story was breaking in that part of the written world known as the blogosphere that Salam Pax was alive and well and e-mailing his posts to a friend and fellow blogger in New York City.

Chapter Twenty-One
Pax

We (the authors) would love to situate Salam Pax for you (the reader). It is, after all, supposed to be our job. We would love to write, for example: 'Salam walked out of his messy bedroom and started up the computer on the desk in the hallway; he was surprised to find an e-mail from the Bahraini ... ' (etc.)

Or perhaps we would be prudent enough to remember that after several weeks of bombing, there would have been no chance of Internet access in his home (or barely anywhere else in the city). (Not to mention the fact that all three computers were inside his room.)

So we might write instead: 'Salam headed down Karada Street (for example), passed the three tanks still stationed in front of the ice-cream shop, ducked into the single functioning web café, paid the prohibitive initial connection fee (five American dollars for one hour, further charges for uploading and downloading), and was surprised to find ... ' (etc.)

We might add that he was worried he would be late for a meeting with his friend Raed. And go on to describe what unfolded in his mind when he clicked on the e-mail marked urgent and waited for it to open, since he could be forgiven for imagining it was coming from the 'government in exile' of Saddam Hussein, informing him that his weblog had indeed been monitored for months, that he was one lucky fuck for not having been arrested and obliged to read a statement of guilt on national television, afterward executed, that in exchange for this mercy Saddam was now expecting him to assist in the efforts to win the hearts and minds of (etc.).

Or perhaps Saddam had been captured by the Bahraini Immigration Authority, in a leaky boat, and had used Salam as a reference to prove that he was a good guy after all and not the ruthless (etc.).

But this was not very likely, either, even if we have just written it, and the e-mail was not from the Ba'athist government-in-exile. All of Salam's revenge fantasies and visions of grandeur would have disappeared with the appearance on his computer screen of the message from the Bahraini Immigration Authority, specifically a fellow named Seyed Samir, who wrote to him in English.

We believe it would please Salam if we attempted to describe him physically ('Hey, me a character in a novel? … woo-hoo.')[36]

We could tell you things we've learned about him over the course of our research: that he sports a goatee. That he likes Björk and does not consider himself to be a good driver. That he likes a Canadian sci-fi writer named William Gibson, whose work we most certainly have not read. That he sees himself in sexual terms as a bear, which we think is cute. That he was undecided about the war — arguing against with American warbloggers and for with Baghdad taxi drivers. Some would say this makes him a fence-sitter, but we're more inclined to think of him as a diplomat. We know he's the son of a Sunni father and a Shia mother, so the fence strikes us as the wise position to take.

All this we could write. One might even argue that it's proper contextualization. But we don't really know anything about the man or his environment that the reader could not find out herself by going to dear_raed.blogspot.com and reading what's there. We don't even really know for certain how he felt about becoming involved in our story, though we have secured his blessing for its telling.

---

36 Though it's not a novel at all.

We know Salam Pax only as Aline knew him: from the words he used to post on the web for everyone to see.

And from the transcripts of e-mails we have between him and Seyed Samir.

And then between him and Aline.

And finally between him and Neil.

A blog is the movie of your life, with subtitles, only it's the subtitles that do all the moving in your movie and not the image above. Also, you're the producer, director, DOP, editor and, most importantly, subtitler.

We did ask Salam to tell us about himself. Sent him a brief questionnaire. He wrote to express delight in the project and to say he would get back to us on the questions, but he never did and in truth we did not expect him to. He's a very busy man now, spreading the word on living in an occupied city. Preparing, we've heard, to leave it.

Anyway, it's not the fashion these days to provide descriptions of characters in books. You're supposed to learn about them from their actions.

And these are all the actions we have left to convey:

+++

Date: Fri, 9 May 2003 10:03:16-0500
From: seyedsamir@batelcom.bh
To: salampax@urukpost.com
Subject: Urgent Request

Dear Mister Salam Pax,

This is Seyed Samir of Bahraini Immigration Authority. Good afternoon. We currently have in custody two young people who stowed away on a ferry ship being towed to a shipyard on the northern coast of our country.

They were followed by six more young people piloting an expensive yacht.

All visitors claim to be Canadian.

The stowaways had in their possession ten astonishingly well-preserved cuneiform tablets relating the story of *The Epic of Gilgamesh.*

We suspect, reasonably, that these ten tablets were recently stolen from either the Baghdad Museum or else an archaeological dig in Iraq. The stowaways say they are theirs.

You have been cited as a person who might hold information related to our case. I would be most gratified therefore if you could contact me at your earliest convenience.

Yours Sincerely,
Seyed Samir,
Bahrain Immigration Authority

+++
Date: Fri, 9 May 2003 10:31:19-0500
From: salampax@urukpost.com
To: seyedsamir@batelcom.bh
Subject: Re: Urgent Request

Dear Seyed Samir,

Whaaa?

I confess I know nothing about stolen artifacts. I spent the last several weeks sitting in a downstairs room with the rest of my family, fingers placed firmly in my ears.

+++

My Dear Mister Salam Pax,

First, I would like to thank you for being so generous as to reply so promptly, especially when one considers how I seem to have been accusing you of something!

In truth, I am not accusing you of anything, neither smuggling nor anything else.

Rather, I am told you might have in your e-mail archives several innocuous messages, dated from the second and third weeks of March, from a young man in Montreal named Joyce I. Aline. Do you have such messages?

That is all I have to ask for the moment. I would, however, like to take this opportunity to convey my best wishes to you and your family. May Allah continue to protect you and allow you to live safely in your house, your city and your country.

Yours Most Sincerely,
Seyed Samir,
BIA

+++
Dear Seyed,

I *do* have messages from a Canadian, saved from the time you mention in mid-March. However, this Canadian is not a 'young man' but rather a 'young woman.' Her name is Aline Irwin.

I'm confused. Her e-mails are all about *The Epic of Gilgamesh* and her name is similar. I'm very confused now. I am forwarding them to you. Maybe someone could explain.

+++
My Dear Salam,

Please do not be distressed. I have confirmed the source of the e-mails you have forwarded as the very same J. I. Aline, who is with me here in custody.

It is of interest to me that J. I. Aline would identify himself as a woman in his e-mails to you. It strikes me as a very simple matter for users of the Internet to represent themselves as something other than what they truly are.

Given this new and fascinating line of inquiry, I have two further questions for you:

1. What evidence can you give that you are who you say you are? Who you say you are, according to my notes, is not a man in cahoots with international smuggling organizations, but rather Salam Pax of Baghdad, AKA 'The Baghdad Blogger,' who sometimes works for an architecture firm, employed by a man named Evil Boss Creature. Good friends with one fellow named Raed and another identified only as G.

+++
My Dear Seyed,

You forgot to ask your second question.

+++
Dear Salam,

Forgive me for neglecting to post my second question and thank you for pointing out the error. The second question is the following: If you are who you say you are, why would you keep the e-mails of this alleged woman from Montreal named Aline Irwin? She would have been a stranger to you, writing of matters that were of no concern to you. Why not simply deposit them in the trash?

I infer from the brevity of your previous message that you might think I am accusing you of something. Let me repeat, I am not accusing you of anything. Answers to both these questions will simply be of the greatest assistance to our work here at the Bahraini Immigration Authority.

Yours Most Sincerely,
Seyed Samir, BIA

+++
Seyed,

Isn't it obvious? The girl who turns out to be a boy had a crush on me. Why wouldn't I keep them? I have a better question — a question for Aline Irwin himself — which is why would a guy pretend he's a girl to write to me when he knows full well that I'm queer?

You have to understand: most e-mails I get are from American armchair warriors who want to kill me. Most of the rest want to talk politics. Your Aline Irwin wrote instead about the exploits of some crazy girls' book club in Montreal. It was exactly what the doctor ordered, my friend!

As for your other question, I've pretty much become an expert at ignoring it. But consider this, Seyed: If I were an international smuggling kingpin, do you think I would have time to construct a web personality and build upon it, day after day, for all the months my site's been up?

Listen: it's crazy the superhuman exploits that you people think I'm capable of. I've even been credited as the author of the Riverbend Blog. So I'm apparently masquerading as a woman myself. It's really quite flattering, but how is it even possible?

No, really, you all seem to think I'm the most prolific novelist in the history of the world. Even if I were, I'm sure I wouldn't have time to scheme a heist at the Baghdad Museum. I haven't even been there since I was five years old. Perhaps I started planning it then. ('Hey, Mrs. Wahabi, can we go look at the Sumer Room again?')

It's unbelievable.

+++

[Here follows a lacuna in the text of Seyed's correspondence — presumably excised by Aline — in which (we believe) Seyed cites details from Aline's missives to Salam about the Lacuna Cabal's re-enactment of The Epic of Gilgamesh, *specifically the startling revelation of the origin of Romy's spiky haircut. Seyed had mistrusted Romy precisely because of her lack of hair, and the discovery that her hair had been an axiom of self-sacrifice apparently so moved Seyed that he cast all further doubt to the wind. He went so far as to briefly consider arresting Coby and Du on a point of honour, but opted against it.*

Nowhere, apparently, is it revealed what Seyed later told us: that he had by this point received a report by the Suez Port Authority, confirming statements made by the Danes that the stowaways had been discovered before docking at the entrance to the canal. The Port Authority had even discussed with the Danes their plans to circumvent protocol and return them personally to Canada.

Nor is it mentioned anywhere that Seyed had also by this time discovered the fitzbot, clutched to the chest of Neil, and that every attempt to separate them was thwarted by the creature itself. In

short, full corroboration to accompany a leap of faith. As Yann
Martel has illustrated more dramatically elsewhere, when the facts
have been established and the outcome is the same, sometimes belief
is a matter of preference.

Seyed goes on to apologize to Salam for the embarrassment he
may have caused by perusing the more personal details of the one-
sided correspondence, but since Aline has already attempted to
excise this part of the story, the less said about it the better.]

+++
Dear Mister Pax,

Thank you for your prompt assistance in this matter. You have
been most helpful. On the strength of your evidence, the claims
of our young Canadians have been verified.

I will urge them, however, to consider handing over custody of
these priceless artifacts to the state of Iraq, since it seems clear
to me that, even if they have not recently been stolen, they were
at some time in the past.

You had a question for Joyce Aline. It seems he also has a question for you. I will now proceed to hand over my address and
server to this young man. It has been a pleasure to correspond
with you. I have appreciated your frankness and your honesty.
And so I remain,

Yours Sincerely,
Seyed Samir,
BIA

+++
Muchos nachos, hombre. Do what I can.
Salam.

+++

Salam,

Maybe you'll remember me. Well, I guess you do, since you kept my e-mails. What a relief! Thanks for that. You've gotten my friends and me out of a lot of trouble. Believe it or not, you were our only hope.

[Here follows another lacuna — also presumably excised by Aline. We believe it contains a substantial amount of personal information conveyed from Aline to Salam, as well as the essential history of the Lacuna Cabal, presumably emphasizing the role of Neil Coghill the Real McCoghill and his identification with The Epic of Gilgamesh.*]*

Essentially, he needs to speak to a wise man.
Aline.

+++

I'm not a wise man. You should take a look at the state of my bedroom. You should ask my mother. No, you should ask my *father.* He'll tell you: I'm not a wise man.
Salam.

+++

You won't help us?
Aline.

+++

I did not say that. I'm simply trying to tell you that you're dealing with a fourth-rate wise man here. Then again, I guess you're getting me at a cut rate too. If you can accept that, I'm willing to give it a go.

What do you want me to say to the kid? Does he have an e-mail address?
Salam.

+++

Say whatever you like. I can accept that. Thank you. Tell him about the war. Tell him anything. I don't know. The main thing is, you're from where the epic is from. And he knows it. Oh, but he doesn't have an address. Seyed Samir's will still have to serve. I have an address, though, before I sign off. Mine is alineirwin@gmail.com, fyi. xo Aline.

ps Thank you, Salam Pax

+++

Shall I start now?

Salam.

+++

Go ahead.

Neil.

+++

Hey! This is already turning out to be harder than I thought. It's confusing to see 'Seyed Samir' there at the top of all these e-mails from different people.

Salam.

+++

Why don't we forget about it then?

Neil.

+++

No, my friend, you won't get rid of me so easily.

Salam.

+++

You have a made-up name.

+++

That's right. How did you know?
Salam.

+++

b/c it means Peace Peace. Not likely it's real.

+++

But it's a good one, don't you think? As a nom de plume?
Salam.

+++

It's all right.

+++

Um … I understand you're looking for the oldest man in the world.
Salam.

+++

No, that's okay. I'm not actually looking for the oldest man in the world.

+++

What a relief! Well, I'm glad. Tho I do think that if I take care of myself, and, you know, don't step on any land mines or sign up for any wars, or get murdered by anybody, or get my heart broken, or catch any of these terrible diseases that are going around, I *will* be the oldest man in the world. It's not easy around here, though, I have to admit.
Salam.

+++

Where are you?

+++
Baghdad.

+++
You really are? How do I know you're telling the truth?

+++
You know, I'm getting very tired of that question.

+++
I'm sorry.
I believe you.
There's a war going on there, isn't there?
Neil.

+++
If I'm not mistaken, the President of the United States has declared an 'end to major combat operations.' Yes, there's a war going on.
Salam.

+++
Are you safe?
Neil.

+++
For the moment. It's useful to be a bit of a coward. Though I've just done a very un-Salam thing and signed up with my friend Raed to take a tour though the south of the country to see how things are with the people down there. I was supposed to meet with him and talk about it a half-hour ago. He must be furious with me.

+++
Do you want to sign off?

+++
No, I love it when Raed gets furious with me. Then I get to watch his brain derail as he makes these strange choking noises for a few minutes. It's very entertaining.

I'm told you don't talk much these days. I'm curious whether that's still the case, or whether you don't consider writing to be talking.

+++
I don't consider writing to be talking.
Neil.

+++
Ah. Well, I'm flattered that you're writing to me, under the circumstances. You are in Bahrain?
Salam.

+++
Yes.

+++
Have you had a look around?

+++
I can't get out of the shipyard. We're here illegally. We don't have passports.

+++
How very 007 of you. I'm curious, though: Did you know that the island you're on is traditionally considered to be where your

282

man Gilgamesh ended up when he went looking for that guy? That Noah guy?

+++

You mean Uta-napishti? This is the island? Are you shitting me?

+++

I'm not shitting you. Are you shitting me? Are you telling me you came all this way and you didn't even know you were coming to the right place?

+++

It's not the right place. Not for me.

+++

Me no understand, Neil.
Salam.

+++

I'm not trying to emulate Gilgamesh. These people around me are confused. My plan was to take the place of my sister in the underworld so that she could escape and go up into the sky and be with the gods. But then the people from the tugboat came and took me away from there so I don't know whether she's back down there or not.

+++

Well, that's different from what I heard. Sounds like you have a problem.

+++

Yes. Anyway, I couldn't be Gilgamesh even if I tried. I was a pretender.

+++
Why a pretender?

+++
I'm too young.
Neil.

+++
Too young? But my friend, don't you know what 'Gilgamesh' means?
Salam.

+++
What do you mean?

+++
Not what 'I' mean. What 'Gilgamesh' means. <g>

+++
That's a bad joke.

+++
Oh I know. But the point is, names have meanings. 'Gilgamesh' means 'the old man is a young man.' Didn't you know that?
Salam.

+++
Oh. Anyway, it's too late. I already switched stories.
Neil.

+++
To Inanna's Descent, apparently. Nice one. Probably the scariest story in the history of the world.
Salam.

+++

How did you know that's what I was talking about?
Neil.

+++

— Contestant Pax for 200 points: I went down to the underworld
to visit my sister. She stripped me, killed me and hung my body
on a nail. Who am I?
— That would be the goddess Inanna, your worship.
— Contestant Pax, you are correct.

+++

They don't call game-show hosts 'your worship.'

+++

How do you know? Maybe they do here. Maybe it's how
Saddam's judges make some extra cash. *Made* some extra cash.

I know your story, Neil, because I studied architecture in Vienna
and they taught us all kinds of shit. I was the Mesopotamian in
the bunch, so they made sure I knew everything about my history.

Let me tell you about Inanna's Descent, my friend. I know you've
got a writer's frame of mind, so you're probably a literalist. You
imagine your sister going into the underworld and being forced
to take off all her clothes until she's naked, and then her twin
sister, who's gone down there before her, who lives there in fact,
strikes her dead and hangs her on a nail.

You probably imagine the nail she's hanging on. You probably
picture it vividly in your mind before you fall asleep at night, or,
more to the point, when you wake up in the middle of the night
and the whole world is asleep except for you.
Salam.

+++

I do imagine the nail she's hanging on.

Neil.

+++

My friend, I don't want to disappoint you, but that story was never meant to be taken literally. I don't want to ruin it for you, I really don't. I don't want to be that guy behind the curtain in *The Wizard of Oz,* but I have to tell you: Inanna's Descent is a story the Sumerians came up with to try to explain the cycle of the seasons. They looked at the world — they saw things die in the fall and come to life in the spring, and they wanted to explain it.

So, as far as that goes, Inanna has to go to the underworld in order for there to be winter. And when her brother[37] takes her place, she comes up and then it's summer. They go back and forth like that, all through time, and the thing you have to understand is: they do it willingly. Nobody's forcing anyone to do anything. I don't want to disappoint you, but they do it so that you can eat your vegetables.

And there's another thing you probably don't know about that story: there are several different versions. The way the story developed over time, the brother who takes Inanna's place eventually becomes king of the underworld. He goes by several different names. The name you might be rather familiar with is Gilgamesh.

So you don't have to choose between those two stories, my friend. Those two stories are both stories of the same man. The old man is a young man. The young man is a boy. The boy's

---

37 Salam presumably knows it is really her husband and is taking liberties for Neil's sake.

name is Neil Coghill, who, I'm given to understand, is the Real
McCoghill.
Salam.

+++

You're from the place where the stones are from, right?
Neil.

+++

That's right. So you should listen to me, because I'm telling you.
I don't want to be mean, but, my friend, you have to remember
that people die. They die all the time. It's happening all over
these days. Especially here. People die and you love them and
you mourn them and the best thing you can do to honour their
memory is to live your life the best way you can. I know you're
just a kid, but that's why you have to get yourself out of the
underworld. My friend, let me tell you: you don't belong there.
You've got your whole life to become king of the underworld.
Salam.

+++

Can I tell you what I think, though?
Neil.

+++

Sure.
Salam.

+++

My sister Ruby had a computer, but before she died she erased
everything on it except one document that was written in big, big
fat letters, and what she wrote was:

I WANT TO GO HOME.
I'M TIRED AND WANT TO GO TO BED.

I WILL NOT GO TO BED EARLY BUT LATE.
I WENT TO BED EARLY. BUT DID NOT GO TO SLEEP.
I STAYED AWAKE AND DOZED ALL NIGHT.
THIS A.M. WAS LIKE NOTHING ON THIS EARTH.

And it scared both of us. Both me and Runner. I'm sorry if I scared you too, writing it with the big letters. It's because she couldn't see very well anymore. She was going blind. I was scared and I think Runner was scared too but she stopped being scared so that I wouldn't be scared.

The thing is, I think she stopped being scared by making herself sick the way that Ruby was. And by not being scared, she would be able to stop me from being scared. That's the way I think she did it. She did it for me.

So she didn't let me be scared for six months and then she died too.

In the end, I think she wanted to go home too.

So how can it not be my fault?

+++
It's not your fault, Neil.

+++
I just told you: it *is* my fault.

+++
Kids always think things are their fault.

+++
This is different. The facts speak for themselves.

+++

It's a fact that kids always think things are their fault.

+++

I've given you the facts. And I still can't get that note out of my head. So I'm worse off than ever.

+++

You should remember that note represents a single moment in time.

+++

I think she felt that way all the time.

+++

Of course she didn't. It stands to reason. That's what writing is. It's moment to moment. Look at me, for example. I can never figure out what I'm feeling: one day I'm all 'Drop the bombs!' and the next I'm all 'Excuse me but don't you think you should clean up this mess you made?' But that doesn't stop me from writing it all down.

I mean, hey, sure, if you're dying and you have a bad day, maybe you pin a note up on the fridge or the computer screen that says something like, you know, 'I want to go home.' But then a moment comes when you think, I don't have no place to go. Home is here, in my heart. As long as you're looking out through your eyes at the people you love, then you're going to be all right. Unless you're looking up at someone you hate and he's gloating over you while you die. That would be different, I guess. That happens here. It didn't happen to either of your sisters, though, did it? I'm betting it didn't.
Salam.

+++

No, it didn't.

Neil.

+++

I imagine your sisters died very close to people they loved. Is that right?

Salam.

+++

That's right.

Neil.

+++

And they knew it too. There's no better way to go, my friend.

. +++

But why did they have to go at all?

+++

I can't answer that one.

Salam.

+++

I wish they didn't have to go. I miss them a lot and I don't know what to do. I thought taking Runner's place would work. I don't know why I can't be Harry Potter. I know Harry Potter's not real, but still.

+++

Hey Neil,

I had a friend die once. Got shot in a car. And I had another friend disappear and I never heard from him again. Except that

I would see him at night from time to time, in the dark, and it has made me hate the idea of war.

Gilgamesh loved war. Even when he made friends with Enkidu, he still loved war. He still went out and killed Humbaba, and the Bull of Heaven, for no reason other than the sport and the glory of it. Only when Enkidu showed him his death's head and the worm fell out of his nostril did Gilgamesh start down the road to becoming a peace-loving man.

I don't mind if you live in the underworld, Neil. I don't mind if you live in a cave. But the things that you've seen, that you know, are the kinds of things that we need up here in the world. There are lots of stupid people up here. Believe me. I've heard from a good deal of them. And there are lots of wise people too, like you. I'm not saying you're the only one. But we could still use one more. So I really hope you come up and live in the world instead of your cave, Neil.

Who's Harry Potter?
Salam.

+++
Harry Potter is a boy in a book.
Neil.

+++
Raed is really going to kill me, but I've got one more thing to do before I go.

It seems to me, my friend, that you're ailing. You're my ailing friend. And where I come from there's a folk remedy for those who are ailing. It goes all the way back to the Quran apparently, though I'm no expert on THAT, believe me, so I don't know for sure.

But it goes something like this: You walk around the sick person seven times to take away his illness.
Salam.

+++
You think I have an illness?

+++
You're sick in the head, my friend. It's obvious.

+++
And you would solve that by walking around me seven times?
Neil.

+++
That's what the old women tell me.
Salam.

+++
But how would you do that?

+++
I have my ways.

+++
I'm in Bahrain and you're in Baghdad.
Neil.

+++
You also have, I gather, enormous faith in the written word.
Salam.

+++
What's that supposed to mean?

+++

It means, my little man, that I have a plan.

Some while back, in this gradual, growing conversation between you and me, I forwarded an e-mail, subject heading 'Walking around Neil,' to a blogger I know in London, England, whom I know to be a notorious nighthawk.

He proceeded to forward the message to another blogger in Reykjavik, whom I don't know, but that hardly matters when the life of a child is at stake.

The Icelander forwarded the message to a blogger of your country, a Newfoundlander, though I believe she's a separatist, so I suppose I really shouldn't say she's from your country.

The Newfoundlander sent it on to a good gothamist friend of mine in New York City, whereupon it made no fewer than four stops in the good ol' U.S. of A., from NY to Wyoming, from Wyoming to Seattle, from Seattle to Honolulu, unrepentant nighthawks all, otherwise this would have taken several hours.

From Hawaii, the missive zipped over to Wellington, New Zealand; from there to Sydney; from Sydney to a sporadic and uncommitted blogger by the name of Joey in the Philippines.

Joey rerouted it up to Japan, which was a bit of a sidetrack, but I wanted to include a banjo-playing blogger in Tokyo by the name of Banjo Boya, because Banjo Boya's been in the blogging business pretty much from the beginning, and I wish to pay homage to my compatriots as much as to you, my friend.

Banjo Boya wound up tight and hurled your message right across China to a catcher's mitt in India.

From India it jumped to a woman in Iran who happens to be Raed's girlfriend.

Raed's girlfriend sent it to Raed and Raed sent it to me. Which means he's not mad at me. That makes one single jagged revolution around the earth. I sent it off again and it's just come back to me for the sixth time. I just sent it off again.

Now I'm waiting for the seventh. When the seventh comes, I will forward it to you and we'll be done. I'm sure the fifteen of us can take on your grieving. I know I've got a little mourning of my own to do, when I get around to it one of these days.

And I'll tell you, my friend, there are no people more sociable than people who are mourning. If you happen to walk past a room full of people in mourning, you should join them because they're probably lonely. And you're lonely too, my boy. You're lonely too.

✝

When Neil got the e-mail, subject heading 'Walking around Neil,' he scrolled down through the miles of forwarded addresses, seven times fifteen, until he came to the message at the bottom, and the message at the bottom said,

Neil Coghill the Real McCoghill,
    (What else did you think I was going to say?)
    Don't go drifting. Don't wander too far in search of the wind. Come up out of your cave. It's been spring for more than two weeks. Take comfort in the handholds of your friends, your women's book club. What's it called? The Lacuna Cabal? And you can add all our names to the Lacuna Cabal. All fifteen of us, from London, Reykjavik, Newfoundland, U.S.A., N.Z.,

Philippines, Japan, India, Iran and moi. Return to your life, Neil. Return to your life.

Pax

✝

And then when Neil came out of the computer office with Romy (who'd been permitted to sit with him) at his shoulder, he was still clutching the fitzbot to his belly, as if it were a favourite toy. The fitzbot seemed to be clutching him back. Neil seemed to have forgotten it was there. Coby felt an impulse but let it go.

Everyone had been so focused on Neil in the preceding hours that they only now began to look clearly at one another. Romy told Aline he looked like a man. Aline said he was a man and told Romy she looked like a dyke. Romy said she was a dyke. Missy mussed Neil's hair and said, 'You stupid kid. You scared the shit out of us, you know.'

And Neil, muffled inside anyone's embrace, said, 'I know.'

Dumuzi said, 'You know, you dethroned me.'

But Neil was still uncertain. He looked up at Dumuzi and said, 'I found her. I found Runner. She's a goddess.'

'She is a goddess,' Missy agreed.

'She sure is,' said Romy.

'Yes she is,' said Priya.

'Yes she is,' said Aline.

Coby said, 'Uh,' and Dumuzi said he'd go along with that.

Neil said, 'I wanted to take her place in the underworld.'

'Come on, Neil,' said Romy. 'You can take her place in the world.'

✝

And now it is April 2007.

Anna Lighter is standing at a podium. There are ten cuneiform stones, perfectly preserved, on display at her feet for the audience and academic advisors to see. She is completing a lecture on the significance of *The Epic of Gilgamesh* in the modern world. There is a young boy standing beside her. And Jennifer H. and Danielle D., co-authors of the book *The Girls Who Saw Everything*, are sitting behind her, looking very pleased with the proceedings. As it turns out, they have been able to help Anna with her research and she has been able to help them with theirs. It has been a fruitful relationship all round.

Anna speaks out to the audience with a greater formality than she has ever mustered: 'As you observe these stones, which have kindly been re-loaned to us by the Baghdad Museum, I'd like to finish with a quote from the beginning, the very beginning, from the Huluppu Tree, the Sumerian creation myth.'

And then, in a gesture the audience does not expect, she hands her microphone over to the boy beside her, who steps forward to the podium. If you look down at your programs you will see his name is Neil Coghill, the contributor of the so-called Coghill Tablets. How young he is! In an unbroken voice, he reads from the sheet in front of him:

In the first days, in the very first days,
In the first nights, in the very first nights,
In the first years, in the very first years.

Neil steps back and Anna takes her place again at the podium, Jennifer and Danielle behind her silently weeping.

'Thank you,' she says. 'That is the end of my pr— my presentation.'

Notes

The Coghill Version of *The Epic of Gilgamesh* is a fictional rendering of this ancient story in which many liberties were taken. Translations of *Gilgamesh* consulted were two Penguin editions, by N. K. Sandars and Andrew George. George's translation is distinctive for its placing of ellipses where there are lacunae in the tablets, and for its presentation of several versions of the epic.

The quotation on the last page of the novel is from *The Huluppu Tree*, translated by Samuel Noah Kramer and Diane Wolkstein.

The novel's title is inspired by the version translated by Robert Temple.

The quoted statements of Prof. Bruce Kuklick of University of Pennsylvania and Prof. Jan Walls of sfu have not been altered. All that changed was the recipient of their knowledge.

Salam Pax gave me permission to use him as a character. His blog is real and can still be seen at http://dear_raed.blogspot.com/. However, the thoughts and feelings I attribute to him, as well as the content of his e-mail exchanges, are fictional.

The web page http://pov.blogspot.com/ is one of thousands of abandoned blogs on the Internet. I don't know who the author of it really is.

The *Nindawayma* is a real boat in the Vieux-Port de Montreal. Since March 2003, it has been moved to another location in the port and continues to deteriorate.

Opinions expressed in this book about the works of Richard Adams, Margaret Atwood, Barry Callaghan, Leonard Cohen, Marian Engel, William Gibson, Barbara Gowdy, E. L. Konigsburg, Ann-Marie MacDonald, Michael Ondaatje, Salam Pax, Philip Pullman, J. K. Rowling and Russell Smith do not necessarily represent the views of the author.

Acknowledgements

This work began as a play commissioned by Bill Glassco and the Montreal Young Company, to be directed by Chris Abraham.

While still a play, it received a couple of workshops by the 2003 graduating class of the National Theatre School: Jessica Carmichael, Jesse Dwyre, Lwam Ghebrehariat, Michelle Girouard, Kate Hewlett, Benjamin Johnson, Shira Leuchter, Shirley-Sharon Marquez, Gareth Potter, Daria Puttaert, Amy Jo Scherman, Suzanne Smith and Adrienne Zitt. These actors, along with director Chris Abraham, left their marks indelibly upon the characters they played and the topography of the novel.

Other thanks: Hilary McMahon, Prof. Jeffrey Tigay, Graeme Somerville, Camille Stubel, Michelle Monteith, E. J. Scott, Carly Street, Allan Hawco, Steven McCarthy, Greg MacArthur, Aviva Armour-Ostroff, Kate Hemblen, Diana Donnelly, Manon St-Jules, Amy Price-Francis, Rafal Sokolowski, Ryan Hollyman, Amy Rutherford, Paul Fauteux, Shawn Campbell, Shawn Riedle, Sam Earle, Coby Stubel, Eva Brebner of the Christ Church Cathedral in Montreal, Jenny Boully, Martin Garside of the Port of London Authority, Kent Malo, George Wharton, Thomas Alley, Carl Wilson, Joel Reardon, Greg Edmonds-Brown, Julie Burch, Cynthia Kelly, Colleen Lashuk, Hugo Dann, Kilby Smith-McGregor, Matthew Payne, Margaux Williamson, Tracy Broyles, Czehoski Restaurant, Amiel Gladstone, Kent and Martin Dixon, Greg Spottiswood, Sherry Bie, Ker Wells, Ivana Shein, Jonathan Garfinkel, Tamara Crist and the Ontario Arts Council's Works in Progress program.

Anne Carson and the Boys' Choir of Lesbos provided early inspiration for this book. Coach House editor Alana Wilcox provided late, great taste, as did proofreader Stuart Ross.

About the Author

Sean Dixon is a writer and actor. His plays include *The Gift of the Coat*, *Billy Nothin'*, *The Painting*, *Aerwacol* and a solo show, *Falling Back Home*.

As an actor he has appeared on stages across the country, from Toronto's Factory Theatre to underneath the Burrard Street Bridge in Vancouver. He helped to found the innovative nineties Winnipeg Theatre Company PRIMUS and is Playwright-out-of-Residence for Victoria's Theatre SKAM.

His writing has appeared in the *Globe and Mail*, *This Magazine*, *Canadian Theatre Review*, *Brick* and on CBC Radio. A play collection, *AWOL*, is published by Coach House Books and a YA novel, *The Feathered Cloak*, will be published by Key Porter in the fall of 2007. He lives and plays banjo in Toronto.

Typeset in Gilgamesh
Printed and bound at the Coach House on bpNichol Lane

Edited and designed by Alana Wilcox
Author photo by Katerina Cizek
Bookplate by Evan Munday, derived from an original 1930s-era
    bookplate and used by special permission of Alpha Delta Phi
    at Cornell University
Cover design by Stan Bevington
Back-cover painting by Julie St. Amand, *Au coin d'la Rue*,
    encaustic on canvas, 30 × 40 inches,
    courtesy of Louise Lipman Contemporary Art

Coach House Books
80 bpNichol Lane
Toronto, Ontario M5S 3J4
Canada

800 367 6360
416 979 2217

mail@chbooks.com
www.chbooks.com